WINNIPEG
WITHDRAWN
NOV 19 2008
PUBLIC LIBRARY

Everything You Want

For Us
est. 1967

Everything You Want

Barbara Shoup

Woodbury, Minnesota

First Edition
First Printing, 2008

Book design by Steffani Sawyer
Cover design by Gavin Dayton Duffy

Flux, an imprint of Llewellyn Publications

The Cataloging-in-Publication Data for *Everything You Want* is on file at the Library of Congress.
ISBN-13: 978-0-7387-1227-7

This is a work of fiction. Names, characters, places, and incidents are either the product of the author's imagination or are used fictitiously, and any resemblance to actual persons, living or dead, business establishments, events, or locales is entirely coincidental.

Flux
Llewellyn Publications
A Division of Llewellyn Worldwide, Ltd.
2143 Wooddale Drive, Dept. 978-0-7387-1227-7
Woodbury, MN 55125-2989, U.S.A.
www.fluxnow.com

Printed in the United States of America

One

Friday night, party time at Indiana University, and I'm holed up in the psych lab with Freud—my assigned goose in an experiment we're doing in my Psych 101 class. I know. What about rats? Or guinea pigs. That's what *I* figured Psych 101 would be about. But I had to get this weird professor who has a thing for the territorial behavior of geese, which as far as I can tell is to try to kill anyone who gets near them. Hardly endearing: Freud hisses every time he sees me. Right now he's staring at me with his beady little red eyes, like why don't you just leave me *alone*? But I can't help feeling sorry for a fellow living being caught in the wrong place, so even though he doesn't seem to like me all that much, I've taken to hanging out at the lab, where I just sit by his cage and keep him company. I read, or write in my journal—complaints, mostly, about how much I hate college, and nostalgic crap about better days. But I keep a lab book open beside me, and if the door opens and someone comes in, I put it on top of my journal, so it looks like I'm taking down data. It's better than hanging out alone in my dorm room. Or worse, hanging out not-alone in my dorm room with my roommate, Tiffany, and her boyfriend, Matt, where I am constantly reminded of my own boyfriendless, virginal state.

Which leads, every time, to thinking about Josh Morgan—*never* a good thing to do. What's he doing right now? Who's he with? Did he see me coming up the hall toward the elevator in Ballantine Hall the other day, or did he just turn and head for the stairs because he was tired of waiting for it to come? What if, somehow, we'd ended up on the elevator together, by mistake? Would he have said something? Would I have?

Give it up, I tell myself. It's over. Ha. Like it ever *was*.

Which is how I've justified just not mentioning to Tiffany that Josh happens to be a pledge in Matt's fraternity. God. Just the thought of her in possession of that piece of information makes me go *la, la, la, la. la, la, la, la, la, la* inside my head.

"Six days till Mom comes to get me next weekend," I

say to Freud. "One hundred forty-four hours—give or take a few—and I'll be at home, in my own room."

As if he cares.

I stay till nine, when I'm sure Tiff and Matt will have gone out for pizza—or whatever it is they do when they're not making out in our room. The dorm is dead, just us dateless wonders and a few geeks who like staying in to study on Friday night. I close the door behind me and climb up to the top bunk. Actually, it's kind of nice lying there in the dark. The smell of home on my pillow. Strains of all the different kinds of music people are listening to blending to make their own strange song.

I'm done with Freud, I tell myself. It's ridiculous to have a relationship with a goose. It's a good thing that Thursday will be the wrap-up of our experiment. He'll be sent out to the country, where he can terrorize cows and pigs for a change. I won't have to feel responsible for him anymore.

Then Thursday comes and, leaving class, I overhear Professor Harmon tell someone they're going to kill all the geese we used in the experiment. The geese are wrecked, he says. They can't be used in the same experiment again.

Even if I hadn't spent all those lonely evenings in Freud's company, I think I'd be freaked out. I mean, Jeez. It's one thing to annoy a bunch of geese so some college students can learn something they could just as easily have learned by reading a book. But to kill them because they can't be used for the same experiment again? That's not right.

So I wait until everyone's gone and go up to him. "You have to *kill* them?" I ask.

"Yes," he says, slipping his lecture notes into his backpack.

"That's terrible," I say. "Can't you take them to a farm, or something like that?"

"Nobody wants geese," he says. "They're mean, as we have just so aptly proven."

"But what will you do? I mean, how do you kill them? And *then* what?"

"Lethal injection." He hoists his pack over his shoulder. "Then we incinerate them. But if you want *your* goose, Miss Hammond, you're welcome to it. If you can take it now."

Freud squawks plaintively. Now, suddenly, he wants to be my friend.

I could take him to the canal near our house in Indianapolis, I think. There are plenty of mean geese there already; he'd feel right at home. I could take him when Mom picks me up tomorrow. The tricky part would be explaining my plan to her in the split second between the time she sees the goose and the time she goes ballistic.

"Miss Hammond? I have a student waiting in my office."

"Could I borrow a cage?" I ask. "I'll bring it back Monday morning. I promise."

He nods wearily.

"Okay, then. I'll take him."

I'm too embarrassed to get on the bus with Freud, so I lug the cage across campus. It's the end of October, a beautiful day, leaves drifting down, fluorescent against the blue sky, but I shuffle along, head down, praying I won't run into anyone I know—especially not Josh and that Heather-type blond girl I've seen him with lately. On a campus with thousands of people on it, you'd think the odds of my even catching a glimpse of him would be pretty low; but I see him all the time. Not that he sees me all that often. I've got some kind of radar where he's concerned and usually manage to take a quick turn down an alternate path or step into a classroom building before I come into his view. When necessary, I skulk into the woods, like a spy. Carrying Freud, though, this could be difficult, and I am deeply relieved to get to the dorm without having to resort to such tactics.

I sneak up the back stairs, sprint for my room. The door's locked, which probably means Matt's there. So I knock before opening it and, sure enough, there's the usual clunk: Matt leaping from bed to chair.

"It's me, Emma. I forgot my key."

"Coming," Tiffany warbles.

Waiting for her to get decent, I remind myself that although Tiffany's a ditz and we have zip in common, she is truly nice. A perky, small-town girl, her idea of paradise is to drive up to Indianapolis and spend the whole day at Castleton Mall, shopping at The Limited and stocking up on cheery little items at the Hallmark store: cute knickknacks and posters with those floaty, pastel, lightbulb-looking figures spouting words to live by like "Today Is the First Day of the Rest of Your Life."

Her side of our room is full of that shit, which makes for a kind of schizophrenic environment. On my side there's a framed photo of the meadow outside our ski house in Michigan just after a snowstorm, and a glass dish of Petoskey stones

I collected on countless beach walks at Sleeping Bear Dunes. There's a Harley-Davidson poster with a picture of a Sturgis just like my dad's, and a Steamboat Springs poster with a girl riding horseback in the snow, a pair of skis balanced on one shoulder. And this other, incredible poster I bought at the Metropolitan Museum when I went to visit my sister, Julie, in New York. It's of this gorgeous, *built* sculptor whose marble figure of a woman is coming to life. It kills me, that painting. The sculptor's muscles, the marble woman pinking beneath his fingers. The day I got to school, I unrolled it to put it up. Tiffany took one look at it and said, "Whoa! He is *buff*!"

Now she opens the door, one hand smoothing her disheveled hair. At the sight of the goose, she gives a little scream and both hands fly to her mouth to stifle it.

"It's my psych goose, Freud—" I begin.

Tiffany pulls me inside and closes the door. "Emma, we're not supposed to have animals in here. It's against the rules."

"He's not an animal. He's poultry," I say.

Matt snorts.

"Anyway, I have no choice," I go on. "If I hadn't taken him today, they were going to kill him. But don't worry. I'm going home tomorrow and I'm taking him with me. If we get busted before then, I'll say I kept him here against your wishes. Okay?"

Tiff rolls her eyes, but doesn't argue. She's used to my weirdness by now. Plus, she can hardly complain if I have a guest in our room for one night when she and Matt have it to themselves for a love-fest nearly every weekend. In fact, it's her idea to put the cage in the closet with her afghan over it, which makes Freud fall asleep and stay asleep till morning.

When I wake up, I realize I should feed him. But what do geese eat? All I know is that when Mom took Jules and me to feed the ducks along the canal when we were little, we fed them breadcrumbs. So I go down to the cafeteria and get some nasty white bread, which I ball up into bite-size pieces. Then I fill his water dish, put the afghan over the cage again, and head for class, hoping he'll go undetected until it's time for me to leave. My plan is to be waiting for Mom in the dorm lobby, the cage out of sight, so I can explain about Freud before she actually sees him.

But a half-hour earlier than I expect her, I hear a knock on my door. When I open it, both she and Dad are standing there. They might be college students themselves, dressed the way they are, in Levi's and jeans jackets. Dad's got on a Harley baseball cap. Mom's blond hair is short and spiky, and she's wearing a tie-dye T-shirt with a big peace sign on it.

Their expressions are *quite* parental, however.

Okay, the room smells a little ripe. Freud isn't house-trained. And he gives one of his nasty squawks when he sees them, then hisses.

"Emma," Mom says. That's all. But it's a tone of voice I know from my childhood.

I try to explain. "It's my psych goose. They're going to kill all the other geese we used in the experiment. My God, they give them some lethal injection, like prisoners on death row! Then they incinerate them."

"Who?" Dad says. "What the hell are you talking about?"

"My psych professor," I say. "He told us they were going to kill the geese. The others could be dead right this second, for all I know."

Mom sits down on Tiffany's desk chair, as far away from Freud as she can get.

"I'm not planning on *keeping* him," I say. "Do you think I'm totally out of my mind?"

Silence.

"I have a perfectly logical plan. I'm going to take him to live down on the canal. We're giving him a ride, that's all."

"Emma, it smells terrible," Mom says.

Dad says, "Look. The goddamn thing is shitting even as we speak. We're going to put it in the car with us?"

"An hour," I say. "And we can crack the windows, okay? What do you want me to do, take him back over to the lab and let him be murdered?"

He opens his mouth to say yes, then closes it. He shakes his head, picks up my duffel bag, and starts down the hallway. Mom picks up the laundry basket full of dirty clothes, and follows him. I hoist my pack on my shoulder, pick up Freud's cage, and join the parade.

"Behave," I mutter. "I got your ass off death row."

"Awwwk," he says, and waggles his snaky red tongue.

It's a quiet ride home. When we finally get there, I go inside only long enough to dump my stuff in my room; then I walk down the street toward the canal, carrying Freud in his cage. There's an old hollowed-out tree I have in mind, a place near where Mom used to take Jules and me to feed the ducks when we were little. We stayed clear of it then, because the geese that lived in it squawked and pecked at anyone who came too close.

I approach cautiously, opening the door of Freud's cage and setting it down at a distance from the tree, which turns out to be a good idea because the two geese standing near the hollowed-out tree aren't about to cut Freud any slack for being one of their own species. They stand perfectly still and stare at him menacingly with their ugly little red eyes. He stares back—then in a sudden move that scares the crap out of me, flies out of the cage toward them, squawking and hissing.

I pick up the cage, back away. "You guys work it out," I say. I get halfway down the block, extremely grateful for having brought this absurd episode of my life to a close, and then glance back to see that Freud is waddling after me. I try again. And again. Each time, he follows me home, squawking like a wronged child.

If Josh was with me, we'd think this was hilarious—that is, the Josh I used to know. We'd think up some wild scenario about liberating the goose, like when we convinced his little cousin, who he babysat for sometimes, that her goldfish Mary Anne was only sick, not dead, and if we brought it to the canal and let it go its mom would find it and make it better. I can still see the three of us walking up the street, Josh carrying the fishbowl with the dead fish floating on the surface of the water. "Tell her goodbye, nice knowing you," he said to Allison, when we got to the bridge.

Alone, all I can think to do is put Freud back in the cage, drive him a mile or so up the canal path, and abandon him there instead. At home, I retire to my room pleading exhaustion, and collapse on my bed. Through the window, I can see the swing Dad made and hung from the maple tree before I was born. I can see the playhouse Mom bought for Jules and me when she got her first teaching job. She put up blue-and-white-checked wallpaper inside, made calico curtains for the windows, and bought us two little wicker chairs. We never played house in it, though. We used it for secret projects and reading, or we gave plays, using the little front porch as a stage. Sometimes we played Nancy Drew in it, solving neighborhood mysteries. Jules, of course, was always Nancy Drew. I was Beth, George, Ned Nickerson, Hannah Gruen—or a criminal, whichever Jules decided. Later, when Jules abandoned me for high school, I made the playhouse into Wonder Woman's lair. I'd sit out there for hours at a time, all alone, wearing the red patent leather go-go boots Mom had found at a garage sale and a pair of Dad's old yellow terry cloth wristbands, my lasso at the ready, patiently waiting for the forces of evil to appear so that I could lay them flat.

Now it seems to me that I have no hope of controlling *anything*. A dangerous, counterproductive thought, which I allow to spiral into a big fat pity party of one, until Mom looks in to ask if I want to go out to dinner with them.

"No, thanks," I say. "I'll just have a frozen pizza or something. I've got a paper on *The Canterbury Tales* due Wednesday, and I don't even have a first draft."

She looks skeptical, but doesn't press me.

As soon as I hear the door close behind them, I go back to Mom's studio and just stand there in the dark, breathing in the sharp scents of paint and turpentine, mixed with the scent of dried roses wafting up from the glass bowl of potpourri that sits on a table—and also some indefinable scent, which is us, our house, our belongings. It's my favorite place in our house. A long, narrow room, its inner brick wall was once the house's outer perimeter, its two entries once windows onto the backyard. It was added on when I was two, as a family room; but I have only the vaguest memories of the time before Mom made it her own. It's perfect as a painter's studio: nearly all windows, most with a northern exposure. In one corner, there's a desk always piled high with school work, and above it a big bulletin board covered with drawings, postcards, buttons, quotes—mostly things that her high school art students have given her over the years. In the other corner, there's a couch and an easy chair; a cozy space for sketching, reading, or dreaming.

I don't even turn on a light, just sink into the couch and close my eyes, wishing I could stay here in this place where everything is so familiar. Not go back to school, not go anyplace.

No.

What I *really* want is to be my six-year-old self, coloring quietly in this corner while Mom works. To show her my picture when we're both through, to have her total attention while I tell her the story of what it's about and feel the warmth of her delight in what I made.

Or to be fourteen again, bursting into the studio after raiding the kitchen with Josh, both of us flopping onto the couch where I sit now, making Mom laugh with some story about what happened at school or at cross-country practice.

"Imagine yourself on a modern pilgrimage," is the topic of the paper I actually do have to write. "To what sacred place would you travel?" the assignment sheet asks. "Why? With whom? What might you experience along the way? What relic might you bring back? How might the experience change you?"

It would be dorky and way too revealing to write about a pilgrimage to my own childhood, though it's the pilgrimage I'd most like to make—Mom, Dad, and Jules traveling with me. We'd stop at the places and moments we loved, all the sad, confused layers of myself peeling away like onion skin until my own small, true self was revealed. That's what I would carry back with me, if I could: the person I was before I even knew Josh Morgan. I'd let her tell me what I should do about—everything.

Instead, I think up something clever about myself as a New-Age Wife of Bath. It's boring, though. My eyes keep closing. Then suddenly it's morning. Somehow I've ended up in my own bed, and there's Dad standing in the doorway of my room, glowering.

"Emma," he says. "That goddamn goose is back. It was in the driveway when I went out to get the paper a few minutes ago. You'd better get up and do something about it."

Two

Believe me, I try. But no matter where I take Freud along the canal path, he finds his way back to our yard. He's still there when I leave to go back to school on Sunday afternoon. Monday, Mom calls the Humane Society, the zoo, two petting farms, and a liberal grade school that promotes hands-on experiences with pets. No dice. Then one of the neighborhood dogs goes after him and she has to put him in the garage.

Dad's garage, I should say. His haven. A place where thousands of dollars of tools are fanned out in the drawers of shiny red mechanics' toolboxes, where the shelves are lined three-deep in STP, where there's a CD player and cable TV. Where Dad's Harley sits at the ready, waxed and gleaming, and a bulletin board displays snapshots of every car he's owned since he was sixteen. He is not pleased when he gets home and finds Freud there.

"The dog was about to kill him," Mom says.

"So what?" Dad shrugs. "Natural selection."

I hear this and more from Mom when I make the mistake of calling home on Thursday. Then on Sunday around noon, while studying, I glance up and there she is standing in my doorway.

Shit. She's bringing Freud back and I'm going to have to figure out what to do with him—that's my first thought. Then, I swear, my heart stops. Mom wouldn't just *appear* like this, no matter how mad she is about the goose. Something awful must have happened, too awful to tell me on the telephone. But then she says, "Emma, your dad's waiting in the car. Come on. Hurry! We have something wonderful to tell you."

So I grab my jacket and follow her, trying to decide whether to be relieved that no one's dead or annoyed at Mom for being so mysterious. Not to mention the two of them showing up, uninvited, when I'd decided to gut out the weekend alone.

But I have to laugh when I see Dad jamming to the Rolling Stones in the car, the stereo up full blast. He turns it down—slightly—when I get in. "Anything you've been wanting lately? Your mom and I were just wondering."

"Sure," I say. "New skis, a Jeep, a puppy. A body transplant, a boyfriend. Like you drove all the way down here to find out about that."

He grins. "Actually, we did. The skis, the Jeep—no problem."

"Uh-huh, yeah. Why is that?"

"Because we're millionaires," he says. "Or we will be first thing tomorrow."

"I'm so sure," I say. "Come on, really. What are you doing here?"

Mom turns around, and you'd think from the look on her face that the angel Gabriel had just appeared before her. "Emma," she says, "*Emma*. Oh my *God*. We won LOTTO CASH! The big jackpot: fifty million dollars."

We're heading for the airport in Indianapolis to pick up Jules before I can stop screaming and calm down enough for Mom to say, "We don't actually get fifty million dollars, Emma. There's taxes. Then you choose a lump sum, or ... " But Dad interrupts her to tell me the story.

"Friday morning," Dad says. "I'm walking over to my office from the parking garage with a guy I know, bitching about the goose, and we stop at the newsstand in the lobby so he can buy a *New York Times*. With the change, he gets a couple of LOTTO CASH tickets. 'Big jackpot this week,' he says to me. 'You ought to get a few. Or are you figuring on the goose to stop shitting and lay the golden egg?' And I think, what the hell. G-O-L-D-E-N. Six letters. So I number the letters of the alphabet, match them up, and buy a ticket."

"So he goes out to get the paper this morning," Mom interrupts. "And suddenly he starts yelling and I think, if he says *one more* word to me about that damn goose..."

"I told you," Dad says, " I take back everything I said about the goose. I love that fucking goose. He's my man!"

Mom laughs hysterically.

"Hel-*lo*," I say. "And then?"

"Oh. Well, he was yelling because we *won,*" Mom says. "He wanted me to bring him the LOTTO CASH ticket to be absolutely sure. I'm like, *what* LOTTO CASH ticket? So he gives me the paper and says, 'Stay right there,' and gets the ticket—so I can read the numbers out loud. So he can compare them. You should've seen him, Emma. Honest to God, Mr. Hard-Nosed Lawyer. I thought he was going to have a heart attack."

"Hey," Dad says.

"You were totally freaked out."

"I was not freaked out. I was happy."

"Ha," Mom says. "Look at you right now."

"What?"

She glances pointedly at the buttoned pocket on his denim shirt, which he touches about every two seconds, then throws up her hands as if in surrender. "Oh. It's *not* the LOTTO CASH ticket you keep checking on, it's a compulsive patriotic gesture—" She places her hand over her own heart and starts saying the Pledge of Allegiance.

"It's a hell of a lot of money," Dad says.

Rather testily, it seems to me.

To avoid further discussion of this matter, I ask, "What about Freud? Are you building him a little dream house? Giving him his own credit card?"

"He's gone!" Mom says. "Emma, it's the weirdest thing. I let him out of the garage yesterday morning and he walked straight down the driveway, turned left, and headed for the canal. Like he'd stayed for the sole purpose of driving your dad crazy enough to buy that LOTTO CASH ticket, and now—" She waves her hand to finish the thought.

"I have to admit that I was ready to kill you for bringing that goose home," she goes on. "But now it's clear to me that you did it because you are a kind and good person. An exemplary person! Our winning LOTTO CASH is clearly a reward from the cosmos for having raised you so well."

I just smile—a serene, cosmic smile. Wait till Jules finds out, I think. Not only are we fabulously rich, but I'm one-up on her big time. Maybe for life.

Not that I don't love my sister. I do. It's just that she does everything right. She was valedictorian of her high school class, graduated *magna cum laude* from college, and now she's living in New York trying to make it in musical theater. She'll probably succeed at that, too. She's a great dancer—and she's beautiful: tiny, with curly blond hair and blue eyes. Okay, she's also nice. And really quite amusing.

When she gets off the plane later that afternoon, I ask, "How was your flight?"

"Horrible," she says. "Turbulence. Jesus! It was like being on the Beast at King's Island. For two hours. No lie! And all I could think was, oh *perfect*, the plane crashes when I'm on my way home because Dad won fifty million dollars, and I'll never get to spend a single cent."

When we get to the car, where Mom and Dad are waiting, her first words are "Well, when do we shop?"

But it's nearly five o'clock—and Sunday, so the mall will be closing at six. There's nothing to do but spend the next sixteen hours in a state of agitation, waiting to be rich. Dad disappears into his garage to commune with his automotive equipment. Mom calls in sick on the substitute hotline, then goes to her studio to make lesson plans to drop off at school early the next morning.

Jules and I watch *Singin' in the Rain*, the old videotape of it she's had since she was a freshman in high school. She takes it everywhere with her. Instant Valium, she calls it. She swears it's impossible to watch that movie and stay anxious about *anything*.

It's a nice fantasy: people singing and dancing their way to romance. Mainly, though, I like the way it always makes Jules so happy. Now, like always, she jumps up and does the rain dance with Gene Kelly, tipping an imaginary umbrella, belting out the words to the song.

When it's over, she collapses on the couch, grinning. "Suppose I could get Dad to give me the money to remake this movie?" she asks. "Starring *me*?"

We get giddy, trying to one-up each other casting the male lead. Matthew Broderick, Brad Pitt. George Clooney, why not? She hits the rewind button and we watch Gene Kelly dance backwards to the beginning of the movie.

"It's just so weird to think we *could* remake a movie if we felt like it," she says.

"Or buy a Lear Jet. Or a Rembrandt."

"Who's buying a Rembrandt?" Mom asks, carrying in two greasy pizza boxes and setting them on the coffee table.

"We're just fantasizing," I say.

She smiles. "Remember how you guys used to play 'Rich' when you were little? I'd save up all the magazines and catalogues and you'd cut out pictures of everything you wanted, making up stories."

"Mine would always be clothes and makeup," Jules says. "Hotels and swimming pools. Pink convertibles and diamond bracelets." She wrinkles her nose. "Ugh. Do you think I was overly influenced by Barbie? Like, permanently damaged?"

"Clearly terminal," I say.

Jules raises an eyebrow. "Well, *you* had a death wish," she says. "As far as I could tell, everything you wanted was likely to kill you. Motorcycles, skis, speed boats."

"Dogs," I say. "I always put a trusty dog in my adventures. And, Mom, remember the time we cut up the art catalogues and made our own museum?"

"I *do*," she says. "I believe we had a Monet—that Japanese bridge with wisteria; Matisse's red room. And the Chagall with the man and woman lifting off in a kiss." She shook her head, bemused. "We were so greedy with that imaginary money, weren't we? But right now just the prospect of new sable brushes and all the cobalt blue my heart desires seems like absolute heaven to me—which pretty much shows I'm nowhere near getting my head around the concept of *really* being rich."

"Just do your best, Mom," I say. "That's all anyone ever expects of you."

She bonks me on the head with a stack of paper plates. Then she goes to the back door and yells for Dad, who comes in looking more, rather than less, agitated than he did earlier.

"I keep thinking about that little trailer we lived in when we first got married," he says to her. "How we'd keep the furnace on low to save money and every fucking night the back door would fly open and it would snow right on our bed."

Said trailer was where they'd ended up because Mom got pregnant with Jules while they were still in college. There is this rather hilarious—but exceedingly long—story about the considerable trauma surrounding their wedding.

I look at Jules, who rolls her eyes. She sees it, too: Mom and Dad looking moony, the way they always do when they talk about that time. They're on the brink of launching into telling the whole story right from the start: how Mom was sitting at a table in the Commons the first day she arrived on campus (the very campus where I'm now a miserable freshman) and Dad walked through the revolving door, took one look at her and, bam, fell in love.

One of us has to break the spell or we'll be here all night, the two of them reminiscing, when what we need to do is think about the future. So I say in my firmest voice, "*Dad.* You should be thinking about Corvettes."

He grins. "As a matter of fact, I am—1962, 327, 4-speed. Red and white, with a red leather interior. Might take a while to find one in mint condition. Meanwhile, maybe I'll pick up a new one. Can't have too many Corvettes."

"So true," I say. "Too much of a good thing is—*not.*"

That night, waiting to be rich, we are giddy, dreaming.

Dad will have his Corvettes; Mom, her sable brushes and cobalt blue; Jules, tickets—really good ones—to every single Broadway show she wants to see. I'll ski every ski resort in the world. Chase snow, like surfers chase surf. Maybe I'll start in that cool place in Switzerland where they filmed the James Bond movie—the one with Roger Moore, where he seduces the teenaged ice skater and gets hounded by Nordic biathletes. I'll practice my French in St. Moritz, where all the movie stars go. Get some of those really expensive sunglasses and people will probably think I'm—*someone.*

I can't sleep that night, running it all through my mind. I feel half-sick with anticipation, like I used to feel on Christmas Eve when I was a kid. At three o'clock, I creep out to the kitchen to scavenge some leftover pizza, and there are Mom, Dad, and Jules sitting at the table, drinking coffee, looking as bug-eyed as I feel.

"Yo!" says Dad.

Mom smiles, weakly.

Jules sighs. She's wearing these idiotic flannel pajamas that have little pink poodles with wings and haloes all over them. Her hair is sticking up every which way; there are dark circles beneath her eyes—which only make them look bigger. God. Even when she looks bad, she looks adorable.

I strike a pose, play a little air guitar, and sing a few bars of "Gimme Some Money." My favorite song from *This Is Spinal Tap*.

Nobody laughs.

"Elvis used to hire out a whole bowling alley or a movie theater when he couldn't sleep," I say. "He'd call up the Memphis Mafia and get them all out of bed and make them come over and bowl with him. Or whatever."

Nothing.

"Once, in the middle of the night, he jetted from Memphis to Denver in his private plane because he got hungry for a certain kind of peanut butter."

"Thank you so much for sharing," Jules says. Then she gives me that look. The one that says, "Please shut up now."

So I do. I get my piece of pizza and pop the tab on a Diet Coke, which sounds like a little explosion. I slump into the empty chair: mine. Crazy, how we go to our regular places at the table no matter what. We'd all probably go right to them if a crazed killer broke in and waved us into the kitchen with a loaded gun.

I do not share this observation with my family. Clearly, they are in no mood for conversation, no matter how witty and observant. You'd think this would annoy me. Instead, this weird, almost scary happiness floods all through me. Not because we're about to be rich. Because here we are, all of us together around the kitchen table, the way we used to be.

Three

We're waiting at the door of the lottery office when a man comes to unlock it, at exactly eight o'clock. He doesn't say a word, just waves us in. I suppose we're not the first dazed people he's ever seen at opening time on a Monday morning.

Dad unbuttons his shirt pocket, takes the ticket out. "I believe this is a winner," he says.

The man, Bob-Something, smiles then, and leads us to a room with ugly plastic chairs and a television blaring

Good Morning America. He takes the ticket from Dad, saying we can wait here till it's verified.

"Oh, God," Mom whispers the second he's gone. "Counterfeit lottery tickets. I never even thought about that."

"There's nothing wrong with the ticket," Dad says.

"Yeah, well, what if that Bob guy doesn't even work here?" I say, just to mix things up a little. "What if he's heading out the back door right now, even as we speak?"

"Ha, ha," Jules says.

Mom, Dad, and Jules sit across from us, their hands in their laps, mute as crash test dummies. Above them are photos of LOTTO CASH winners. There's a young, earnest couple, a little boy with a terrible bowl haircut standing between them. A church lady, dressed in a flowered dress with a Peter Pan collar, her hair swept up and sprayed into a silver pompadour. One big fat guy, in bib overalls, looks like he just fed the pigs and drove in straight from the farm.

What are they all doing right now, I wonder?

"Mr. Hammond?"

Bob gestures us into his office, where he confirms that the ticket is valid and explains the options. Dad can take the whole amount paid out annually over twenty years, or a lump sum of twenty-five million dollars now—minus thirty percent in taxes in either case.

"Lump sum," Dad says. "Bring it on!"

"You got it," Bob replies.

He leaves the office and returns in about five minutes with a huge cardboard replica of a check. "Mac Hammond" is written after "Pay to," and on the next line, "Fifty Million Dollars." There's a PR guy, Clark, who takes a picture of Bob handing Dad the actual check for $17,500,000 with me, Mom, and Jules holding the big fake check in the background. Then he interviews Dad with a video camera rolling, probably for the TV news.

"Any plans, sir?" he asks. "Will you be quitting your job?"

"Are you kidding?" Dad says. "Anybody who wins fifty million dollars and keeps working has got to be crazy!"

Everyone laughs, except Mom, who still looks stunned.

We go from the lottery office to the bank, where Dad has a cashier's check cut for a million dollars to give to his father. He arranges for ten new hundred-dollar bills to be delivered to the woman at the newsstand who sold him the ticket, and, on his banker's advice, puts the rest of the money in a money market fund until he figures out what he wants to do with it. Then he calls his secretary at the law firm from his cell phone.

"Janet?" he says. "Yeah, it's me. Listen, I'm not coming in today. I'm calling in rich." He grins at us. "Nope," he said. "Not sick. Rich. R-I-C-H. I'm rich. That's why I won't be there." He tells her about winning LOTTO CASH.

"I've got her on the clock," he says, hanging up. "Janet's better than instant messaging. Two seconds from now every single person at Reynolds, Nash, Archer, and Boyd is going to want to be my best friend." He smiles like a Cheshire cat. "Okay, let's go tell Dutch the news."

"Oh boy," Mom says. "Get ready."

I know exactly what she means. Gramps is—well, *himself.*

Nothing like you'd think an old guy would be. He wears his silver hair a little long, over his collar. He wears jeans and cowboy boots everywhere he goes. He loves to dance, loves to ski.

He has a Harley, too—but not like Dad's sleek black Sturgis. His is a big touring bike, turquoise, with white saddlebags decorated with silver and fringe. It's so loud you can hear the engine two blocks away, and, when I was little, I'd listen for him coming and run out to wait in the yard, jumping up and down with excitement until he roared up. When he climbed off the bike, knelt down in the grass, and put his arms around me, he smelled like leather and sunshine.

He lives across town, in the little box of a house Dad grew up in. He didn't change it a bit after Grandma died, though the curtains and slipcovers are faded now and her antiques are dusty in the places Gramps' cleaning tool of choice, a feather duster, doesn't reach. He spends most of his time in the garage, anyway—a wreck of a place, with tools strewn everywhere and old file cabinets full of stuff he's never gotten around to throwing away.

That's where he is when we pull up, coffee mug in hand, contemplating a greasy engine part on his workbench. His face lights up at the sight of us.

"What's up?" he says—yells, really. He has the loudest voice of anyone I know. He's hard of hearing, and I guess he thinks everyone else is, too.

Dad gets out and gives him a bear hug. "Got something for you, buddy."

"What's that?"

Dad grins and hands him the check.

Gramps looks at it, puzzled. "What the—?"

"It's yours," Dad says. "No shit. I won LOTTO CASH."

"My ass," Gramps says. "Is this some kind of joke? What the hell's going on here?"

"No joke, Gramps. " I say. "They came and dragged me away from school yesterday when they found out. Jules came all the way from New York. We cashed in the ticket this morning and came straight here from the bank."

Gramps looks at Mom, who never plays jokes on anyone.

"Well, goddamn," he says when she nods yes. "Goddamn. How much?"

"Fifty million bucks," Dad says. "So start getting your bike in shape. As soon as the good weather comes, we're heading west. And you can go ahead and squander my inheritance, okay? Dad? Dutch?"

"Goddamn. *Goddamn*!" Gramps says, over and over. "I always said you were smart," he finally says. "I always told your mom you'd be a rich man some day." As proud as if Dad's winning LOTTO CASH is a personal accomplishment.

The mall is next on our agenda. Right off, Mom stops to admire a beautiful little Persian rug displayed in a store window, then marches in and buys it for her studio without a second thought. At the Gap, she hands me outfit after outfit. "Here, try this. Try that," she says, not even looking at the price tags. At Ann Taylor, Jules finds a black miniskirt she loves, but can't decide on a sweater to go with it. She lays out three: more than a hundred dollars each. Dad says, "Get 'em all."

Victoria's Secret, the Body Shop, Banana Republic. I feel like a housewife who's won one of those shopping contests—the kind where you get to run up and down the aisles of a supermarket throwing as many T-bone steaks and frozen turkeys and cans of jalapeño dip into your cart as you can until a buzzer tells you to stop. Only it's clothes and bubble bath and CDs we're picking out. And there's no buzzer; we just have to quit in time to get Jules to the airport for her flight back to New York.

"Okay, I want you to start looking for a decent apartment," Dad says when we drop her off. "Preferably one without rodents." He hands her a fistful of hundred dollar bills. "And here, see a show. Eat. Whatever."

"Dad," she says, then gives him a quick, fierce hug.

We watch her head down the concourse, pulling the new suitcase she bought for all her new stuff. An hour and a half later, I'm heading back to school in a fabulous yellow Jeep Wrangler, stereo blaring, the credit card Dad gave me in my new Coach wallet, still trying to comprehend that from now on, I can have everything I want. Do whatever I want to do. All fall I've been telling myself: college is a ticket to real life. Suck it up. And I have. But I don't need a ticket to real life anymore. I'm rich! I have a lifetime pass.

I feel this huge weight lift from me. I can get the hell out of this place, I think. Never see fucking Josh Morgan *again*. I could drive right past the IU/Bloomington exit right now—take the first road west and stay on it until I hit the

Rockies, where I'm always happy. Up in the mountains, skiing, I feel lean and quick and pure. I could rent a little cabin near Steamboat Springs, be just like that girl in my favorite poster, riding my horse through knee-deep snow, carrying my skis balanced on one shoulder. Boys might even be different in a place like that. They might like a girl who can beat them racing, someone who can take care of herself and won't nag them about stupid shit all the time.

Then a nagging voice inside my head reminds me that *I* didn't win LOTTO CASH. The money belongs to my parents. *And if you start something, finish it,* the voice adds for good measure.

Get a grip, I tell myself. Money or no money, I can't just quit in the middle of the semester. Mom and Dad are never going to let me get away with that. Plus, it's an idiotic idea to run away to Colorado just so I won't have to see Josh. Like that would make me forget him. So I exit with a sigh, drive to my dorm, and drag myself up three flights of stairs, carrying the two shopping bags full of all the stuff I bought at the mall.

Four

I'm so tired by the time I get to the top of the steps that I feel like lying down right there and taking a nap. The only thing that keeps me going is the smell of pizza, which seems to be coming from my room.

I can hear Jules' voice in my head, the sisterly warning she gave me before I left for school in August about not gaining the "freshman fifteen." Well, I've gained that and more. I've been living on junk food. Plus, I haven't run or gone to the gym since summer. Getting back in shape is definitely something to put on the list of goals for my new life—whenever I manage to get one. And, being rich, I can hire a hot, buff personal trainer and pay him whatever it takes to kick my butt, keep me on task. Meanwhile, why should I starve myself?

"Emma!" Tiffany screams when I open the door. "My God, are you all right? I've been absolutely worried to death about you. I heard your mom came yesterday and you left in a rush, and I said to Matt, oh no, did something awful happen? Didn't I, Matt? Wasn't I worried to death?"

"We were kind of worried," Matt says. "Is everything okay?"

I start laughing hysterically.

"Emma?" Tiffany says.

"I'm sorry, I'm sorry," I say. "I didn't even think about calling you. But—well, let's just say things are *definitely* okay. In fact, you guys aren't going to believe what happened."

"What?" Tiffany thrusts the pizza box toward me. "Here. Want some?"

I take a piece, take a huge bite. I get a Coke out of our little refrigerator.

"*Emma*!" Tiffany says. She and Matt are staring at me, waiting for me to speak. "Where were you? What happened?"

"Okay. Are you ready for this? My dad won LOTTO CASH. Fifty. Million. Dollars. No shit! That's why they came to get me. So I could go with them when they cashed in the ticket this morning."

"Oh, my *God*," Tiffany says.

Matt says, "Emma, are you serious?"

"Totally," I say. "I know. I thought it was a joke when they told me. But it wasn't! He won—and because of *me*! Well, because of Freud. You know, my psychology goose."

"That hideous goose from your psych class?" Tiffany scrunches up her face, like she's actually smelling Freud's rank *odeur*.

"Yep. The goose you guys may remember you made fun of me for rescuing."

"Emma, exactly how does a goose win LOTTO CASH?" Matt asks.

I explain the G-O-L-D-E-N thing, which leaves him looking only slightly less skeptical. "Anyhow," I babble on, "my sister flew in from New York yesterday so we could go shopping. Then my dad bought me this Jeep." I go to the window and pull the curtain back. "Look, you can see it in the parking lot. Way back there, under the streetlight."

"That is so *cool*," Tiffany says. "Oh, and it's yellow! I love that."

"You guys can borrow it any time you want," I say grandly. "A mobile love nest."

Tiffany turns beet red. Matt laughs and shakes his head. He still doesn't quite know what to do when I say something outrageous, though he's getting better at not treating me like a girl. I didn't make a big deal about it when we first met and he treated me like he treats Tiffany—gentlemanly, but careful and a little condescending. I just let him see that I didn't *need* for him to open doors for me or not swear in my presence and, after a while, he started treating me like a regular person, at least most of the time.

Of course, as Jules is always pointing out to me, making boys treat you like a regular person doesn't do much for your love life. Like I haven't figured this out myself. I mean, look at what happened with Josh. And boys here are hardly breaking down my door. The only shred of possibility for a date I've had all semester was Tiffany's idea to get Matt to fix me up with one of his fraternity brothers, which completely terrorized me. All I could think of was Josh finding out and giving the guy some friendly advice. Like, get out of it if you possibly can.

"Sure, uh-huh," I said about the first ten times she offered. "Supposing Matt tried to talk some guy into taking me out on a blind date, what would he say to describe me? She's large and blond? She's got a really *fun* personality? I ask you, is that not the kiss of death?"

Tiffany said, "You are not large, Emma. You're tall. And you're very pretty. If you just paid a little attention to yourself, you'd look great."

After a while, I took to saying things like, Dang! I promised Brangelina I'd babysit this weekend. Or, I'd love to, but I absolutely cannot break another date with Johnny Depp.

"Oh, Emma," she'd say. And she'd go back to doing her nails, or whatever.

You've got to love Tiffany, though. It occurs to me now, scarfing down the last of the pizza, that as determined as she's been to help me get a social life, she'd never in a million years even think to say, "Gosh, Emma, I know you can get some dates now that you're rich."

God. It occurs to me that I probably *could* get some dates because of it. There's a depressing thought! Supposing some guy ever does ask me out: how will I know it's really me he's interested in, and not the money? Suddenly, I feel electrified. *What if finding out about the money gave Josh second thoughts about me?*

"Emma?" Tiffany says. "Are you okay?"

"Yeah, yeah," I say. But I'm not, because I'm thinking about Josh Morgan *again*, tumbling backwards to meeting when we were on the cross-country team together freshman year in high school, what a kick Josh got out of the fact that I decided to run the same distance as the boys in practice. We bonded instantly, ran together on weekends and off-season, hung out at his house or mine, talking, watching movies. We raced go-carts together, rode miles and miles on our bikes. For three whole years, I counseled him through romances with cute, bitchy girls. I understood when he cancelled something we'd planned to do to be with them, listened when they broke his heart.

"You're the best, Emma," he'd say. "All girls should be like you."

I knew what he meant. More importantly, what he *didn't* mean. Girls should be fun and easy to talk to, but also small and cute, with bodies to die for. Still, I couldn't help falling in love with him. I couldn't help being hopeful that one day he'd wake up and see that he loved me, too.

Hadn't Mom always said real love was no more than a

charged friendship? And hadn't she always said that both real love *and* real friendship depend on people trusting each other enough to share how they feel?

That's what got me in trouble. I really believed that.

His parents were getting a divorce, and they'd sent him away to work as a camp counselor the summer before our senior year. Maybe it was missing him so much that made me tell him the truth about how I felt when he came back, maybe it was thinking that, loving him, I could somehow make up for what was happening in his family. I didn't even know I was going to say it. I just did. Then I burst into tears.

I swear. I feel like I'm going to cry right now, just remembering it. The moment floods into me. Josh just sitting there, dumbfounded, staring at me for the longest time. Then bumbling around, telling me what a swell person I was, just not *that* kind of person, at least not for him, not now anyway—and finally bolting from the car and practically running up the sidewalk to his house. He spent the next week avoiding me. I said I was sorry; I tried to talk to him. I said, really, it was okay if he didn't feel the same way. He was my best friend and that was the most important thing in the world to me. That was when he started being mean.

No way I'm going *there*. Not now. I look at Tiff, leaning back against Matt on the narrow bunk. He turns on her little TV with the remote, channel surfs. She looks sleepy. What would it be like, I wonder: that kind of comfort with a boy, the feel of your body against his? On the other hand, they act like an old married couple already. I don't want *that.*

What do I want, though—aside from being fifteen and best friends with Josh Morgan again? Life as a no-max credit card: yeah, it's a fabulous thing. But what I *really* want is a way out of the life I'm in. I want to care about something and someone enough to give my whole self to it, to see it through. I want not to be lonely.

None of which has a thing to do with money.

Except—and I feel a sucker-punch of dread—being rich, I no longer have any excuse for maintaining the status quo. We're millionaires, but so what? I'm still my old, clueless self. And now I'm going to have to *do* something about it.

Five

An elementary education major, Tiffany believes that the door of our dorm room offers an excellent opportunity to develop her bulletin board decorating skills. She keeps a stash of construction paper in her desk, also stencils, stickers, various seasonal decorations, and a world-class selection of markers. So I'm not too surprised when I get back from class the next afternoon and see a huge sign stuck on our door:

CONGRATULATION$ EMMA!

The cutout letters are green, of course. There are visual aids, too. Magazine pictures—a mink coat, diamond jewelry, a Ferrari, a chateau in the Alps. All this draped with toilet paper printed to look like money. Where in the hell did Tiffany find *that*?

I hear voices inside, giggling, and I know a celebration awaits me. I imagine myself like one of those cartoon characters who's just placed a bomb, tiptoeing away in an exaggerated fashion, then bursting outside, running—somewhere, anywhere—as fast as my legs can carry me. As a matter of fact, I'm truly considering escape, but Tiffany has bat's radar. She flings open the door and drags me inside.

"Surprise!" everyone yells.

Then they all start talking at once.

"Oh my God, you are so lucky!"

"Fifty million dollars!"

"That is so cool!

"What are you going to *do*?"

Get the hell out of here is not what they want to hear, so I avoid the question altogether. I don't even attempt to explain that we didn't actually get the whole fifty million, which I'd tried to explain to Tiffany and vowed never to try to explain to anyone else. Like seventeen million dollars is so different from fifty, *really*? Like whoever I might try to explain it to is going to say, "Oh, *seventeen* million dollars. That's no big deal at all." I just dig into the feast of junk food they've assembled.

Taco chips with salsa, Cheez-Its, double-fudge brownies. This I can speak about with honest enthusiasm.

I chow down, listening to the girls talk about what they'd do if *they* suddenly became millionaires. Clothes, cars, swimming pools, fabulous houses. One of them says she would drop everything and go straight to Cancun.

"That's what my parents are doing," I say. "Well, St. Maarten. Same difference. Sun. Beach. Total self-indulgence. They leave Saturday morning; they'll be there till the day before Thanksgiving. They're probably packing even as we speak."

"And you're not going with them?" the girl asks.

"Duh. *School*," I say.

She laughs. "Like you really have to worry about that anymore."

"Yeah," I say. "That's the great thing about money, you know? If you have enough of it there's nothing in the whole wide world you have to worry about."

"No kidding." She sighs with envy.

Well, I think. So much for college being a place fraught with irony.

By the end of the week, I'm in a bad funk. Thanks to the combination of Tiff's big mouth, plus the CONGRATULATION$ EMMA! on our door, everyone in our dorm and half the people on campus know what happened to me. "Hey, you're the millionaire!" perfect strangers say in the lounge or dining hall. Or bathroom, for that matter. Or walking through Ballantine Hall.

Worse, people start hitting me up for money. Not for

themselves, nobody's quite as crass as that, but for a thousand and one good causes. Welfare mothers, migrant workers, innocent men on death row need my help. There are Afghan women trapped in burkhas, starving children in Darfur. Great white whales are nearly extinct; rain forests are dying.

People I've never met—and some I have—accost me on my way to class, petition me by phone or e-mail, stuff flyers in my mailbox, slide them underneath my door. Some are polite, even apologetic; some try to lay a guilt trip on me; some are rude, some pathetic. Once, in a study carrel at the library, I'm startled by a pale, earnest girl who thrusts a photograph of baby seals being clubbed before me and bursts into tears. Not the worst strategy, since I write a check for fifty dollars, just to make her go away.

After another whole week of this kind of crap, it gets so that every time I approach our room and see CONGRATULATION$ EMMA on our door, I feel sick at heart. The Friday before Thanksgiving break, I snap. I walk right past our room, on through the hall, down the stairs, and drive to the mall, where I buy the tackiest door-sized Thanksgiving turkey decoration I can find. I could buy two CDs for what I pay for it. But then I could buy two CDs *and* the door decoration if I felt like it. Or twelve CDs and the decoration. Or twelve CDs and the decoration and a yacht.

In any case, stealthily, guilt-ridden, I dismantle Tiffany's tribute and install the turkey in its place. I stack the green letters and the magazine pictures neatly, fold the money toilet paper, and put it all on her desk. Who knows what incarnation we'll see them in next?

I should study. Instead, I put Alanis Morissette on the stereo and throw myself on the bed in a funk that deepens considerably when Tiffany bursts into the room like a character from *It's a Wonderful Life*.

"It's fabulous," she says. "It's so perfect! Our door. Oh, Emma, I was so stressed out walking back from my history test. It was a total bitch, and I'm dreading the final. It made me so *happy* when I saw the turkey on our door! In no time, my mom and I will be baking pumpkin pies together. Matt and I will do nothing but hang out every day. Seeing that silly turkey just put everything right in its place!"

She plunks down on the bed beside me, hugs me despite my fetal position. "Emma, I mean it, you're the best. And guess what!" she rattles on. "This friend of Matt's, Gabe Parker—well, his fraternity brother really. Anyway. He's a journalism major and when Matt told him about you guys winning the lottery, he said it would make a cool story for the *Daily Student*. So he's going to call you." She leers at me. "He's very cute," she says. "Very. Very. Cute. He's going home this weekend, but he'll call you Monday, he said. So you can talk before Thanksgiving break." She segues in her mind-boggling fashion to some tidbit of dorm gossip, and I do my usual "mm-hmm, mm-hmm," all the while having a complete and total anxiety attack.

He knows Josh, I think. How could he not know him? They live in the same house together. Shit. For all I know, the two of them are talking about me right this minute.

Josh: You're interviewing Emma Hammond?

Gabe: I'm doing a story on her for the *IDS*. You know, about her family winning all that money. Do you know her?

Josh: (Shrug.) I went to high school with her.

Gabe: Yeah? What's she like?

Josh: Guffaw.

"He'll *like* you," Tiffany says. "Gabe. Why wouldn't he like you? He told Matt he really wants to meet you."

"He wants to meet the *story*," I say. "Not me."

Which makes me feel pissed off at him. Totally irrational, since we've never even met. Nonetheless, I get so worked up over the whole thing that I act like a spoiled brat when he calls on Monday. "I really don't see why you want to interview me," I say. "*I* didn't win anything."

"Come on," he says cheerfully. "Matt told me about the psychology goose. That's definitely a story people on campus would want to hear. So can we meet? Go get coffee?"

I don't want to be in the *Indiana Daily Student*, I hate coffee, I'm unfit for civilized company. But Tiff will be crushed if I don't go. And, okay. While I'm over the idea of love at first sight, part of me wants the illusion of having a coffee date with a fraternity guy. "Yeah, okay, I guess," I say, against my better judgment.

Tiff is positively beatific when she hears we're having coffee on Wednesday afternoon. "I just knew it would work out," she says. "My God. What should you *wear*?"

Before I can argue that it doesn't really matter what I wear—it's an interview for the *IDS,* for God's sake, it's not like he asked me to the prom—she opens my closet and stands there, tapping one foot, staring at my clothes with a pensive expression. Even with the addition of my LOTTO CASH purchases, there aren't many options. Jeans and cargo pants, shirts and sweaters. There's the one skirt my mom made me bring, black wool, its Nordstrom tags still attached. Tiff plucks it from the rod.

"You can wear this with black tights," she says. "And your black Doc Martens. That'll be cool." She rummages some more and finds a stretchy gray and black striped rib-knit top I bought last summer in a hopeful mode.

"I'm not wearing that," I say. "It makes me look fat."

"Emma, you're not fat. Here, try it on and you'll see."

Actually, it doesn't look as bad as I thought it would. It's just that I'm used to baggy clothes, and this sweater makes me feel—exposed. The skirt looks decent, too. And the clunky Docs have a slimming effect on my legs, which makes me hate them less than usual.

But I just shrug when Tiff says, "See? I told you."

She gives me a crash course in makeup, or tries to. But I stab myself with the mascara wand three times and make such a mess of the eye shadow that she says she'd better do my makeup herself for the actual date.

"It's not a date," I remind her.

"What*ever*," she says. Oblivious.

Six

"I feel like Barbie," I say, when Tiffany's dressing me on the actual day I'm going to meet Gabe Parker for coffee. "All I need is a pair of those teensy weensy spike heels."

"Ha," Tiff says. "You would kill yourself on *any* spike heels. Even *I* am not that hopeful about your feminine potential."

"Hey!" I say.

Tiff raises an eyebrow. "Focus, Emma," she says.

The "date," as she persists in calling it, is still three hours away. But we both have class in an hour, so she's getting me ready now. It won't hurt for me to go to class dressed up for a change, she says. And who knows who might notice me walking through campus and think, who's that girl?

She straightens my skirt, polishes a scuff on my Docs with a Kleenex, then steps away from me, head tilted, lips pursed, assessing. Then she comes back at me with a dab of eye shadow, spritzes an errant curl. Moments later we set out together, Tiff chattering as we go. When we get to the place where we'll split to go our separate ways, we stop and she puts her hand on my arm. "You look beautiful, Emma. You really do. Just be yourself, okay? It'll be fine. And e-mail me about how it goes, okay? Matt and I are leaving for home right after my class, so I'll be gone when you get back."

I salute, which makes her laugh and roll her eyes.

"Have a great Thanksgiving!" I call out as she walks away.

I head toward Ballantine, like I'm heading for my class, but as soon as I know Tiff can't see me I turn and take a path through the trees back to the dorm. I can't wear all this makeup. It feels like a mask on my face. I wash it off, and there I am again, in the mirror. But now my hair doesn't look right. I don't mean it doesn't look good—Tiff made me wear it down and did something amazing with a round brush to make it curl at my shoulders. I mean it looks, well, like I took too much trouble with it. Like this so-called date is a big deal to me. So I pull it back in a ponytail, the way I usually wear it.

By the time I leave for the Daily Grind, I've talked myself out of the skirt and sweater, too. They're folded up at the bottom of my laundry bag, replaced by jeans and a baggy sweater. My only hope now is that Tiffany was wrong about how cute this Gabe guy is. Maybe he looks like Matt, who *she* obviously thinks is cute, but in my opinion is kind of bland. Not that it matters, I remind myself. This is not a date. It's a stupid college newspaper interview.

Unfortunately, however, Tiff was dead-on about him. Gabe Parker has dark curly hair and chocolate brown eyes. That olive skin that makes you look tan, even in the winter. He's sturdy, like my dad. He's wearing a gray Phi Delt sweatshirt—that's how I know him.

"Gabe?" I say, to be sure.

"Yep." He smiles. "Emma?"

I nod, then stand there like a dork until he gestures toward the chair across from him.

"Oh," I say, and sit down so fast I bounce.

I have this weird feeling in my stomach. I feel lightheaded. Plus, it's like someone just turned up the treadmill of my heart. Is this how Dad felt the first time he saw Mom, I wonder—then immediately think, *shit, shit, shit, do not even go there*. And try to concentrate on my surroundings.

The Daily Grind is a dark, battered kind of place, nothing like the cheery Starbucks up the street. The barista looks like a vampire, the clientele looks seriously underfed. What little light there is filters in through the posters and notices taped to the grimy windows. I've only been here once before. Early this fall, I went to a reading with a gloomy, poetic girl from my dorm. I thought maybe I'd meet someone who liked to talk about books, maybe even get inspired to write down some of the stuff floating around in my head. But it was incredibly tiresome: a bunch of intense, humorless people wearing black, sitting around smoking and drinking espresso. Then this anorexic grad student read a bunch of really bad poems about the six months she spent in a mental institution.

I'm having a total flashback, and before I know it I'm telling Gabe Parker all about it. "One of those brain-scan poets," I say. "You know. Thank you for sharing your derivative anger and the shock therapy you had as a result of it. Jesus. When she was finished, the conversation naturally turned to Kafka. Doesn't it always? *The Metamorphosis.* I mean, what's to say? It's about a fucking cockroach."

Gabe laughs. "Matt told me you were funny."

That stops me cold. What else did Matt say about me, I wonder? Or, worse, Josh Morgan. Not to mention the fact that I've just been making fun of the place Gabe chose. He probably comes here all the time, I think. He was probably at that poetry reading and loved it. Jeez. He probably writes poetry.

Which, unfortunately, when added to his fraternity creds, only makes him seem more attractive.

"So," he says. "You want a cup of coffee?"

"Latte," I say. Because I know it's the kind with the most milk in it. I take out my wallet to give him some money, but he raises his hand to stop me.

"Expense account," he says.

An obvious lie. But his tone of voice tells me there's no point arguing. So I just sit there, breathing in the smell of coffee, listening to the hiss of the espresso machine, trying to calm myself down while he's at the counter ordering. Okay, I fantasize a little, too—about how people glancing in the window might see him bringing me a cup of latte and assume he's my boyfriend.

Gabe sets the latte down in front of me and I dump a couple of sugars in it, then raise the cup to my lips, hoping not to grimace with the first sip. My mom never liked coffee till the first time she went to Europe, I remember. Maybe travel would turn me on to it, too—and help my image. Espresso at a coffeehouse in Vienna. Café au lait in a Paris café. Preferably with a large chocolate mousse. I make a mental note to add the Grand Tour to my impending plans for self-improvement.

Okay. Pay attention, Emma, I tell myself. Be here now. I look at Gabe, sitting across from me, an inquisitive expression on his face. He has regular coffee, black. A jumbo cup of it.

"I'm kind of a coffee junkie," he says, gulping some down. "I smoke, too."

Is he apologizing? Making a joke? Asking if I care if he smokes now? Clearly, I have the social skills of a newt. All I can think to do is push the ashtray toward him.

"Thanks," he says, and lights up—then pushes the pack toward me.

I wave it away with a spastic gesture that mirrors exactly my state of mind.

He grins. "My plan is to quit when I'm old. You know. Thirty."

Which makes me laugh, in spite of my discomposure.

"Okay." He flips open his notebook, trades the cigarette for a pencil. "What slant should we take here? *Poultry Rescue Brings Cosmic Result*?"

I can't help it. I groan. "You realize," I say, "that no matter how you write what happened, I'm going to sound like a crazy person."

"It's a great story," he says. "You'll sound funny, that's all."

"No, I'll sound like a crazy person. But I said you could do the story. So, okay—" I shrug. "What do you want to know?"

He's quiet a moment, then sets his pencil down. He takes a drag from his cigarette, and I can't quit looking at the bluntness of his fingers on it, the dark hairs curling around his wrist. "Emma, we don't have to do the story if you're going to be embarrassed by it," he says. "Really. It's not that big a deal to me. We can just sit here and drink coffee. Talk about something else." He grins *again*. "Kafka—?"

"No way," I say. "The last thing I need is someone overhearing me say I think Kafka is hilarious. Major collegiate faux pas."

He laughs. "Okay then, we'll do the traditional thing. What's your major?"

"English," I say. "I'm a totally self-indulgent person, with no serious life goal other than to figure out how to spend as much time as possible immersed in novels—which, looking on the bright side, isn't quite the serious character deficiency it was before I got fabulously wealthy. That's off the record, by the way. My bad character."

"You don't seem so bad to me," he says.

I feel my face flush, realizing he probably thought I was fishing for a compliment. I rush into telling him the funny story he's come to hear. It seems better, easier, than attempting a real conversation.

"It must be weird," he says when I'm through. "It would make a great reality show, you know? Give people a huge chunk of change like that and—"

"What?" I ask. "Watch them all self-destruct?"

He looks mortified. "I didn't mean that," he said. "Just that it must be ... *interesting* when something like that happens all of a sudden. Is it? Has anything changed because of it? Or maybe that's too personal a question—"

I shrug. "Nothing's changed. Not *really*. Nothing that matters, anyway. It's weird, mainly. I mean, it's so *much*. If I try to imagine the actual money, I see those bank robbery movies. You know, guys opening suitcases stacked full of it. Like green bricks.

"And it's awful how everyone knows about it. You wouldn't believe how many people have hit me up for every kind of cause. Save the Whales. Save the—whatever. God, sometimes I get the feeling it's all anyone is thinking about when they're with me. I don't mean you," I add quickly, blushing again.

Gabe waits for me to go on. He's closed his notebook,

stubbed out his cigarette, and is leaning toward me as if we're having that real conversation I decided to avoid. The thing is, I really want to tell him how freaked out I am about the money. About *everything*. I believe what he said about not caring about the story. But I'm scared of him, scared of how he's making me feel.

So I shrug again. "I don't know. Probably it's too soon to tell what being rich is *really* going to be like. But, hey? Don't you want to know what I'm going to *do* with all that money? That's the question most people ask."

"Sure," he says. "What?"

"Beats me," I say. "I don't have a clue."

I meant to be funny, but my voice came out all wrong. Worse, I know that if I say one more word I'm going to start crying.

"Are you okay?" Gabe asks. "Emma?"

I nod. I drink down the last of my latte. Look at the pack of cigarettes on the table and consider taking up smoking. Anything to keep from having to try to talk to him anymore.

He talks at me for a while. He probably wouldn't know what to do with all that money either, he says. He's really not that into *stuff*. It would be cool to take off for Nepal, hang around in Katmandu a while, climb to the base camp of Everest. Or maybe hitchhike through Europe.

He shrugs. "But wherever you go, you're still you, right? Eventually, you have to come home to your real life."

Fine for you, I want to say. But what if "you" is *me*? What then?

But I can't say that, and we fall into an anxious silence.

Finally, Gabe glances at his watch. "Well. It's after five," he says. "I guess we should go?"

Who can blame him, I think. I wouldn't want to deal with me either. I stand and take a deep breath, hoping my voice won't go south on me again. "It was nice meeting you," I say.

"Hey, hold it." He grabs his jacket. "I'll walk with you."

It's better once we get outside. I don't have to look at him. We amble up Kirkwood in what passes for a companionable silence. He smokes. After a while he says, "I can see how it would be annoying. People making such a big deal about the money."

"It's not that," I say. "It makes me feel stupid, that's all. Like, because I have it, I'm supposed to know what to do." I glance at him. "Don't put *that* in the story."

"I told you before, Emma. I don't have to write a story."

"Ha!" I say, attempting humor. "And you want to be an ace reporter? I hate to tell you, but there's no Pulitzer Prize for being nice."

He stops suddenly, puts his hand on my arm. "Listen, I'm sorry," he says. "I think I've said something that upset you."

He *is* sorry. He's nice, too. I'm the one being a pain in the ass. But I'm not up to trying to redeem myself. Just then, a bus rumbles up and stops beside us. The doors sigh open. I look at Gabe. He's about to apologize again. Or worse, try to help me.

"It's not your fault," I say. "Really."

I step into the bus; the doors close. I have no idea where it's going.

It's hot inside, the windows steamy. It's almost empty, but I go all the way to the back and slump into a corner seat, where I try not to think about Gabe Parker. Or worse, what he might say about me if he sees Josh when he gets back to the fraternity house.

"Is she, like, a little—"

"Whacked?" Josh might say. "Listen, whatever you do, just don't let her get a crush on you. Believe me, you'll be sorry."

Two small comforts:

1) Maybe being attracted (*major* understatement) to Gabe Parker means I'm finally over being in love with Josh—or could be, if...but there's no way, no possible way Gabe Parker is attracted to me too. So forget that.
2) This one's more reliable. If Josh and Gabe actually do have a conversation about me, Josh will stick with what a loser I am. He'd never in a million years tell Gabe the truth about what happened between us, especially what a shit he was after I told him how I really felt about him—the rude remarks he made whenever I passed him in the hall, or the way he made fun of me every time I raised my hand to answer a question in class. How, at our high school parties, he'd get blotto and hit on some freshman girl right in front me, how he quit the cross-country

team, which made everyone, including the coach, freeze me out until *I* quit a week later—then how he joined back up the very next day.

Just thinking about all this brings back my own incredible stupidity in a flood. How dumb it was to convince myself that telling him that I loved him was the only honest thing to do, that I *had* to do it, because we'd always been honest with each other. How dumb to believe that we could just go on the way we'd been before, best friends, if he didn't feel the same way.

Even so, I still can't believe he turned on me the way he did.

There *were* extenuating circumstances, I remind myself for the millionth time: his parents were in the midst of an ugly divorce, his whole world was falling apart—then I pulled the rug out from under him and he lost me, his best friend. Psychologically, it makes sense—though it still doesn't make me feel any less miserable or ashamed. It doesn't keep me from remembering the absolute worst thing that happened, either. I see myself in the locker bay, just like it was yesterday, screwing around, shadow-boxing with Ryan Farber.

As usual, I got a little carried away, whacked him harder than I meant to, and he put up his hands and stepped back, laughing. "Help me, man," he said to Josh, who I was mortified to realize was standing nearby. "She's killing me."

Suddenly, everyone was staring at the two of us. Josh was looking at me like, you dipshit. I felt like I was about ten times my size, like one of those balloon figures in a parade. I'd act like it was a big joke, I decided. So I laughed. I punched him lightly on the arm and said, "Ha! You can't take me either."

And Josh decked me. No lie: he hauled back and punched me right in the face. Next thing I knew, I was on the floor. My nose was gushing blood. Everyone was freaking out all around me.

Except Josh. He was just standing there with this look on his face, like he couldn't believe what had just happened. Then he turned and walked away.

Lisa Chochrun scooped me up and helped me to the nurse's office. Ms. Riley made me lie down with a wet cloth over my face, while she dragged out of Lisa what had happened and then called the principal's office. Pretty soon I heard on the intercom, "Josh Morgan, come to Mr. Bergen's office immediately. Josh Morgan, to Mr. Bergen's office."

Josh was in deep shit, needless to say. He would've gotten expelled, but the second my nose stopped bleeding and Ms. Riley released me, I ran upstairs, burst into Mr. Bergen's office, and begged him not to make a big deal about it because it was at least partly my own fault. He held firm, till I started sobbing. But he made Josh apologize.

"I'm sorry I hit you, Emma," Josh said. He didn't look one bit sorry, though. He looked mad as hell. Especially when Mr. Bergen launched into a lecture about how it just wasn't acceptable to react to girls in a physical way.

As miserable as I was, I could see the irony in that. If the thought of reacting to me "in a physical way" hadn't totally repulsed Josh, we wouldn't have had this problem in the first place. The sad thing was, I knew him so well, I knew he saw the irony, too.

Before, when we were friends, we'd have listened to this crap, then laughed our heads off later. But I knew that would never happen again. At best, we'd be polite to one another. And I missed him so much that moment, I thought I would die.

Like I miss him right now—and always will. Ha! So much for the idea of being smitten with Gabe Parker solving that. I feel like crying to think that I will never, *ever* get over Josh, and maybe I actually make some pathetic sound, because a guy sitting a few rows in front of me turns and gives me a weird look.

"It's good to remember how much loving Josh hurt," I tell myself sternly. *Hurts*. Not to mention the disastrous consequences. So don't even *think* about Gabe Parker. He's way out of your league, just like Josh is.

The bus makes a loop around campus. I ride past my dorm twice, then once more to be absolutely sure that Tiffany will be well on her way home with Matt. It's dark now, and the first snow of the year has begun to fall, fat, lazy flakes that drift down, settling on the shoulders and heavy backpacks of students who trudge along, returning from their last classes before Thanksgiving break. The big houses along Fraternity Row look hazy and picturesque, like an advertisement for college life.

I'm glad to be going home for Thanksgiving break myself, though I wish we were having Thanksgiving at our ski house in Michigan, like we usually do. It sort of pisses me off that Mom and Dad planned their trip to St. Maarten so they'd get back late last night and wouldn't feel like making the long drive. But the truth is, when I think of going, it's not me *now* that I imagine. It's the little-kid me, standing at the dining room window, waiting for Dad to come home so we can leave.

Weird, how vividly I remember what it was like then. Standing so close to the window that my breath made little wet circles on the frosty glass, my jacket already on, my red backpack, stuffed with books and games, at my feet. My teddy bear, Lori, peeking out the top of it, the red and green scarf I knitted for her tied jauntily around her neck. There were secret treats in the backpack, too, Milk Duds that Mom didn't know about. Later, when Dad turned the stereo up loud, I'd crawl under the blankets in the back of the Subaru, open the box as quietly as I could, and let the little caramel candies melt in my mouth, one by one.

You big baby, I tell myself, blinking back tears. The next time the bus goes by my dorm, I get off and step into the snow. I cross the street and go in the side entrance, avoiding the dorm's lobby where I might run into girls from my floor. I take the stairs instead of the elevator, peer through the door that opens onto the hallway to make sure the coast is clear, and sprint for my room, retrieving my backpack and duffel full of dirty laundry before heading home.

Seven

When I get home, Mom and Jules are vegged out, watching a movie on TV. "The Corvette got here this morning," Mom says, rolling her eyes. "Your dad's been out in the garage all day, communing with it.

"You go out there," Jules says. "He's already dragged us out a million times, making us look at every little thing."

It's a great car: 1962, 327 engine, 4-speed. Cherry red. Mint condition, with its original red leather seats buffed to perfection. The car of his dreams. He spent practically the whole week after he won the money tracking it down on the Internet, and had it transported from some obscure town in Utah so it would be here when he got back from St. Maarten.

When I open the garage door, he's bent over, rubbing some invisible spot with a chamois cloth. Gramps is on a bar stool, attending. But when he sees me, he sets the can of beer he's been drinking on Dad's workbench to engulf me in a hug that leaves me breathless. Dad throws his arm around my shoulder and gives me a squeeze.

"What do you think?" he asks, gesturing toward the Corvette, as proud as if he were introducing a new, third child in the family.

"Nice ride," I say. "Have you had it out yet?"

"Oh, man," he says. "It goes." Then he launches into a long, mind-numbing recitation of all its glories, Gramps occasionally interrupting to put his two cents in.

When I've marveled over everything, from the Ram's horn manifold and reverse-flow muffler to the original hubcaps, not to mention the Corvette shift knob Dad bought at a junk yard when he was sixteen *just in case* he ever got it together to buy the car to go with it, I ask Gramps if he's on the lookout for one too.

"Nah," he says. "Too damn small. I've got something else in mind."

"Yeah? What?"

He produces a Winnebago brochure from his back pocket and hands it to me. "Take a look at this."

"You're buying an RV?"

"Thinking seriously about it," he says. "I got a buddy down in Florida, and I'm thinking I might head down there after the first of the year. Hook up in his yard for a few weeks. Then maybe head west in March. You know, see the Grand Canyon. The whole shebang." He nods at the brochure. "What do you think?"

"'An unprecedented level of excitement, sophistication and style,'" I read aloud. "That's you all the way. Plus, it comes with 'elegant brocade bedspread with coordinating pillow shams.' You should definitely go for it."

"Yeah, yeah," Gramps says good-naturedly. "Which one, though?"

"Chieftain!" I say. "What else?"

He beams. "Think so? I've been kind of leaning that way."

"Absolutely," I say.

"I'm with you," Dad says. "I told him, just don't start wearing Hush Puppies and Sansabelts, like the other old farts who drive around in those things."

"Fat chance of that," Gramps says. "Hell, I'm way too old to change. I figure I'll be wearing these cowboy boots and blue jeans when I get to the pearly gates. Saint Peter's got a problem with that? Shoot! I'll go the other way." He's quiet for a moment, then says rather wistfully, "Boy, your mom would've had a ball with all this dough."

"Tupperware stock would definitely be on the rise," Dad says.

Gramps snorts.

"So, what else are you in the market for?" I ask him.

"Maybe a little Mustang convertible," he says. "Tow it behind the RV. Pick up gals."

"You wish," Dad says.

Gramps laughs. "I bought Margaret a new car. Hers went on the blink. Old Buick. Ernie bought it right before he died—ten, maybe twelve years ago now. She was always having trouble with the damn thing. Big gas guzzler, too."

"Margaret *let* you buy her a car?" I ask.

He grins. "I just bought it and parked it in her driveway with the keys in it. Nice little red Camry. Sun roof. Zippy engine."

Gramps' next-door neighbor Margaret is a sharp, no-nonsense lady, always perfectly turned out in slacks and matching sweaters, her stiff white hair sitting on her head like a helmet. I can just see her standing in the driveway, her hands on her hips, steaming about some interloper parking in her driveway.

"She didn't call the police when she saw a strange car there?"

Gramps grins wider. "She was about to when I went over and came clean. You know Margaret. She tried to argue with me. She's says, 'For heavens sake, Dutch. You can't buy me a car. It's not right.' I said, 'Yeah, well, I just did. I've got more goddamn money than I know what to do with, and if I want to buy you a car there's not a thing in hell you can do about it.'"

"So how many chocolate cakes has she brought you since then?"

"A few," Gramps says.

It makes me happy to think of fussy Margaret tooling around in a zippy little car, and even happier to be hanging out in Dad's garage just like old times. And later, to be gathered around the kitchen table, eating carry-out Chinese, everybody talking a mile a minute.

Mom and Dad look great, tanned. Dad's wearing a LIFE'S A BEACH T-shirt. Mom shows us some postcard-size watercolors she made while she was there.

"They sunbathed *au naturel,*" Jules says. "Is that a trip or what?"

"No way," I say. "Mom, did you? Really?"

She looks a little sheepish. "There's not much of a walking beach there, so we went over to Orient Beach, thinking we could walk there. We didn't even know part of it was a nude beach."

Gramps looks startled. "Nude?"

"In the buff," Jules says. "It's a French island, you know."

We all crack up at the expression on Gramps' face.

"It's not what you'd think," Mom says. "I mean, it *was* strange: this whole long beach, with lounge chairs and umbrellas. Bars and restaurants. And everybody stark naked. But it wasn't a bunch of perfect bodies. There were a few of those, of course—girls wearing nothing but gold chains around their waists, hunky gay guys playing badminton. Mostly, though, they were people our age and older—every kind of body you can imagine. It was wonderful. The feel of the sun and breeze on the whole surface of your skin."

She sighs, glances at the bare maple tree framed by the

kitchen window with a bemused expression, as if she's not quite sure how she got back to this entirely mundane place. "It's so *beautiful* there," she goes on. "The resort where we stayed was in this little scoop of harbor dotted with sailboats, with these sort of friendly green mountains rising up on either side. Turquoise water, all these pretty pastel houses. Honestly, it's paradise."

"You could move there if you wanted to," Jules says. "Live *au naturel.* Did you ever think of that?"

"Live there!" Mom looks alarmed. "Good God, I don't even want to think about anything as drastic as that. Just suddenly *having* all this money is plenty weird for me right now. I still can't make any sense of it."

Dad leans over and puts his arm around her shoulder. "You don't have to make sense of it. Remember? You just have to enjoy it."

"Right," she says. She doesn't look convinced, though, and segues into a long description of the island women in African dress, their beautiful black hair clicking with bright beads, who set up small tents on the beach where they stand braiding the hair of tourists, their fingers flying. They'd call back and forth to one another, and to the tourists walking past. When they talked they sounded like they were singing.

"'Lady, braid your hair?'" Mom says. "'Lady, you want to take a bit of the island home wit you?' It was funny. All these girls on the plane coming home with their African hair."

Jules shudders. "White girls should not even *consider* braids," she says firmly. "Ugh. All you see is their scalp."

"I'll write that down," I say. "In my Book of Rules to Live By."

Jules sets her imperious gaze on me, the one she's used to keep me in my place since the day I was born—and it makes me unaccountably happy.

Thanksgiving dinner the next day makes me happy, too. The usual gargantuan feast, no surprises. We eat till we can hardly move, then Mom gets the bright idea that we should walk the calories off by going down to the canal to feed Freud, so we do—except for Gramps, who heads home to ponder life on the road in the Winnebago he's now decided for sure to buy.

Freud's personality hasn't improved any. He comes waddling at us, squawking.

"Whoa," Dad says, tossing breadcrumbs Mom didn't end up using for the dressing. "We bring gifts."

Freud stops, his neck an arrow pointing at us, hissing.

It's funny, really. Dozens of ducks start hurrying up from the water, quacking, happy to get the bread we throw out to them, but Freud won't touch it. Like he's thinking, jerks! They're millionaires on account of me, and they're bringing me *stale bread*?

When we get back, Mom and Dad sit Jules and me

down and Dad says, "Your mom and I want to talk to you about some arrangements we've made."

"What arrangements?" I ask.

Money, it turns out. Dad goes to his den and returns with two intimidating folders, which, he tells us, hold information that explains everything in detail. "For the time being," he goes on, "all you need to know is, you've got a million dollars each. The money's been invested, though; and—until you're thirty—you can only spend the interest it earns. After taxes, that'll probably average out to be around seventy thousand dollars a year."

Of course, I have to be a smart-ass. "Only seventy thousand a year?" I moan. "God, Jules, how will we ever survive?"

Of course, she starts to cry. "You're already giving me an apartment," she wails. "Now you're giving me money, too? *Dad*, I'm grown up. I'm supposed to be taking care of myself."

"Calm down," he says. "Will you? And listen to me. We're rich, okay? All of us. Your mother and I just expect you to be sensible with what you have, that's all." He looks at me. "Both of you."

He launches into a lecture about how seventy thousand dollars a year might seem like a lot, but it's easier than you'd think to go through that kind of money in no time flat. Then, suddenly, he stops. "Oh, fuck it," he says, grinning. "We're Scrooge McDuck! We've got money out the wazoo! I don't give a damn what you do with it."

"Within reason," Mom says.

"Absolutely! Within reason." Dad grins. Then he goes

to the kitchen and brings back a bottle of champagne, apparently purchased for this moment.

He pops the cork. Jules lifts her glass toward me. "Maybe *we* should go live in St. Maarten," she says.

"Maybe," I say. "A nice little villa could be very groovy—set up like we used to set up the backseat of the car on the way to Michigan: one side yours, one side mine, and *nobody* crosses the line. On the other hand, why stay in one place? I'm thinking, why not take a whole year and follow the sun all over the world? Better yet, follow the snow! Skiing in New Zealand in August. Would that be cool, or what?"

"Hey!" Dad says. "I'd sign up for that!"

Late that night, sleepless, still heady with all the possibilities, I get up and head for the kitchen, thinking I'll make myself a turkey sandwich and top off the perfect day. But I hear Mom's voice coming from the living room and stop in the hall to listen.

"But why *now*?" she says. "I can't help thinking about what it might've been like if we'd gotten the money when we were younger, when Julie and Emma were still at home. We could have given them so much more."

More what, I think? I mean, we weren't rich before we won LOTTO CASH, but I can't remember anything I really, really wanted that I didn't get because we couldn't afford it.

Dad, ever practical, points this out to her now.

"I know that," she says. "It's just—" her voice wobbles. "I always wanted a big, wonderful house for them to grow up in. With window seats in their bedrooms and a screened-in porch for reading away summer afternoons. It's dumb, I know. But sometimes I think of all the things I meant to do better with Julie and Emma and wonder if it would've made a difference raising them in the house I always *imagined* we'd have. If *I'd* have been different. Better."

"Jules and Emma are great kids," Dad says. "I don't see how growing up in a different house could have made them any better. It wouldn't have made life perfect."

"I know that," Mom says. "I know. I just—worry about them, that's all. Julie all by herself in New York. And Emma's been so miserable in Bloomington. Sometimes I want to tell her, 'Just come home.' I can't stand to see her feeling so lost. So not like herself. But she has to—"

This is the trouble with eavesdropping, I think. I can't say, "*What*? I have to do what?"

Still, I know. I have to grow up, is what she means. I have to learn how to have a life away from them.

"She'll be fine," Dad says. "She'll figure out what she wants to do and do it. And making a living isn't a factor anymore, so she can do anything."

"Mac," Mom says. "Can't you see the money makes it *harder*? I mean, it's hard enough just being young. Trying to figure out who you are. But to have no limits! To be able have anything you want, do anything you want?"

"It's a high class problem," Dad says, dryly.

Which would be funny, except Mom suddenly bursts into tears.

"Abby," Dad says, alarmed. "Jesus. *Abby*."

"It's just so *confusing*," she wails. "Ever since we got the money, it's like I can't remember who I am. I don't know what to *do* with it. Or myself."

"Listen," Dad says. "We just have to make a few decisions together in the next few weeks, that's all. Then I'll do the money like I always have. Just think of me as your Yoko Ono, okay? She managed John Lennon's money, why can't I manage yours? What's the big deal here?"

"I hate being stupid about money," Mom says. "I hate it that you just assume I can't—"

"I don't assume you can't understand money. If you decided you *wanted* to understand it, I'm sure you could. But—"

"But I'd rather go back to work on Monday," Mom interrupts. "Like a *crazy* person."

"Whoa!" Dad says.

Instinctively, I take a step backwards. My body wants me to keep going, every muscle is telling me I don't need to hear this. I shouldn't hear it. But I keep listening.

"You lost me, Abby," Dad goes on. "What are we talking about here? What do you mean, you'd rather go back to work like a crazy person?"

"Crazy as in, 'Anybody who wins fifty million dollars and doesn't quit his job is crazy,'" she says. "You said it. The day we won the money, you said it to the guy in the lottery office."

"I didn't mean *you*," Dad says. "Jesus, I was just talking to the guy. Joking. We'd just won fifty million dollars. How the fuck did I know what I was saying?"

"Well, you said it."

"Fine, okay. I said it. What I don't understand is why you're bringing it up now. I just meant—come on, Abby, you know what I meant. I liked practicing law. I was good at it. But it was never anything but a job to me, a way to make a living. Teaching isn't like that for you. It's all hooked up with your painting, all of a piece. All I'm saying is you didn't choose your work based on how much money you would earn doing it."

"*Oh*?" Mom says. "Like *you* had to do to support us?"

"Abby," Dad says. "This is getting to be a really stupid conversation."

It's quiet a long time. I really should retreat now. I shouldn't have stayed as long as I have. But I can't *not* listen. And when Mom finally speaks, her voice low and full of tears, I take a step closer to the living room so I can hear her.

"I just keep thinking about what you said to the guy in the lottery office, and the more I think about it the more I think you were right. I mean, I can do whatever I want, and I'm going back to *school* on Monday morning? It does seem crazy."

Dad wisely doesn't comment on that.

"There must be something I'm supposed to *do* because of the money," she goes on. "Like, maybe, quit teaching and just paint. See how good I could be."

"You should do what you want to do," Dad says. "Whatever that is. The money's not a sign or an omen. It doesn't *mean* anything. It's just—luck. We were lucky. That's all. If the money means anything, it just means we never have to think about money again."

"Mac," Mom says. "Money is *all* we think about now. We'll always have to think about it. It's going to change us, it already has."

Her voice sounds harsh, like a warning, and I don't stick around to hear where the conversation will go from there. I don't want to know. I just slink back to bed and lie there, still sleepless, washed in moonlight, the happiness I'd felt for the last twenty-four hours collapsing all around me.

Eight

I sleep till eleven the next morning, then curl up on the couch in Mom's studio trying to read, but she ranges around, moving this, dusting that, glancing now and then at the unfinished painting set on her easel, as if hoping it might somehow surprise her. Finally, she sinks into the easy chair and stares at me until I look up from my book.

"I've had two epiphanies about the money," she says. "Well, so far."

"Number one?" I ask.

"The cosmos remains the same," she says, grimly. "You can have all the money in the world, and you still have to do things like go to the grocery store. Or at least think about food. You still have to exercise, if you don't want to get fat. That sort of thing."

"Okay," I say. "And number two?"

"All those people who win the lottery and say they're just going to keep on doing what they've always done? If anybody ever bothered to track them down and see what came of it, I'd bet what they'd find out is that people who *have* to work, which is virtually everyone, are never going to forget that *you* don't. Even if they're your friends, they can't help resenting you, at least a little. Honest to God, Emma, every time I walked into the teachers' lounge those few days before your dad and I left for St. Maarten, conversation just *stopped*."

"They were talking about you?"

"Yes," she says. "They were. And I'll tell you something else. I'm pretty sure that what they were talking *about* is how pissed off they are, because I'm making them look bad. Choosing to stay when I don't have to—well, it's as good as saying all the petty rules, all the stupid, asshole things administrators do to make your life miserable don't really matter. The work itself should be enough."

"Well, isn't it?" I ask. "I mean, for you?"

She sniffs, blinking back tears. "I don't think it can be anymore. That's the worst part. Because the work isn't the same. My students were so thrilled by what happened to me, it was all they wanted to talk about. What was I going to *do* with the money, they wanted to know—and expected me to tell them something wonderful and romantic. They wanted it to be like TV."

"The girls in my dorm are like that," I say.

But she's up, pacing, again; I guess she doesn't hear me.

"It's so *boring*," she rattles on. "Thinking about money all the time. And it's not going to change. How could it, when I'd always be taking time off to go...wherever? I'm going to quit," she says, abruptly. "Really, I have no choice. The truth is, I *don't* want to teach every day. I can't. Your dad and I—" She waves her hand vaguely, to indicate... *plans*.

Okay, here's the moment I could tell her that I'm kind of a mess myself. Scared, like she is. Struggling to figure out who I *am*. But Jules comes bouncing in to remind me it's time to take her to the airport. There's an audition Monday morning and she absolutely has to get back to New York so she can work with her vocal coach to prepare for the singing part of it.

"Do you think Mom's acting weird?" I ask in the car. "You know, about the money."

"Mom's always weird," she says.

"Has she shared any of her... epiphanies with you?"

"'The cosmos doesn't change, people do?'" Jules asks.

"Yeah."

"Well, she's right," Jules says. "You know how Mom is like a dog with a bone trying to figure out how to think about certain things. Then she gets them worked out. Like, when I decided I wanted to be a cheerleader and she freaked out until she realized I'd probably hate it and quit. Which I did. Problem solved. She'll figure out how to deal with the money, don't you think?"

"I guess." I consider telling her about my eavesdropping on Mom and Dad the night before, but why worry her? Anyway she's probably right. Mom will freak out, then figure out how to think about it, what to do.

We ride a while in silence, and I wait for Jules to grill me about my social life, like she usually does. To advise me in her big-sister voice to get out more, meet people. To suggest the theater department *again*. Not acting. Certainly not singing or dancing. I could be a stagehand, or a props person, she always says. In Jules' view, the theater is a perfect world in which there's a place for everyone, no matter how geeky or weird. Theater people would embrace me; they embrace everyone. I'd find one friend, then another. But theater doesn't really interest me. Books are what I love, the problem with them being that they're the perfect escape from the real world in which I'm supposed to be finding my place.

But Jules doesn't try to tell me what to do. She just leans back, her eyes closed, breathing in the music on the radio. She gives me a quick hug when we get to the airport.

"Love you. Buck up," she says.

Then she hops out of the Jeep and strides away from me, back into her life—and even while she's still in sight, I'm sucker-punched by how much I miss her.

God. I thought I was over that. It's been ten years since Jules left me behind for high school—a totally normal, reasonable transition, I remind myself. She discovered theater and dance. Who wouldn't rather be in that world than hang out with her little sister? It wasn't her fault I was so dependent on her—or that I screwed up in high school so much I don't have a life now.

I beat myself up mentally about that for a while, high school, worrying every little moment of the Josh fiasco like you'd worry a broken tooth, moving from there right into a litany of fresh embarrassments about college that take me to the coffee "date" with Gabe Parker and the potential for a variety of humiliations in the near future.

I am in no mood to go to the party Lisa Cochrun is having tonight, that's for sure. In fact, just thinking about it makes me feel like I've got a light case of the flu. Josh will be there, I know. Plus all the others in the group I used to hang around with—until I screwed things up with Josh and made everyone so uncomfortable they started avoiding me like the plague.

It's tempting to call with some excuse, or just not show up. But I don't want to hurt Lisa's feelings. She was the only one who stuck by me, even when the things were at their worst with Josh. Over time, she actually managed to create an uneasy peace among us so that, by commencement, we were all at least speaking again—Josh and me included, though barely.

Ever the peacemaker, she babbled on over the phone last week when she called to congratulate me for being rich, filling me in on everyone she'd seen Homecoming weekend. Meredith was in heaven at Purdue, where there were about ten boys for every girl; one semester at Antioch had turned Heather into a hippie. Cara loved Smith. Lauren wished she'd gone farther away than DePauw, because her parents kept coming down to visit her. Sara was in love with a grad student. Ryan Farber actually had a girlfriend.

"We missed you," she said. "I'm having this party the Friday of Thanksgiving weekend. You'll come won't you? Please? Everyone's dying to see you."

Stupidly, I said okay.

What I think now is, Ha! If it's true they're dying to see me it's because they want the scoop on me suddenly being a millionaire. Probably, they're wishing they'd been a lot nicer to me when Josh was being such a jerk last year—this little satisfaction somewhat balances my dread about seeing Josh tonight, and makes me remember what Mom used to say when they were being so awful to me about him: "You'll see, Emma. They'll be punished! They'll grow up and have to spend the rest of their lives being *themselves*!"

But if their terrible suffering has begun, it's not apparent to me.

Stepping into Lisa's rec room is like stepping right back into high school. Barenaked Ladies blasting on the stereo. The girls cloistered on the sofas, gossiping. The boys playing pool.

Josh isn't among them, I notice with relief.

Lisa jumps up from the couch to give me a big hug, and the other girls follow. They actually do seem glad to see me, which makes me feel guilty about hoping they were unhappy. Because the truth is—yeah—they were bitchy and mean when I got sideways with Josh last year, but I was, still *am*, my own worst enemy. Like my favorite English teacher Mrs.

Blue used to say, wryly quoting Mark Twain when someone did something truly idiotic, "'Be yourself is the worst advice you can give to some people.'" Trouble is, I've never been able to figure out how to be anything else.

Even now, I can't resist doing a comedy routine about winning the lottery. I tell about Jules flying in from New York to go shopping at the mall. About Dad calling in rich, Mom's meltdowns and epiphanies, Gramps' intention to hit the road in a new Winnebago.

When I tell about my new Jeep, Ryan Farber says, "Your old man says you can have any car you want and you get a Jeep? Man, you should have hit him up for a Ferrari."

"You would want one of those dick cars," I say.

There's a moment of shocked silence, the kind I've been expert at creating all my life. Then Ryan laughs, gives me a bear hug. "I love you, Emma. No shit, I do."

"Yeah, yeah," I say. "Everybody loves me now I'm rich!"

I try to sound nonchalant, but I'm embarrassed by what I've said. And as if that weren't bad enough, there's Josh standing at the foot of the basement stairs, watching me with a look on his face that makes me wish I could just vaporize myself to a whole other dimension. It's not pity, not quite. But it's close enough to make me avoid talking to him, to get the hell out of there as soon as I can, claiming I have another party to go to.

A bald-faced lie.

I'm home, feigning sleep, by the time Mom and Dad get back from dinner with some friends. And thinking about something else Mrs. Blue once said: Everything's a story. “Your life is one story,” she told us. “You’re the main character in it. But you’re a character, major or minor, in the stories of dozens of other people, too: parents, siblings, relatives, friends, enemies. You may even play some part in the stories of people you don’t know, people who notice you or know of you for some reason.”

It blew my mind at the time. I’d walk past some poor bag lady downtown and try to imagine her imagining me, hours later, while she lay sleepless in some awful shelter. I’d spend whole evenings wondering whether I was a major or minor character in whatever scene my friends and I were living, whether I was a major or minor character in each one of their lives.

I think about a book I read, *Wide Sargasso Sea*, which tells the story of *Jane Eyre* from the point of view of Mr. Rochester’s crazy wife. Weird, the way what happens seems so completely different through someone else’s eyes. It makes me wonder how Josh would tell the story of what happened between us. But I don’t really want to know.

Nine

"Well, how was it?" Tiff asks the second I walk into our dorm room Sunday evening.

"Fine," I say. "You know, the turkey thing—"

"I mean *Gabe*," she says. " You didn't e-mail me about your date like you promised you would. So how *was* it?"

I'm over reminding her it was an interview for the *IDS*, not a date. Tiffany's made up her mind I had a date with Gabe Parker, and there's no point in trying to change it.

I set my duffel on my desk chair and start unpacking my stuff.

"*Emma*!"

"We had coffee together," I say. "I told him about winning. He was very nice." No *way* am I going to tell her the truth about how I felt when I was with him, how the whole time I was home he kept creeping into my mind.

"And cute?" Tiffany leers at me. "*Very* cute? Didn't I tell you?"

"Cute?" I say. "Yeah. I guess. So, how was your break?"

"Good," she says. "Except I ate too much."

"What, you went up to a size 2?"

"Don't try to sidetrack me, Emma," she says. "Did you *like* him?"

"Gabe?" I shrug. "Sure. I liked him. I said he was nice."

"Arrgh." Tiff throws herself backward onto her bunk, but I know she's only temporarily deterred. She'll grill Matt next time she sees him, then go at me again.

Which is exactly what happens. "Matt said Gabe told him he thought you were really cool," she says, the next day.

She's a terrible liar. Gabe Parker might have said I was nice, or funny—just to be polite. Maybe he actually did think I was nice or funny. But cool? Absolutely no way. So why do Tiff's words give me this scary little twist in my heart?

"He *did*," she says. "Really."

I ignore her.

Thank God finals are looming. In the next few weeks, everyone, Tiffany included, is studying nonstop and I'm beginning to think we may make it to Christmas break without any further discussion of my social life—or lack thereof. Then after my very last class, I come back to the dorm and there's Gramps in my room, chatting with Tiffany.

"First road trip!" he says. "Brought the Chieftain down so you could check it out. She rides pretty darn smooth and, man oh man, wait till you see the interior."

"Look," Tiffany says. "You can see it out the window."

I peer out. There it is, a large tan-and-brown-striped vehicle dwarfing the cars in the parking lot. "Wow," I say weakly. "You made the right choice with the Chieftain, Gramps. Definitely."

He beams.

"We've been dying for you to get back," Tiffany says. "Dutch says we can drive it over to the Phi Delt house to show Matt, and then he'll take us all out to dinner."

Characters in books are always blanching when something shocks them, and I'm pretty sure blanching is exactly what I do now at the prospect of a cruise over to the Phi Delt house in the Winnebago, followed by dinner—which I strongly suspect will include Gabe Parker, if Tiffany has anything to do with it. I'm certainly speechless, scrambling to come up with some excuse for why this plan is impossible. But if Tiffany and Gramps are a challenge one at a time, together they're a force of nature. It's fruitless to argue with them. Still, I feel like a zombie following them down the hall and out to the parking lot.

Gramps is wearing jeans and a plaid shirt, with a silver and turquoise bolo tie; his cowboy boots, of course, and his awful Harley jacket—black leather, with fringe on the sleeves and an eagle in flight painted in full color on the back. He has a springy step, just like Dad's. Tiff and I have to hurry to keep up with him.

He hops up the steps of the Winnebago and opens the door. He grins, gesturing us in like a *maître d'*.

"Oh! It's just like a playhouse," Tiffany says, glancing into the living area. She plops down in the white leather passenger seat and swivels it around a few times.

If either she or Gramps notices I'm a reluctant participant in this adventure, neither of them mentions it. Gramps starts up the engine and they chatter away in the front seat like old friends. I strap myself, prone, on one of the leather couches—and suddenly remember touring the Lisa Marie, Elvis' personal airplane, on a family trip to Graceland years ago. He was terrified of flying, the tour guide told us, and there were heavy, gold-plated seat belts that buckled across his bed. We thought it was hilarious at the time, but now I think of Elvis strapped into that bed high in the sky in the dead of night, and I know exactly how he felt.

Of course, Tiffany—Miss Manners—called to let Matt know we're coming. He and Gabe are out in the yard throwing a football, waiting for us, when we pull up. I could *kill* her right now. I swear to God, I'd give back every penny of the lottery money never to see Gabe Parker again, let alone try to act like it's the most normal thing in the world to be buzzing over to the Phi Delt house in a recreational vehicle with my *grandfather*.

Just in case I thought what I felt about him the first time was a fluke: *not*. I practically groan out loud when I see him. Jesus. He's wearing baggy khakis and a black sweater with a white T-shirt showing at the collar, James Dean style. He waves, and I wave back in spite of myself. Then I panic as he and Matt jog toward the Winnebago. What am I going to *say* to him?

Tiff grabs my arm and yanks me out the door and down the metal stairs, letting go only to throw her arms around Matt as if she hasn't seen him for a year.

"Hey, Emma!" Gabe says.

"Hey!" I say back.

Then we freeze: wax models in the Museum of Awkward Social Moments.

Gramps stands in the doorway of the Chieftain, king of the road.

"This is my boyfriend, Matt," Tiff tells him.

Gramps steps down, and the two of them shake hands.

"And this is Gabe Parker." Tiffany beams. "He's doing the story on Emma for the *Indiana Daily Student* I told you about. You know, about winning the money."

"Well, how about that!" Gramps gives him a wink. "After we take a look at the Chieftain, I'll tell you some stories about Emma you can use. She's a crackerjack skier. Probably won a hundred medals, skiing. I'll bet you didn't know that."

"No kidding!" Gabe says.

He smiles at me. That *smile.*

Could it be real? Could he be impressed that I'm a ski racer? Could he actually be glad to *see* me? This thought throws me into such a state of agitation that I cannot say a single word in response. I can't even look at him. He's a nice person, I tell myself. He was nice at the Daily Grind, and he's just being nice now—which only makes me feel worse about being struck dumb in his presence, because on top of everything else I'm afraid he's going to think I'm a stuck-up snob. Let me die right now, I think. Before Gramps decides to tell him how I loved to run around naked in Jules' dress-up wig when I was two.

And then, as if things aren't already as bad as they can get, a bus stops next to where we're parked, and Josh Morgan gets off of it.

"Hey." Dutch turns to me. "There's that boyfriend of yours. What's his name? Jake?"

I definitely blanch this time. No doubt about it. "Not Jake, Josh," I say through clenched teeth. "And he is *not* my boyfriend. He never was my boyfriend. He was just a—*friend*. And he's not even that anymore."

But Gramps is already heading for him, grinning.

"Mr. Hammond?" Josh says.

"You guys *know* each other?" Tiffany asks.

"We went to high school together," I say. "That's all."

Gramps returns, Josh in tow with that deer-in-the-headlights expression.

"Hey, Emma," he says.

"Hey," I say back, repeating what appears to be the only exchange I can manage with a person of the male species.

I feel Tiff's eyes on me, beady with curiosity. I feel Gabe looking at me, too. Until Gramps-the-Oblivious invites all of us to come aboard the Chieftain for a tour. Josh takes a half-step back, then I actually *see* him remember there's no arguing with Gramps once he makes up his mind. I see the resignation settle in, see him gird himself and decide there's really no option but to follow the rest of us up the steps.

Inside, I'm crushed against Gabe in the miniscule space just behind the cab. His solid arm against my shoulder makes me feel faint. Meanwhile, Gramps blathers on about the chassis and wheel base, the rear axle ratio, and how much horsepower the engine has. He pushes a button and a faux cabinet slides back to reveal a TV screen. "Mobile theater unit," he says. "And look here." He pushes another button and the wall behind one of the leather couches moves about a foot outward. "Extender. Isn't that something?"

"Cool," Josh says.

Encouraged, Gramps moves on to show off the ingeniously built cabinets in the galley kitchen and the way the built-in table can be neatly transformed into a single bed. I pray he won't tromp us all back to the bedroom with its "elegant brocade bedspread and matching pillow shams," but of course he does.

He does not—thank you, Jesus!—make some joke about picking up "gals."

"So what's your first big trip?" Josh asks.

Up to Michigan with us at Christmas, Gramps tells him. Then Florida. West, in the spring.

"That sounds *so* fun." Tiffany cuddles up to Matt. "We

should get one of these when we get married. Pile all our kids in and go—anywhere we want."

"Absolutely!" Matt says "Yeah. Sure. We should!" But he looks freaked out at the prospect, though I can't tell if it's the idea of buying an RV that freaks him out, or being married with a bunch of kids to drive around in it.

Meanwhile, Gabe hasn't said a word. In fact, he seems ominously quiet. He can't possibly be jealous of Josh. But maybe he hates his guts, and finding out I used to be friends with him is the third strike in the relationship we'd never have had anyway—the first two being how I look and who I am. More likely, Matt just "forgot" to mention that I'd be coming along with Tiffany and the person with the Winnebago—and now here he is, stuck in said Winnebago with *me*.

I wonder if he's written the *IDS* story and when it will run, but I'm afraid to ask him because I'm living in dread of the moment I'll open up the paper and see it there. Still, I should say *something* to him—if for no other reason than to be polite. But I just stand there, mute as a goldfish. Worse, I can't quit looking at Josh—his floppy blond hair like a skateboarder's, his long, lanky body—and thinking of him stretched out on the sofa in Mom's studio and me curled up in the armchair, talking about ... everything.

Oh, what a surprise: both Josh and Gabe beg off coming to dinner with us. Matt does, too. Finals, they say. A boatload of studying to do. So it's just Gramps, Tiffany, and me at the Pizzeria. The two of them have a bang-up time, laughing and telling stories, but I'm so stressed out by then that all I can do is eat: a whole stromboli, an order of breadsticks, and two pieces of the pepperoni pizza that Gramps and Tiffany are sharing.

"Your grandfather is the cutest thing," Tiff says when he drops us back at the dorm and heads for home. "I swear, if he weren't fifty years older than me, I might've just stayed in that Winnebago and run off with him! Speaking of which—"

"What?" I say.

"Gabe?" she prompts.

"You might run away with Gabe instead?"

"Ha, ha," she says. "You know what I mean, Emma. I *told* you, Gabe told Matt he really liked you after you guys had coffee together. So why didn't you even talk to him?"

"He didn't talk to *me*," I say. "If he's so crazy about me, how do you explain that?"

"He's shy," Tiffany says.

I roll my eyes.

"He is. Really. Why would he have come out if he didn't like you? Didn't you see the way he waved at you? Not to mention how he *ran* over to the RV the second we pulled up."

"He was being polite, that's all."

"Uh-uh," Tiffany says. "I know when boys are being polite. He was glad to see you." She arches an eyebrow. "*Also . . .*"

"Also?" I echo.

"Yes, also. As in, do you think Gabe might have been a *little* taken aback by the fact that Josh Morgan and your *grandfather* seemed to be the best of friends? I mean, *I* was totally flabbergasted myself. So was Matt. Emma, I can't believe you never even mentioned you knew one of his fraternity brothers so well."

"I don't really know him that well," I say. Which is not exactly a lie.

She casts me a skeptical glance, but lets it go—which would be a relief to me if I didn't know *her* so well. It's not that she's not interested in getting to the bottom of me and Josh, she's just not going to get sidetracked trying to figure it out now. Focus is her strong suit. She's made up her mind that Gabe Parker likes me and, once finals and a fabulous all-Matt-all-the-time winter break are behind her, she's going to do whatever she has to do to prove she's right.

Ten

As for my own winter break: I return home to more of Mom's theorizing about the unchanging nature of the cosmos.

I should say, first, that she is not a big fan of Christmas.

1) She's not religious, so it feels phony to her to celebrate what is allegedly a deeply religious holiday.
2) She feels manipulated by the fact that the true

meaning of Christmas in our culture has become buying and accumulating *even more stuff* and there's no real way you can opt out without looking like a jerk.

3) She hates shopping. Period.

So I am not surprised when she shares the observation that Christmas is yet another proof of her theory.

"It comes every year, doesn't it," she says in a fake cheerful voice. "You go out and buy a bunch of stuff nobody wants or needs. Right? It's the American way."

I just look at her. I've dragged myself to the kitchen, poured myself a bowl of Froot Loops. Jesus, I'm barely awake. But I still know exactly where this is going. Please. *Spare me*, I think. She needs moral support on the inevitable trip to the mall, and that moral support is going to be me.

Sure enough, within an hour we're trudging from store to store, me playing yes-man to her gift choices. "Brilliant," I say. "Absolutely." Jules or Dad or whichever friend or relative will *love* it. Eventually, we collapse on an empty bench and people-watch a while. Shoppers hurry by, their arms hung with bags. Teenagers flirt, braces flashing. "White Christmas" plays, then "Home for the Holidays."

Nearby, a young couple not much older than I am struggles with a baby stroller. He's tall and gangly, dressed in black leather and chains. She's got on ripped-up jeans and a jacket with "GRRRL POWER" painted on the back of it. Her hair is dyed platinum, cut short in little spikes. She wears dark red lipstick. When she turns to put the baby in the stroller, I can't help laughing. It's a beautiful little girl, dressed in a pink snowsuit with furry white trim, smiling a two-toothed smile.

"Look!" I whisper to Mom. "You won't believe this!"

"Oh!" she says. Then her eyes fill with tears.

As the couple passes by us, the girl says, "Okay, Damien. Remember, fifteen dollars per person. That's it. Now, what do you think for your mom? Lotion from the Body Shop? Or maybe we could find a nice pair of earrings on sale."

We watch them make their way down the broad hallway; then, abruptly, Mom stands up and strides after them, fumbling in her purse as she goes. I'm so startled that I just sit on the bench and watch her catch up to them. She taps the girl on the shoulder. The girl turns and looks at her, kind of belligerently, like, *What?*

Mom says something I can't hear. Then she takes a handful of bills from her wallet and thrusts them toward the girl. Shocked, the girl takes them. Then she just stands there, watching Mom hurry toward the mall exit like a hit-and-run driver. Then both she and the boy call out at the same time, "Thank you. Ma'am! Hey, thanks a lot!"

But Mom is already halfway to the doors. She doesn't look back.

"I'm sorry," she says when I catch up to her, lugging all our shopping bags. "But I looked at those kids and suddenly remembered how your dad and I saved quarters in a jar for Julie's first bicycle—that little pink bike with its pink-flowered banana seat and high handlebars with pink and white streamers. It just killed me, you know? To think that no present I could ever buy for anyone ever again would matter the way that bike mattered. So why even try—"

"How much did you give them?"

"I don't know." She waves her hand. "A couple of hundred dollar bills. Three, maybe. A fifty, some twenties. The poor girl was so mortified that she didn't know what to do but take it. I was babbling about how they reminded me of myself when I was young and Julie was a baby. It was the *baby* that made me do it," she says in a wobbly voice. "That pink snowsuit and her fuzzy hair, like a halo. I know it was a crazy thing to do."

"It was a little crazy, yeah. But it was nice."

I get her out to the car. She's in no shape to drive, so I take the keys and slide into the driver's seat. I start the engine, hoping for something dopey and cheerful on the Oldies station she always listens to—but, no. The DJ's talking to a woman whose postcard was just pulled out of the hopper in the Christmas Wish Contest. What she wishes for is a La-Z-Boy Recliner. For her husband, she says. Because he works "real hard" and she wants him to be able to come home to his own special place to relax and watch TV in the evenings.

Mom bursts into tears. "It's just so—*depressing*," she says when she's calmed down enough to talk. "You do think it's depressing, don't you, Emma?"

"Yeah, it's pretty depressing," I say.

But when we get home and Mom tries to explain this to Dad, he says, "What's so depressing about a La-Z-Boy Recliner?"

"Being so poor you can't just afford to go buy one if

you want one," Mom says. "Not to mention, that woman actually believes a La-Z-Boy Recliner will make her husband happy."

"Maybe it will make him happy," Dad says. "Hey, you're always talking about things being cosmic. This seems like the perfect example. We get fifty million dollars, this guy gets the La-Z-Boy Recliner of his dreams. You want to talk about depressing. Depressing would be if things had been reversed."

This cracks me up. It's so—Dad. Even Mom smiles, and then she tells him about giving the money to the punk couple—already embellishing it in a way that makes me know it will become one of those stories we always tell: The Time Mom Gave Away Money in the Mall.

It's nice the way Dad listens, grinning. The way he puts his arm around her and gives her a squeeze when she's through, and looks at her with an expression on his face that lets you know what a good person he thinks she is and how much he loves her.

The trouble is, I'm left wondering if she really is okay.

I need to talk to Jules about this, I think. But she steps off the plane on Christmas Eve, bursting with joy, and why would I want to put the damper on that? She's in love, and his name is Will. She met him in September, before we were rich, the night she worked her very first shift as coat-check girl at the Sherry Netherland Hotel.

"And *dog*-check girl," she says, telling us the whole story at dinner. "Right? I've been there maybe an hour when this old couple comes in and sets a cage with a cocker spaniel in it on the counter. Sasha, the girl I was working with, tags it and gives the old guy a token, like checking a dog is the most normal thing in the world. Is that nutty, or what? Anyway, I'm still laughing hysterically when I look up and there's this guy standing there, his jacket over his arm. He—Will—looks at the cage, then he looks at me, smiles—God, he's got the greatest smile, you won't *believe* his smile—and says, 'Fur coat starter kit?' And I'm hooked. I'm totally in love.

"I told myself, don't even go there. He's probably here to meet his girlfriend. But he wasn't. He kept coming out to the lobby—supposedly to see how Pookie was doing. And he stayed till closing time, sitting at a corner table all alone. It totally got to me, you know? Him sitting and waiting all that time, half asleep."

"He could have been a serial killer," I say.

Jules looks beatific. "I know, *I know*. I didn't have the faintest idea who he was. But we went for coffee and it was like we'd known each other forever. We couldn't stop talking. He's part owner of this gym and he told me all about that. And I told him, well, *everything*.

"I can't wait for you guys to meet him," she says. "Tomorrow! He's coming in at noon, I invited him to come up to Michigan."

Mom sets the water pitcher down with a clunk.

I freeze, a forkful of steak halfway to my mouth.

Dad says, "Michigan?" Like it's another planet.

"It's okay, isn't it?" Jules says. "I'd have called, but we

just decided this morning. I mean, I suddenly realized I just couldn't stand to be away from him for a whole week."

"Of course, it's okay," Mom says. "But you've been seeing him since *September*?"

Jules flutters her hands, blushing. "I couldn't tell you when I came home because of the money. *Duh*. And compete with that? Besides, I hadn't known him that long. I wasn't sure. Then I was going to tell you at Thanksgiving. But we were all still so—you know, *distracted*. So I decided to wait till everything settled down and I could have your complete and total attention." She beams around the table at us. "Like now."

"Oh, Julie," Mom says in a small voice.

Even Dad looks a little bit chagrined.

Jules doesn't seem to notice. "I swear, you're going to totally adore him," she babbles on. "He's worried about that—whether you will. You know, like him. But I told him, if I'm in love with you, my family will like you. Not that you wouldn't like him *anyway*. He's so—"

"We like him," I say. "Jules, we like him already, okay?"

Mom puts on the Elvis Christmas album, and we open presents. A gazillion of them. When all the packages under the tree are open, Dad stands up. "Okay, Emma," he says, and the two of us go to the garage and get the dollhouse he bought for Mom. It's a Victorian house, lavender-blue with white gingerbread trimming.

"What in the world?" she says, when we set it before her.

Dad says, "You always wanted a dollhouse."

"Open it," I say. "See? It opens out from the front, like double doors, and the roof lifts up to show the attic."

Mom gets down on her knees and opens it. Inside, it's all white, primed, ready to be decorated. There's nothing in it but a miniature Christmas tree, decorated with tiny red balls and candy canes and gold garlands. A tiny star at the top. And a doll family: a mom, a dad, and two little girls with blond yarn hair.

"I can't believe it," Mom says. "It's exactly like the dollhouse I wanted when I was a little girl."

"I know," Dad says. "I remembered that."

She jumps up and throws her arms around him. "Mac Hammond, you are the best person in the world! I can't believe you would even think of giving me a dollhouse!"

"Will took me to see the Rockettes," Jules says, in this tone of voice that says *I know exactly what you mean.* "And the skaters at Rockefeller Center. Then we went to see the Christmas decorations at Saks. It was like a fairyland, all green pine boughs and white twinkling lights. Last night he gave me this glass ball with New York City inside it. There's even a little yellow cab. When you shake it, it snows."

But Mom's not listening to her. She's down on her hands and knees again, opening the little door, peering through the little windows. Jules doesn't care; she's in her own world anyway. And if the longing I feel, the fear that nobody will ever fall in love with *me* are visible on my face, not a single person in my family mentions it. Or maybe they don't notice.

The next morning, Mom fixes our usual Christmas

breakfast of waffles and sausage and fresh-squeezed orange juice, making enough batter for four extra waffles so we can have our traditional waffle toss. For this event, Mom, Jules, and I stand, shivering, on the freezing cold front porch, still in our pajamas and robes. Dad backs his truck out of the garage and parks it in the street, so we can aim the waffles at the bed. Then he joins us on the porch.

"Okay, let's do it," he says.

His waffle goes beyond the truck, into the middle of the street; Mom's flies out of her hand too soon and lands about two feet away from the porch; I throw mine like a Frisbee and it spins sideways and hits the window of the car parked next door. Jules' sails out in a perfect arc, curving right into the truck bed, which makes her even more insufferably happy than she was last night. In fact, she's so daffy I insist on driving her to the airport to meet Will. I'm afraid she'll wreck the car, left to her own devices. And, okay, I'm dying to see him.

I'm expecting the usual: tall, dark, and handsome, nice clothes, expensive haircut. In fact, I have my eye on a guy I think could be Will when this stocky blond guy in jeans and a Hammer Strength sweatshirt comes through the security gate, sees Jules, and breaks into a dazzling smile. He owns a gym; it makes sense he'd be a jock. I don't know why this surprises me. He puts his arms around her, picks her right up off her feet, and hugs her hard. Then he sets her down and they look at each other for what seems like forever.

"Hel-*lo*," I say finally. "Are you guys auditioning for a part on *The Young and the Oblivious*?"

Will laughs and says, "You must be Emma."

I hold out my hand and we shake. Then I herd the two of them through baggage claim, to the parking garage. "Nice Jeep," Will says, which gets him some points with me. He gets more when he likes our neighborhood, which I drive him through, taking the long way home. It's called the Village—it actually was a village a hundred years ago, before the city grew up to it and absorbed it. It has a nice feel. Lots of little shops and restaurants—and the old Whitewater Canal runs through it, where Freud, the famous lottery goose, resides. Will looks anxious for the first time when I mention Freud, and it occurs to me that he might feel uncomfortable about meeting the suddenly rich parents of his new girlfriend.

"Okay," I say, pulling into our driveway. "The parental units await you."

He gives an endearing little groan.

"No problem," I say. "They love you. We all do. Jules said we had to and we always do what Jules says."

He casts me a grateful glance, then smiles—and Jules is right: it is a smile to die for. "All right, then. I'm ready," he says. "No *way* you'd ever want to mess with Julie."

The way he says it—kidding, but in this sort of besotted tone of voice, like maybe he half-believes it—makes me think, yeah, this is going to be okay.

We head up the front walk, Jules insisting she's without a doubt the most reasonable, easy-to-get-along-with person in America, and Will and I laughing, one-upping each other to remind her how perfect she's not.

"You should see the bathroom," Will says. "Desert Storm."

"Yeah, well, has she dragged you to see that *Joseph and His—*" I wave my hands around. "*Coat,*" I say. "Whatever. I never can remember the whole name of that stupid musical, but I'll tell you what. I'd rather be stabbed in the eyeball than ever go see it again."

Jules grins wickedly and breaks into that hideous "Go, Go, Go Joseph" song from it, which she knows I particularly hate because of the way you absolutely *cannot* get it out of your mind.

"See?" I say to Will. "I'm warning you now. That's the kind of thing she'll do to you."

Just then, Mom appears in the doorway and smiles at the sight of all three of us laughing. I watch her taking Will in, deciding, by whatever it is she sees in him—the way he looks at Jules, maybe, and catches her hand, as if just touching her will bring him courage—that she's going to like him.

"Will," she says, and opens the door wider.

Eleven

We caravan to Michigan later that afternoon—Mom and Dad together, Jules and Will in my Jeep. I ride in the Winnebago, with Gramps. I've forgiven him for the mortifying Bloomington visit, and, now that I'm not paralyzed with anxiety about what he's going to say next, I get a kick out of how he acts like a kid with a new toy. I let him crank up my Lenny Kravitz CD to prove how great the stereo is;

then, at his insistence, view *The Great Escape* on his mobile theater unit while he drives.

It starts snowing when we cross the state line into Michigan—big fat flakes that swirl onto the windshield and make it seem as if we're looking at the highway through a white kaleidoscope. Up north, it's cold and crisp. We turn onto the narrow road lined with pine trees that leads into the ski area, and when we turn again and drive down the hill toward our house, there are six deer in the meadow. The sky is black, punctured with stars.

We're up early, on the slopes. When we get back, around two, Dad and Gramps brush the snow off the picnic table in the yard and spread tools and engine parts all over it. They're never without some kind of project, and this Christmas vacation it's restoring an old beat-up snowmobile Gramps bought at an auction in the fall. If you go out on the deck, you can hear them bickering.

"Goddamn it, Dutch," Dad says. "Will you quit beating on it? You're not going to fix it by beating on it." Then there's a crash—Gramps dropping something—and Dad starts laughing. "Jesus Christ," he says. And Gramps goes at the engine again with the wrong side of a wrench, the sound of metal on metal ringing in the cold, dry air. Before too long, Will's out there with them, all three of them drinking beer, swearing, and goofing around.

Mom looks up from sketching and rolls her eyes. "It's a guy thing," she says.

Jules watches through the kitchen window with a moony expression. An expression that's been fixed on her face since Christmas Eve. Will, Will, Will. He's all she can talk about. Doesn't Will ski amazingly well for a person who's only been skiing three times in his whole life before? Doesn't he look fabulous in that orange parka? Isn't he the most truly funny person in America?

Well, yeah, I think. So far, I like Will just fine. He gets our jokes; he likes our goofy ski house with its strange books and posters and flea market treasures. He doesn't mind when I beat him, racing. But it's always been just us in Michigan, and it seems strange with Will here. Not that Jules is ignoring me or anything. In fact, since Will arrived she's been paying more attention to me than she has in a long, long time.

Over the next few days, Jules goes out of her way to make sure the two of us have the chance to get to know each other. Every night after dinner, the three of us head over to the bar at the lodge. Between band sets, Jules and I entertain him with family stories.

"Tell Will about when Mom got pregnant and they went to the doctor," Jules says one night. "You tell it funnier than I do."

"Okay," I say, and tell the story.

Mom and Dad are pretty sure Mom's pregnant—and mind you, they're *not* married—and they decide she needs to go to the doctor, but Mom's too embarrassed to come right out and make an appointment for that. So she makes it for a check-up instead, figuring she'll come clean when she gets there. Meanwhile, she gets this terrible cold. So they sit in the waiting room for almost two hours on the day of the appointment, Mom hacking and wheezing like a TB victim until her name's finally called. Dad's a wreck, waiting for her to come out. Then, when she does, she walks right past him and keeps going.

"So he goes after her," I say. "But when he catches up to her on the street and asks her what the doctor said, she waves a prescription slip right in his face and says, 'I've got strep throat. It's no wonder I feel so terrible. I've got to get this penicillin and start taking it right away or else I'm going to be even sicker than I already am.'"

"She didn't even ask the doctor about—you know?" Will asks.

"Nope. And when Dad asked why, she had this total breakdown, right there on the street. She goes, 'You don't even care how sick I am! My God, I'm really, really, *really* sick and all you can think about is whether or not I'm pregnant.'" I'm on a roll now, wailing like Mom does when she tells the story.

Jules cracks up. "Mom *is* pathetic when she's sick."

"Yeah," I say. "And this was the *crème de la crème* of pathetic, according to Dad."

I'm about to go on to the rest of it: Grandma Hammond freaking out, wanting to send Mom to an unwed mothers' home; their disastrous wedding night, when the pipes burst in the dinky little trailer they'd rented and they were ankle deep in water. But I realize Will's not laughing.

"Your *dad* told you that story?" he asks.

"Yeah. Well, actually both Mom and Dad tell it all the time. They think it's hilarious."

"My parents would never tell me a story as personal as that," he says. "But then, we don't talk much about anything."

I say, "You don't get along?"

He shrugs. "Oh, we get along okay. They just don't have a clue why I'd want to hang out in a gym when I could go to med school, which is what I originally thought I wanted to do. What they still want me to do. You know, get a real life. What can I say? They're nice people, just—boring. The idea of them ever being young, being in love like your parents were—well, I can't even imagine it."

"Are," I say. "Like my mom and dad *are*."

Will looks at Jules and smiles. Jules smiles back. Like we are, they're thinking. God, this is like a cheesy movie. They might as well be surrounded by a thousand points of light.

I fake a yawn. "You guys want to go back pretty soon?"

"I'm fried." Jules reaches for her jacket.

"Me too," Will says. "Boy, being outside in the cold all day really takes it out of you."

Right. Like they're going to go back and *sleep*. Later, I can hear them in the next room. They're trying to be quiet, but there are the inevitable thumps, the muffled laughter. A society of two, just like Mom and Dad have always been.

Sometimes it made Jules and me mad when we were kids, the way their time alone was so important to them. They left us with babysitters, took vacations without us. They refused to devote themselves endlessly to teams and lessons. But as we got older, and a lot of our friends' families fell apart, we saw their closeness differently. We realized it was no small thing that the way they were together let us keep on believing in love.

I still believe in it. I just can't imagine it will ever happen to me. Lying alone in the room Jules and I used to share, I think about Gabe Parker for maybe the millionth time since we met and the hopeless idea that maybe... Stop right there, I tell myself. I make my mind tumble backwards to those early Michigan times when Jules and I were always together.

Saturday mornings, early, Dad would blast us out of bed with the Rolling Stones—"Start Me Up"—so we could be at the ski area the second the lifts started running. We'd be freezing as the old chair lift creaked us up to the top; we'd be clapping our mittened hands together to warm them; laughing, making our breath puff out, white as snow. On top, it seemed like you could see forever: blue-green pine forests, frozen lakes, roads flung across the hills like narrow gray ribbon. Our own brown and yellow ski house, like a doll's house, below. We'd look a long time, then we'd zoom down, our faces burning with the cold wind our speed made.

Jules and I would ski with Mom and Dad for a while; then they'd send us off to ski North Peak where all the kids hung out. We made ski jumps near the edge of the slope, carrying snow out of the woods and packing it hard, then shoveling out the bottom with our hands to give a cliff-like effect. I lived for the moment I would be airborne, sailing up toward the sky. Then, boom, there was the thrill of starting down, hoping like crazy that both skis would touch the ground at the same time, tips apart. If they didn't, if I fell—Jules would collect me, wipe the snow out of my face, and send me back up the chair lift to try again.

Remembering this, my heart hurts, I'm so lonely.

Jules and Will have fallen asleep in the next room, or maybe they're just lying warm and happy in each other's arms. I'm glad for her, I really am. So just suck it up, I tell myself. From now on, it's going to be Mom and Dad, Jules and Will. And me.

Well, that week, me and Gramps. We ride up the chair lift together; we're pool partners, card partners, bowling partners. When we go to restaurants, Gramps introduces me as his date. Okay, I can see why everyone thinks it's so amusing. But sometimes I get tired of the way everything in my family is up for grabs in the comedy department. Doesn't it occur to any of them that, when you're eighteen, the idea of being paired up with your seventy-year-old grandfather might be just a little bit depressing—especially on New Year's Eve?

We go to the Yuma Bar that night, a little country bar out in the middle of nowhere. Inside, it smells like beer and cigarette smoke, snowmobile exhaust, motor oil, and sweat. There's a long bar, where the regulars lounge; a jukebox, heavy on Bob Seger; a half-dozen pinball machines. The tables are covered with faded yellow oilcloth, dotted with cigarette burns. At the Yuma, the Christmas decorations stay up year-round. Twinkling lights are strung around the bandstand and across the mirror at the bar. Ratty silver garlands wind round the rafters.

We haven't been here twenty minutes when a woman at the next table starts flirting with Gramps. She's maybe sixty, perky in an awful Christmas sweater with real bells sewn onto it. He's loyal, though. "Nah," he says when she asks him to dance. "I got a date here." He nods in my direction.

"Go," I say. "Dance."

He raises an eyebrow, like—are you sure?

"You dance," I say. "I don't want to, anyway."

I really, truly don't. I want to sit here, nursing my Dr. Pepper, feeling sorry for myself. But Mom and Dad get up to dance, too. Then Jules and Will. "Dance with us, dance with us," they beg. Gramps and his new girlfriend boogie over.

"Come on, hon." She leans toward me, jingling. "Have some fun, why don't you?"

"No, thank you," I say, not very politely.

I get up and go over to the pool table, where a couple of guys are playing. They're maybe thirty, wearing jeans and down vests and work boots, and smell of the forest. One of them, Dean his friend calls him, has a shaggy blond ponytail and a nice smile.

"So what do you think?" he says to me, tipping back on one heel, surveying the table.

I'm not the greatest pool player in the world, but I know the game pretty well from years of watching Dad and Gramps. "I'd bank it," I say. "Go for the twelve. Right corner pocket."

He steps back and looks at me. "You play?"

"Some."

"Any good?"

I shrug.

He takes a quarter from his jeans pocket and puts it on the edge of the table. "That's yours," he says. "When I take this guy, you're next."

His friend laughs.

"Well, shit," they both say, when I give him a decent game.

This cheers me considerably. We play for an hour or so, alternating partners, not talking much at all, just concentrating on the game. I hold my own. And I don't feel self-conscious, either. Maybe because I know I'm just a kid to them. But then Bob Seger launches into "Feel Like a Number" on the jukebox and Dean says, "Hey, you want to dance?"

I don't, *at all*. But it would be rude to say no, so I take his outstretched hand and let him lead me to the dance floor—much to the approval of my family, who beam at the sight of me. Like, *finally* a guy's paying attention to me. Maybe I'll get out of my funk and join the party. For a woodsy guy, Dean is a surprisingly good dancer, perfectly comfortable on the dance floor. I, however, feel as if somebody just poured me full of lead. I shuffle, trip over my own feet, all the time keeping an eye on Gramps, praying he won't dance over here and start bragging about Dad winning LOTTO CASH.

Smile, I tell myself. At least act like you're having a good time.

Which I guess Dean interprets as encouragement, because he grins back at me, grabs both my hands, and attempts some tricky maneuver designed to end in a spin. But I can't do it.

When he tightens his grip to give it another go, the calluses on his palms feel scratchy and hard and I think of the little crescent-moons of dirt under his nails that I saw when he spread his fingers on the table to hold the cue. Up close, he smells like smoke and sweat and cigarettes.

When the song ends, I mumble an excuse and flee to the restroom. I close myself into a stall and just sit there, ashamed for having ditched Dean the way I did, obsessing over whether or not he'll think I was embarrassed to be with him. Was I? God. I feel like the stupid, rich, college kid I am. I stay in the stall for what seems like forever, listening to the women come in and out, gossiping, talking about the men they're with, or men they wish they were with instead.

Which unfortunately makes me think of Josh and wonder what he's doing tonight, if he's with that Heather-looking girl. And Gabe Parker. He's probably got a girlfriend at home that Tiffany doesn't even know about. I torture myself with that until I hear Jules' voice. "Emma, are you in here? It's almost midnight."

"They're giving out the hats!" Mom says. She hands me one when I emerge from the stall, a cardboard beanie with a red propeller on it.

I put it on, look in the mirror. "Oh, perfect," I say.

"Who's that guy you were dancing with?" Jules whispers. "He was cute."

"Nobody," I say. "I mean, I don't know him."

Back in the bar, the countdown toward midnight has begun. Dean's standing at the pool table, cue in hand, shouting out "Ten, nine, eight..." along with a girl who has bleached blond hair and is wearing a lot of makeup. Mom, Jules and I hurry toward our table, where Dad and Will and Gramps are waiting. When the crowd shouts "Happy New Year" and the band breaks into "Auld Lang Syne," we crush together in a big, amorphous hug.

"To us," Mom says, when the waitress brings around the plastic glasses of champagne.

"And doing whatever we damn well please!" Dad adds.

We drink. Except for Jules and Will, who are kissing and can't seem to stop.

The next morning, I leave for the ski area before anyone else wakes up, and ski myself into oblivion. Up and down, up and down. It's not crowded: just me and a bunch of little kids as crazy as I used to be.

It's snowing hard, and cold. Riding the chair lift, the snowflakes feel like needles scraping my face. My feet feel like blocks of ice—when they feel at all. My ears hurt. But I don't go in. I like being so cold that it hurts. I like the way the tears freeze on my face when I start crying. And the ugly ripping sound my skis make going over the icy patches.

I feel like such a loser. I don't know what I want to do with my life; I don't have a clue about what to do with the million dollars my parents gave me. So far, all it's done is confuse me.

If I could just stay here forever, I think. I close my eyes and try to imagine myself living here, but what I see is a kid on a ski hill, smiling.

Myself, no older than eight.

Twelve

Dad wants to leave for Colorado the day after we get back from Michigan, even though Mom thinks they should wait until I go back to school.

"I'm fine," I tell her. "Really! I'll be fine. It's just a week before school starts. I'm eighteen, you know. I can take care of myself. Jesus, it's not like you haven't ditched me to go on vacations before."

"We're not ditching you," she says. "And this is not

exactly a *vacation*. We'll be in Steamboat Springs probably into March."

"Whatever," I say. "Mom. Please. Just give me a list of things you want me to do when I close up the house to go back to Bloomington. I'll be fine." God forbid I forget to turn down the thermostat and you have to pay a big heating bill, I think. Not to mention the fact that I'll probably be home every weekend, turning it back up again.

"Okay," she says reluctantly. "But do you have a plan?"

"Yeah," I say. "Read, watch TV, eat pizza. It's Christmas break, Mom. What kind of a plan do I *need*?"

I swear to God, she's driving me crazy. I wish they would just *go*. Though I have to say I'm not sure spending the winter in Colorado is the best idea they've ever had. Mom hates the mountains. You can see too far, she says. You can't find a place to settle your eyes. Just a single week of skiing in Colorado has been known to get her seriously out of whack in the past. She's going because spending a winter skiing in Colorado has been Dad's fantasy ever since we went to Steamboat Springs the first time, when I was six.

But I can't worry about that. I'm going to try not to worry about *myself*, just hole up and enjoy a week of not having to think about who I might see and what dumb thing I might say or do in their presence. When Mom and Dad *finally* hit the road the next day, I put my iPod into its neat new portable stereo dock, dial up "Let the Cool Goddess Rust Away," turn it up full-blast, and dance through the whole house, singing at the top of my lungs... because I *can*.

The fact that a blizzard sets in that afternoon only makes things better. I couldn't even go out if I wanted to. I'll have a film-fest, I decide. Start the new year by casting out any remaining bad high school juju through viewing my collection of the all-time best high school revenge movies. *Carrie*, of course. *Pump Up the Volume. Sixteen Candles*, for a little comic relief. It's almost midnight when I microwave the third bag of popcorn and am about to settle in to watch *Heathers*, the absolute pinnacle of high school revenge in my view. Then, hitting *play*, I glance out the window to check out how the blizzard is coming along and see the dark outline of a person standing beneath the street light in the swirling snow. I swear, it seems like he's looking right at me.

It scares the shit out of me. I yank the curtains closed, my heart hammering, and suddenly my mind starts replaying all the people I didn't even know who hit me up for money when they found out I was a millionaire. They weren't bad people. Some asked for really good causes, others were just envious and maybe a little greedy. But there are dangerous people who know about how much money we have, too. Thieves and drug addicts who might look upon a blizzard as an … opportunity. The person out there might have found out somehow that Mom and Dad were leaving. He might be casing the place, considering whether to risk a break-in.

Be rational, I tell myself firmly. Lights are on all over the house. It's obvious there's someone here. Even if the person standing there came with the idea of breaking in, surely he'll change his mind and come back another time, when the house is empty.

Unless he's desperate.

I hear myself let out a little moan. God. Aren't there always terrible, tragic stories about people so desperate they'll do anything to get what they need?

I squeeze my eyes tight, to disappear him. But when I open them, he's still there.

Always call 911 if you think anything's amiss. Mom and Dad drummed this into us when Jules got old enough for the two of us to stay at home alone. But nothing ever went wrong.

I've led a charmed life, I think—which makes the person out there seem all the more ominous. Like it's my turn.

My cell phone is on the coffee table, and I pick it up and dial.

"I don't know if this is actually an emergency," I say when the operator comes on. "But there's a guy standing outside my house. I don't know how long he's been there. I'm home alone."

She takes my address, reassures me that a patrol car will come by and check him out.

"Call if anything changes before they get there," she says.

Which makes me feel cold inside, like my blood has turned to ice. My teeth start chattering, too—not from the cold, though. I've never been so scared in my life.

I peek through the closed curtains. He still hasn't moved.

Maybe ten minutes pass before I see the squad car approaching slowly, its headlights cutting through the snow. The guy doesn't move then, either. He doesn't even seem to see the cop get out and come over to him.

A few seconds pass and I see the cop visibly relax. He gestures towards our house, the guy nods—and the two of them start across the yard. For an instant, they disappear from view, then I hear footsteps on the porch. The doorbell.

I open the door just enough to see the policeman's face.

"This guy says he knows you," he says. "Is that right?"

I open the door wider.

"Emma?" a voice says: Josh Morgan's.

He takes a tentative step forward, but the policeman grabs his arm to restrain him.

"Do you know him, miss?" he asks. "If not, I'll take him in."

"No," I say. "I mean, yes. I know him. Don't take him in."

He lets go of Josh's arm, and Josh stumbles.

"He's loaded," the cop says, his voice disgusted. "He's damn lucky he didn't fall down and freeze to death somewhere. You sure you want to be responsible for him? Like I said, I can take him in for public intoxication."

"It's okay," I say. "Thanks. I'll take care of him."

He takes Josh's arm again, guides him into the foyer. Then shakes his head at the sight of the two of us: Josh soaking wet, pale as snow, shivering; me in flannel pajamas covered in little yellow ducks, my hair caught up with chopsticks on the top of my head.

He doesn't make a report, which I know is an act of kindness on his part.

"Oh, fuck," Josh moans, as soon as he's gone, and slides like Gumby down the wall into a puddle of melting snow.

"Take those wet clothes off," I say. "You'll catch pneumonia."

"You sound like my fucking mother." He laughs, bitterly. "Like my mother *used* to sound. Before she time-traveled back to her adolescence."

"Take off your wet clothes," I repeat. "I'll get you something of my dad's to wear."

Jesus. I meant take them off in the bathroom. I go in there, start a hot shower for him. Then I get a clean towel, a pair of Dad's sweat pants and a sweatshirt, thinking I'll hand them through the door. But when I get back he's not in there.

He's passed out, stark naked, in the hallway.

Was he always so ... *white*? That's my first useless thought.

Then: *be careful what you ask for*. God. Hadn't I longed for this—well, sort of: Josh, completely vulnerable, under my power? I stare at him, at his body. His long, muscular arms and legs, his knobby knees. His tight abs, the patch of blond hair on his chest. His ... other hair, blond, too. And his penis, flopping over onto his thigh. Pathetic.

I wanted him tanned and glistening in the summer sun. *Awake* and vulnerable. Laughing at some joke I'd made. I guess I forgot to tell the cosmos that part.

Meanwhile, what am I supposed to *do* with him?

I kneel down and, tentatively, dab at him with the towel. He shudders, pulls himself into the fetal position. He's covered in goose bumps.

"Josh," I say. Then louder. "Josh!"

His eyes flutter open. "Emma?" he says.

"You're freezing," I say. "Come on. Get up. You can sleep in my bed."

He lets me pull him up from the floor and help him down the hallway to my room. I can't trust him to stand alone long enough to pull down the covers, so I just push him onto the bed and go get some quilts from the linen closet. It's a relief to me to lay them over his nakedness.

I throw Josh's wet clothes in the dryer, turn off *Heathers*, then go lie down beside him on the bed. Not touching him. Just beside him. He's so drunk that if he got sick he could choke on his own vomit, I tell myself. Or wake up, disoriented.

Duh. Of course he's going to wake up disoriented. That's the least of it.

The truth is, I just want to be near him.

I can't sleep, though. How could I sleep?

I don't even obsess too much about what's going to happen when he wakes up and realizes where he is, or what he was doing, drunk, outside my house in a blizzard in the first place. I definitely do not allow any fantasies about what any of this might mean.

I just lie there beside him, dozing and waking to the shock of it all.

It's not till morning that I get scared, thinking about

the time Josh was trapped in the car, vulnerable, me telling him how I felt—the humiliation and heartache that caused. What if he's mad at me for taking him in, seeing him this way? What if it grosses him out to think of me lying all night with him?

The latter, at least, I can avoid. If I get up now, he'll never know I was there.

Carefully, I roll to the edge of the bed, then sit up. I wait, perfectly still, for a long moment before standing. Then wait again, to make sure he doesn't stir, before tiptoeing out of the room into the hallway. I consider a shower, consider washing my hair. But then I'd have to think about what to wear. Whether I'd look good in it, whether I *care* about looking good because Josh is sleeping off a bad drunk in my bedroom.

Fuck him, I think, and remain in my duck pajamas. I do comb my hair, though, and pull it back in a ponytail, which I'd have done in any case.

I eat a Pop Tart for breakfast, turn on *The Today Show*—though I have to admit that the drama playing out in my own life is considerably more compelling than what's happening in Iraq.

I fold Josh's dry clothes, like a good wife. Think about what I'm going to say when he finally gets up. Maybe something clever, *à la* the Talking Heads: "Well? How did I *get* here?"

Or caustic: "So, can I offer you a drink?"

But when he staggers into the kitchen around noon, wrapped in a pink-flowered quilt, his eyes bloodshot, his half-dozen or so cowlicks standing at attention all over his head, he looks so stupid that all I can do is laugh.

"Want some coffee?" I ask, trying to make up for it.

"You can't make coffee," he says. "Anyway, you couldn't... *before*."

I shrug. "People change. *Some* people," I add.

"Can you, now?" he asks irritably. "Make coffee?"

"No," I say. "So?"

He snorts. Then he gets up and starts making coffee himself. He really does look ridiculous, like somebody's grandmother in a pink housecoat, and it pisses me off the way he still knows where everything is in our kitchen.

"Just wondering," I say. "You were standing outside in the blizzard last night, hoping you could come in and be a *jerk*?"

"I don't know *what* I was doing last night," he says. "If you want to know the truth."

"Drinking. We know that."

"Yeah, well." He sits down with a mug of coffee and takes a sip. "*Fuck*," he says, putting a finger to his burned lips.

"Is it a common thing with you now?" I persist. "Drinking till you don't even know where you are?"

"I know where I am," he says. "*Was*. Last night."

"Oh. You just didn't know what you were *doing*."

He glares at me. "I came to tell you I was sorry. If you really want to know."

"Sorry?" I say, astonishingly in control at this turn of events. "*Sorry*?"

"Yeah. Sorry. For high school. All that shit. I've been

wanting to tell you for a while—" He takes another, more careful sip of his coffee. "Then, when I saw you that day with your grandpa, I decided I would. So, I'm sorry. I was an asshole, and I'm sorry. Okay?"

"And you think it still matters to me?" I ask.

"Yeah, I do." He grins a little. "I think you miss me, like I miss you. Even though you're mostly a pain in the ass."

"Fuck you," I say, but I can't help smiling back at him.

"Listen," he says, then. "Do you think I could just hang out here a while?"

Thirteen

His grades sucked, he says. His dad took away his credit card and cell phone—and *sold* the truck he'd given him for graduation. Worse, as far as he could tell, the only thing his parents have agreed on since their split-up was the fact that if he wanted to stay on campus at all he'd have to get a job and move out of the fraternity house into a dorm.

"Did they kick you out of the house?" I ask.

"You mean the basement dungeon I've been relegated

to at my dad's house since the new baby came? Or the couch in my mom's Barbie pad? Fuck. Where's the punishment in that?

"I just don't want to *be* there," he says. "With either one of them. Like my dad's ever even *home*. Which leaves me with Shelley, who's pregnant again and barfing all the time—and hates me, because I don't fit into their perfect little family. My mom's doing a Demi Moore trip, dating some guy about five minutes older than I am.

"You're lucky, Emma," he says. "Your parents are cool. Where are they, anyway? Up in Michigan?"

"Colorado," I say. "They left yesterday. For the whole winter."

"Man, I bet your dad's pumped up about that."

I nod.

"I figured he'd be having a good time with all that dough." He laughs. "How many Corvettes has he bought, so far?"

"Just one. In the garage."

"It's a '62," he says. "Right? A 327, 4-speed."

It kills me that he knows my dad so well. I get up and bustle around fixing Josh some toast, to distract myself from imagining the two of them in Michigan, working on the snowmobile with Gramps and Will. Me watching from the window with Mom and Jules.

"I heard you went out with Gabe Parker," Josh says, after a while.

"I didn't go out with him," I say. "He interviewed me for an *IDS* story. About the lottery."

"Yeah, well. He's a good guy. You ought to go out with him."

"Right," I say.

"What's the problem?" Josh says. "What's wrong with him?"

"Nothing's *wrong* with him."

"Well, then?"

"Listen, Josh," I say. "You've been back in my life approximately twelve hours—eleven of which you were passed out, drunk and naked, on my bed—so let's not get overly personal here, okay? You said you were sorry for being an asshole in high school. Fine. But you don't know jack shit about anything that's happened to me since then, so don't go giving me advice about ... *whatever*."

"Okay." He raises his hands, palms-out, in surrender. "Okay. Your call."

It's a beautiful morning, an after-a-blizzard morning—blue sky, sun dazzling the new snow. After Josh showers and gets dressed, we dig my Jeep out and drive around and around the block in four-wheel drive, mashing down the snow so our neighbors can make it from their driveways to the plowed streets and get where they need to go. I drive awhile, then Josh drives, fishtailing now and then, which is extremely entertaining.

When we get bored with that, we go over to Butler Hill and sled awhile. Then go to his dad's house, get his stuff, and dump it in Jules' room, where he's going to stay till we go back to Bloomington. When Mom calls to let me know they've arrived safely in Steamboat Springs, I don't mention he's here. How, exactly, would I explain it? He was drunk and his homing instincts sent him to our house? It sounds lame, even to me. But the real problem is that any conversation about the situation is bound to lead to the suggestion that *just maybe* Josh's sudden change of heart could have something to do with the fact that I'm now a millionaire.

It doesn't. He said so when we were sledding. Grabbed my arm before I headed down for about the tenth time on my cookie-sheet sled. "Emma," he said. "Listen. It doesn't matter to me about the money. That's not why—I mean, I just want you to know that."

I can't prove he wasn't lying, of course. But I know.

Anyway, I tell Mom about the blizzard and what a blast it was, clearing the street with my Jeep. She laughs and tells me about how Dad hit the slopes fifteen minutes after they got to the condo—even though they'd driven straight through and he hadn't slept in more than twenty-four hours.

"You go back, when?" she asks.

"Sunday," I say. "Classes start the ninth."

"And you're okay?"

"Fine," I say.

For once, I really am. In fact, the next few days, hanging out with Josh, I'm actually happy. I'm not dumb enough to think he's ever going to fall in love with me. It's enough being friends again, watching movies, eating pizza, talking. We go over to the mall and test ride those weird Segway walking machines. Stamp out a huge peace sign in the snow in the park across the street.

He talks a lot about his parents, admits he's been totally

screwed up ever since the divorce—and pissed. But, except for the fact that his crappy attitude is an inconvenience for them, they're both so wrapped up in their new lives that they don't really notice.

The truth is, he says, he's been hurting himself. Not them. Realizing that is what made him decide to get his shit together. He wants to do it. For *himself.*

I always brought out the best in him, he tells me. He figured the first step in getting a life of his own was remembering how to be the person he used to be, when we were friends. But it wasn't until he was drunk out of his mind that he had the nerve to come and find me. Even then, he chickened out and couldn't make himself actually knock on the door.

When he tells me about how his girlfriend broke up with him the day after he gave her the diamond earrings he saved up to buy her for Christmas, and I commiserate and we both laugh about the fact that her name really *is* Heather, I know we really have gone backwards to the way we used to be.

It's also when I get the idea that I could make it a lot easier for him to get his shit together if I bought him a car. What he'd like to do is deliver pizzas, he told me in one of our conversations. You get tips on top of minimum wage, plus you don't have to put up with much bullshit because you're mostly driving.

"If I had my truck, I could do it," he said. "Fucking asshole. I can't believe my dad would take it away—and sell it. Like, he thinks I'm never going to be the kind of person to deserve it again."

Okay. I'm perfectly aware of the fact that if I told anyone, especially my parents, that I was thinking of buying Josh a car, they'd say, "Are you *crazy*?" I don't tell Josh I'm considering it, either. He'd just refuse.

But I look at it this way: if I *didn't* have $70,000 a year that I don't need, and had, instead, only the couple of thousand in my savings account plus the money I earned from my summer job, I wouldn't think twice about spending a few hundred bucks to buy Josh a bicycle so he could get back and forth from his new job. My parents probably wouldn't get freaked out about that at all. They'd probably commend me for being so generous. Josh might be a little embarrassed. But he'd be grateful.

Really, it's a matter of proportion. If I weren't so bad at math, I'm sure I could come up with an algebraic equation that would show how, under the circumstances, spending a couple of thousand dollars on a car was comparable to buying a bicycle. And it's not like I'm thinking about buying him a Ferrari. Or even a truck, like the one his Dad confiscated. Just a nice, serviceable used car.

So, the morning before we're supposed to go back to school, I just do it. Drive over to the used car lot where Dad bought Jules and me cars when we first got our driver's licenses, ask the salesman to show me what's available, then surprise the shit out of him by pulling out my checkbook and writing a check for $3,500 after settling on a very modest ten-year-old Honda Civic. I have a few complimentary donuts while I wait for him to call the bank and make sure the funds are actually available.

"Great. I'll be back to get the car in half an hour," I say, when he returns and happily announces that the funds are there.

"There are papers—" he says. "The title. Registration."

"Oh, right," I say, as if I hadn't totally forgotten about that sort of thing. "Maybe you could draw those up while I go get the person the car is actually for." I write down Josh's name, address. He can fill out his social security number when he gets here.

Draw those up, I think, driving away. Very professional. I'm feeling pretty pleased with myself until it occurs to me that I also forgot about insurance. Josh will need that, too. Probably, we can add six months of it to the bill. I mean, how much could it be?

Josh is still in bed when I get home. I put a Counting Crows disc into the CD player, turn the volume up full blast, and pretty soon he comes staggering out of the bedroom.

"Jesus, fuck," he says.

"It's nearly noon," I say. "Get dressed, okay? There's something I need you to help me with. We can stop and get coffee on the way."

He grumbles a little, but he's game. Even cheerful, after we hit the Starbucks drive-through and he gets a little caffeine in his system.

"What's up?" he asks. "Where are we going?"

"I bought you a car," I say. "We're going to get it."

Dead silence.

"You bought me *what*?" he asks, finally.

"You need a car if you want to get a decent job, so I bought you one. That's all. It's not a big deal. It's not even all that nice. It's a Honda Civic, for God's sake. Like something your grandmother would drive. Beige."

"Emma," he says. "You can't do that."

"Just shut up," I say. "I already did. Look, you're my best friend—even though you've been, well, *on leave* for a while. You're in trouble. Why wouldn't I help you, if I can?"

"How much did it cost?" he asks.

"Never mind," I say. "It doesn't matter. Josh, I told you how much money my parents gave me. Plus, there's millions more where that came from. What do I care about a couple thousand dollars? You can get the pizza job if you have a car. Maybe even get to the point where you don't need anything from your dad at all."

"A couple *thousand*?" he says.

"Thirty-five hundred bucks, okay? No big deal."

He's quiet a long time, drumming his fingers on his thighs—that weird thing boys always do, and you think, what song are they hearing?

"You have to let me pay you back," he says.

I shrug. "If you want to. When you can. Like I said, it's not a big deal to me."

"Well, it is to me," he says. "I'm paying you back."

"Fine," I say. "Your first-born child. Preferably not for a few years."

He laughs then, and I know what I did was okay.

Fourteen

Of course, I haven't done a single thing to get ready for second semester. When I left for break, I was thinking that I might not come back—so why bother? So I spend the first day back in Bloomington buying books and generally organizing my life—in the company of Tiffany, who talks non-stop about what a fabulous vacation she had. I swear, nothing is unworthy of mention: every little gift from

Matt, every cute thing her grandmother said, every fucking Christmas cookie she iced with her mother.

I have to admit I'm glad to see her, though. And our room feels, I don't know, familiar to me—like maybe I sort of belong there.

"That friend of yours?" she says, plopping down on her bed. "Josh—? Matt told me he moved out of the house."

"I know," I say. "His dad made him."

"Why?" Tiffany asks.

"Den of iniquity," I say. She looks baffled, so I add, "Too many parties. His grades sucked, and his dad figured that's why."

"*Well*," she says, personally affronted. "It's not the fraternity's fault his grades sucked. Plus, it's not like there aren't any parties in the dorms."

"He knows that," I say. "Josh does."

Tiff raises an eyebrow.

"I saw him over break," I say.

"*Really*," she says.

"He got into a fight with his dad and ended up staying a couple of days at our house. That's it. Zip. The end."

"He's cute," Tiff says. "He looks kind of like Owen Wilson, you know?"

I shrug.

She sighs deeply.

"It's a totally platonic relationship," I say. "Can we just leave it at that?"

"Okay. *Okay*," she says, but she's lying.

The good thing is, the news of what she sees as a promising relationship with Josh makes her forget all about her determination to fix me up with Gabe Parker. She grills me for information about his life, wants to know every little thing about our—she says the word as if it has quotes around it—*friendship*. She's ecstatic when Josh calls to see if I want to go see the new *Mission Impossible* with him, and it's all I can do to keep her from tying me down and dressing me in something other than jeans and a sweatshirt when it's time for me to go down and meet him. Even after I explain (*sans* explicit details) that I once had a crush on him and it just didn't work out, she persists in considering him an excellent romantic possibility.

I'm glad he's not living in the fraternity house, where she could easily arrange to corner him and give him the third degree about his intentions. As it is, she's got fucking radar for any moment I connect with him for any reason, and oh-so-casually drifts past. Wired for all I know. Nancy Drew goes digital.

The thing is, I don't care. I'm happy.

The first week of the semester flies by. Josh and I see a few movies together, meet at Starbucks a couple of times; but I'm busy with my classes and he is, too. Plus, he's delivering pizzas four nights a week. I'm proud of how hard he's working, how determined he is to get back on track. So when almost a week goes by and he doesn't surface, I don't think much about it. I've got his new Kanye West CD, though, and I'm feeling guilty because I promised to return it as soon as I put the songs on my computer.

I know his schedule. No classes Tuesday or Thursday

afternoons, and he usually spends that time in his room, studying. So I put the CD in my backpack Thursday morning, figuring I'll just drop it off. It's a great day, cold and sunny, and after my last class I walk through campus heading for Josh's dorm, grooving to Pink on my iPod.

Then I see them: Josh and Heather.

They're up ahead of me, walking hand-in-hand. She's tiny and beautiful and blond, like all his girlfriends are, and he has to bend down, she has to stand on her tiptoes when they stop and kiss. All I want to do is get away from where they are. But when I stop short, thinking I'll turn and bolt in the opposite direction, I crash into a girl walking behind me and scatter her books everywhere.

"God, I'm so sorry," I say, bending to pick them up for her.

I don't even realize I'm crying until I stand up to hand her the books and she looks at me and says, "Hey, are you *okay*?"

I bolt then, clearly not okay at all. Because I bolt in the direction of Josh and Heather, instead of away from them. I nearly crash into them as I go past.

"Emma," Josh yells. "Emma."

I keep going. I hear him pounding after me, at least for a little while. But I don't look back. I run like my life depends on it, my books clutched to my chest, my lungs burning. I'm done, I think. Done. *Done*. I knew Josh didn't love me. Not that way. I knew he never would. It's just—

I simply cannot deal with him being with someone else. Not someone like that: a fucking *Heather*. I just can't.

I can't be in the same ... *world* he's in if he's going to do that—and not *tell* me. Not now, anyway.

I'm going to Michigan, I decide. I'm dropping my classes, dropping everything, and going up there where I can be alone and figure out who I can be without him. Fine, if it's melodramatic. Fine, if I have to forfeit most of my tuition and my room is already paid for through the end of the semester. I don't care.

I slow down to a walk once I've decided that and feel, suddenly, calm. Back at the dorm, I get on the Internet and withdraw from all my classes. I write a note: *Tiff—Don't freak out. Please. But I just can't be here right now, so I'm going up to Michigan until I figure out what I want to do. This has nothing to do with you. I swear to God. You're the best roomie anyone could ask for. Love, Emma.*

Then I take down my posters, pack up my books and photographs, empty my drawers and my closet of clothes. It surprises me how little there is. Loading it in my Jeep, heading north, I think maybe something inside me knew all along that I never meant to stay.

I'm almost to Muncie when my cell phone rings. Tiff, crying.

I try to explain. I'm just not ready for college yet. I knew it last semester, but I thought I ought to try to stay. But I just can't. I meant it when I said it was nothing to do with her. She *is* the best roommate, ever.

"It's that *fucking* Josh Morgan," she says, shocking the shit out of me.

"No," I say.

"It is, too. He called over here, asking for you and I could tell he was upset."

"He called?"

"Yes," she says. "And if you don't tell me what happened, I'm going to call him back and ask him. I am! *Emma*?"

"God, don't do that," I say. "*Please.*"

"All right, then. Pull over the next place you can and call me back. All you need is to get in an accident over it. But if you haven't called back in fifteen minutes—"

"I'll call," I say. "Okay? *I'll call.*"

When I do, she surprises me again. She's calmed down, totally rational.

"I know you're unhappy, Emma," she says. "I knew it practically the first day. That's why I was always trying, *you know*—well, anyway. After that day your grandpa came down in the Winnebago, and Josh appeared? I started figuring out why. Jeez, you were a *wreck* just looking at him. Anyone could see that—

"So, what *happened*? It's something to do with Josh. Don't try to tell me it's not."

"I saw him with this—*Heather*," I say.

"That girl he was dating last semester? I thought they broke up."

"They did," I say. "Before Christmas break."

She's quiet a moment. "Was he your boyfriend in high school?" she asks.

"*Boyfriend*?" I say. "Are you out of your mind?"

"You don't need to be crappy to me, Emma. Anyway, why is that such a stupid question?"

"It just is," I say. "I'm sorry. I don't mean to be an asshole. It's just—I don't really know how to talk about—"

"Josh," she finishes for me. "Obviously, he's important to you. Was."

"Jesus," I say. "Have you considered law school?"

"Just say how he was important to you, okay? How hard can that be?"

"He was my best friend in high school, till senior year—till I wrecked everything wanting more. It's a long story. I'll tell you sometime. Honest, I will. But I can't right now. I swear, though, Josh *isn't* why I'm leaving. Not the real reason."

"Is that true, Emma? Really?"

"Yes," I say. "The thing with Josh just made me know it's what I need to do. I need, I don't know ... space."

Tiffany sighs. "Do your parents know you're doing this?"

"No," I say. "They'll freak out if they find out. But they're in Colorado, and they probably won't figure it out, at least for a while, since they always call me on my cell."

"You're *sure* you need to do this?"

"Yeah. I am."

"You'll keep in touch with me, though. Promise?"

I agree, though right now I don't want to be in touch with *anyone*.

It's nearly midnight when I get to our little ski house. It's so quiet here. The sky is black, black, black, sprinkled with stars, and standing beneath them, looking up, I feel lighthearted, full of good intentions. The next morning, I get right out of bed, do sit-ups till I can't breathe, eat yogurt for breakfast. It's a beautiful day, pristine snow twinkling in the sunlight, the beautiful curve of deep drifts. I glide across the meadow on my cross-country skis, then into the woods, where all I hear is the swish of my own skis and the occasional tiny plop of snow falling from the tree branches. I go more than an hour, until I'm soaked with sweat and my legs ache from the constant motion.

I eat a healthy lunch, then set out for the bookstore in Traverse City, where I buy all five of the Edith Wharton novels they have in stock, plus a collection of short stories and a biography. She was rich and spent all her life writing about it, so I figure that studying her will be food for thought. I buy some French tapes to brush up on my high school French—who knows when I might become a world traveler? I even buy a meditation tape, thinking that maybe if I can calm down, guys won't find me so alarming.

I eat a Lean Cuisine for dinner, spend the evening lost in *The Age of Innocence*.

Yes, I think. This is where I'm supposed to be.

Those first days, I like being alone. I like the way I feel, pleasantly sore from so much exercise, my mind full of interesting thoughts. I like *myself.*

Pretty soon, though, I'm feeling guilty about deceiving Mom and Dad. Tiff calls a half-dozen times, and finally leaves a message saying, "I guess you don't want to talk to me. It's okay if you really need to be alone. I'm not mad. But I miss you." Even then, I don't call her back or answer any of the newsy e-mails she's sent. Josh e-mails: "Emma, can we talk?" But I don't answer that either. I don't even *listen* to the message from Josh, just delete it when the number comes up on the screen of my phone. I put my laptop in the closet, and don't check e-mails at all.

Within a week, I'm hitting the "snooze" button two, three, four times before getting up. Then I stop setting the alarm altogether and sleep till I wake up—never before eleven. I eat a donut, drag over to the ski area around one and eat lunch—anything with French fries. I downhill awhile, hang out at the lodge playing video games, then go home and zonk out for a couple of hours on the couch before fixing Kraft Macaroni and Cheese, or worse, and reading magazines or watching whatever stupid sitcoms are on the tube. I write in my journal, but all I do is complain:

Mom's right: so what if you're rich? This place is still a pit, clothes and dirty dishes everywhere. Nobody to clean it but me, unless I want to hire somebody and let them see that I'm a rich, spoiled brat who can't even clean up after herself. Today I didn't even take a shower or get dressed. Gave up on Edith Wharton: the rich women in her books are even more screwed up than I am. Ate toast in bed and finished the stash of Elle *and* Cosmo *magazines Jules left behind. Huge zit on side of nose. More fodder for Mom's cosmic theory of wealth: zits happen. On the bright side: I have no friends here, nowhere to go, so nobody but me will see it.*

Fifteen

I get a job waiting tables at the lodge, which helps some. I'm not always alone. And it's good for me to be there with women whose lives are truly difficult, nothing like my own. I like to listen to their stories. Sometimes I have dreams about them. In one, I line them all up in the kitchen and hand out hundred-dollar bills; in another, I drive out to the double-wides they live in, knock on their doors, and give them checks like I'm the star of some kind of reality show.

They're dirt poor, most of them. They wear cheap clothes from Wal-Mart. Most of them aren't that much older than I am, and they have kids already. Their husbands, if they have them, are usually unemployed. They don't know I'm rich. Well, they don't know I'm fabulously rich. They know I'm not from here, they know my parents own a vacation house in the area, and to them that *is* rich, which I see is true, in a way. Even before we won the lottery, we had a whole lot more than any of those women will ever have.

I swore Jules to secrecy about my leaving Bloomington, and since then she's reverted to her sensible big-sister mode. She calls a lot, usually late. It kind of reminds me of how Josh and I used to drive around at night, talking about everything under the sun. I don't know. Maybe it was the enclosed space, the way when he was driving he had to look straight ahead and mostly couldn't see my face when I was talking that made me feel like I could say anything. I feel that way now, talking to my sister. I tell her about Freud, the real story of spending whole evenings at the psych lab because there was nowhere else to go. I even tell her about Gabe Parker—just the embarrassing coffee interview, not that I haven't been able to get him out of my mind ever since. Nothing about Josh, though. I can't even stand to *think* about that. Still, it's nice feeling close to her. We laugh a lot, puzzle over the sticky ethics of wealth.

"Will's very weird about the money," she confides. "He doesn't like me to pay for show tickets or dinners out. But *other* people! It's like, now they know I'm rich, they think I should pick up the check every single time. And should I? Even when it feels like someone's sponging?"

"Beats me," I say. "Up here in the north woods all alone, how to deal with the money hasn't really been a problem. Though I keep having this weird impulse to give it away."

"Why?" she asks.

I tell her about the women I work with, and how they make me feel.

She's quiet a long moment, and I can almost hear the New York traffic going by outside her window: cars honking, that wheezing sound buses make. Then she says, "But isn't it all relative? I mean, Bill Gates probably wouldn't consider us rich at all."

She's most likely right. But I still feel bad having so much more than the women I work with have, and I'm constantly trying to think of ways to make it up to them—without being obvious. I help bus the tables, take the coffeepot around to everyone's stations. Sometimes, when nobody's looking, I even put extra tip money on a table.

The bartender at the lodge, Harp, is in his twenties, tall and lanky with a sparse goatee and black hair that he wears pulled back in a ponytail. He's been pleasant to me at the restaurant and he always nods in a friendly way if I see him on the slopes or walking with his St. Bernard around the ski area. But we've never really talked. Then one night he follows me out of the restaurant, out the big front doors of the lodge into the freezing cold, and calls, "Emma?"

I turn. He's standing there in just a V-neck sweater, a faded tie-dye T-shirt underneath, his hands in the pockets of his rumpled khakis. He doesn't say anything more, just tilts his head and kind of half-smiles and looks at me. I have no idea how I know what he's thinking, but I do. *What were you doing with Marcy's money?*

"I wasn't taking it," I say. "I was leaving it. You know, so the tip would seem bigger."

But he knows that, too. I can tell by the way he just keeps looking at me with that curious but detached expression. Now his eyes say, why?

"She needs it," I say. "They all do. And I don't need what I make at all. I'm only working here because I can't think of anything else to do." At which point, I start crying. And right there in the parking lot, snow starting to fall, I tell Harp about my parents winning the lottery and how I've ended up a complete and total screw-up because of it. When I finish, I'm shivering; my face, wet with tears, stings with the cold.

"So," Harp says. "*That's* what's driving you to random acts of kindness."

"Random acts of guilt, you mean."

He shrugs. "Effect's the same, isn't it?"

"Yeah, big deal," I say. "A dollar, two dollars. Like that's going to make any big difference to anyone."

"It can." Harp glances toward the lighted restaurant. "Could even be there's something you're supposed to learn from all this. Or are you too into beating up on yourself to consider that?"

"I'm pretty into beating up on myself," I say.

He laughs. "And does it make you feel better?"

I shake my head. My throat feels tight again. I can't speak.

We stand there awhile longer, Harp still showing no effect at all from the cold. He's so calm. I've never known anyone as calm as he appears to be. Who is this guy, anyway? He looks like he took a wrong turn after a Grateful Dead concert years ago and never found his way back. Still, he's smart. I can see it in his eyes. I wonder if there's something that tending bar in this nowhere place is teaching him.

"How'd you know what I was doing, anyhow?" I ask.

He smiles enigmatically. "Mirrors." He pauses just long enough for me to think, okay, this guy is too weird for me, I'm out of here. Then he laughs. "I can see that section of the restaurant from the mirror behind the bar."

I laugh, too.

"I live in the log house where the cross-country trails begin," Harp says. "Got a pool table, great stereo, cold beer. Come over if you want. Any time."

"Thanks," I say. "Maybe I will."

The next day, I dress for cross-country skiing, carry my skis to the wooden arch where the trails begins, and stand there pretending to study the map. *You are here.* A red arrow points to a cluster of triangles: the pine trees that shelter me. Broken lines that signify the dozen or so trails meander out from the arrow into the forest, which is marked by many more triangles and the lacy circles that are deciduous trees. There's Harp's house just to the side of the arrow: a small black square. The actual house, tucked into a stand of birches, looks like a child's drawing of a log cabin. It's the house that Jules and I used to call the Little House in the Big Woods. Sometimes we pretended that we were Laura and Mary Ingalls, skiing away from it toward school or church or to get something for Ma from Mr. Olsen's general store. Or, even better, we were Laura and Mary lost in the great forest with night falling, trying desperately to find our way home.

The house is long and low, with a wide porch that wraps around it. The windows are hung with prisms winking in the morning sun. There's firewood stacked neatly next to the front door, more—a whole winter's worth—in a lean-to at the side. Smoke curls lazily out of the brick chimney into the blue sky.

I really want to visit Harp. I can't stop thinking about what he said to me. I lay awake a long time last night, wondering if my being here might actually have a purpose, and if so, what purpose? I don't have a clue. Now I stand under the arch, trying to work up the nerve to walk across the unspoiled snow in the clearing and shake the cowbells on Harp's front door. What would I say? Hi, if you're not too busy, could you please explain to me what I'm *doing* here? It's all I can think of to say and it seems totally stupid. Not to mention confusing. Even I don't know exactly what I mean by it. "Here" as in the arrow on the map? In Michigan? In this life?

Anyway, he was probably only being nice when he invited me to come by, I think. He probably felt sorry for me. That's the last thing I need. I'm dressed for skiing, and I brought my skis, thinking that I could pretend I was just stopping by at Harp's on my way out to get my morning's exercise. I hadn't really meant to go out on the trails; why start doing something healthful and constructive *now*?

But I feel agitated about having nearly embarrassed myself by my own neediness, and I think maybe skiing will calm me down. It's a perfect day for it: sunshine, blue sky. That nice, crisp kind of cold. So I set out in no particular direction, skiing right past the maps that are placed where various trails merge, allowing the challenges of each path to appear to me in a seemingly random way, as if part of a game.

I feel myself grow calmer, feel the ugly chatter in my mind loosen and drain out of me into the shadowy forest, until finally it seems that there's nothing in the world but this forest and the blue sky above it. The clear, cold air and the warm sun on my face seem to be the same thing. I hear birds calling, the occasional rustle of deer. I look up at the trees. The sight of them, like gargantuan pussy willows because of the way the snow has caught in the crooks of their branches, makes me so purely happy I think I will die.

Stop, I think. Remember this. I bend over and brush the snow from a fallen tree, and the moment I sit down on it, a mosquito flies up, wobbles in the cold air for a moment, and settles on my glove. It can't be real, I think. A mosquito can't possibly have survived into the middle of the winter. I sit still and look at it a long time; it seems more like a quick line drawing of a mosquito than a mosquito itself. But when I raise my hand and blow gently, the mosquito lifts off, flies dizzily to the tree trunk and perches there, proof of its own existence. Proof of anything, everything—or so it seems to me at this moment.

Sixteen

"I saw you heading out to ski this morning," Harp says. "Great day for it."

I nod. I told the other waitresses to go on home and I'm filling the salt and pepper shakers, getting the tables ready for tomorrow's breakfast. He's been taking the clean wine glasses out of the dishwasher, hanging them upside-down on the rack above the bar. Now he stops, leans forward, and folds his arms on the bar expectantly.

I wasn't going to tell him—or anyone—about the mosquito and its cosmic message. But I look at Harp and have this weird idea he knows it anyway, like he knew about the tip money the night before. Which makes me think, why not?

So I say, "I saw this mosquito while I was skiing. A live mosquito! Huge! It flew out from under some dead leaves on a log and landed on my glove. It was—I don't even *know* what it was. The way the woods felt, that mosquito. I was so happy. So *there*. And I know it sounds totally insane, but when I went back out on the trail, it was like it wasn't even me skiing. Like it wasn't anyone at all."

He doesn't laugh. He looks—interested. "There's a word for that," he says. "*Shunyata*. It means emptiness, as in emptiness of yourself. It's a Buddhist idea."

"You're a Buddhist?"

"Nah. I don't buy into the religious thing. I'm interested in some Buddhist ideas, though."

I think he'll say more, but he stands and puts away the last of the glasses. I go around with a box of Sweet'N Low packets, refilling the little ceramic holder on each table. I glance at him when I'm through, but I guess he's decided to ignore me. So is this *shunyata* a bad thing? Yet another clue that I'm a person to avoid?

"Well," I grab my jacket. "See you tomorrow."

He raises his hand in a salute. But when I'm halfway across the parking lot, he opens the door and calls out to me. "Hey, Emma! Want to come over to my place and play some pool?"

I stop. But I can't help thinking, wouldn't it be a little crazy to go off into the woods in the middle of the night with a guy I barely know? Then he catches up with me, throws his arm around my shoulder in a friendly way.

"Come on," he says. "You're lonely."

The way he says it, like it's just a fact of life—nothing to be embarrassed by or ashamed of, nothing that can actually be fixed by a game of pool—tells me he understands loneliness. He's inviting me be lonely with him, which is better than being lonely alone. And so I go with him.

It's nice, crunching along the snowy path not feeling like I have to think of something smart or witty to say, and when his house appears, strung with twinkling white lights, it seems right to be there. Harp opens the door, and his big, furry St. Bernard lumbers up from where she's been dozing in front of the fireplace. He bends and ruffles her fur.

"Lani," he says. "Short for Thulani. It means 'peace.'"

He gestures me toward an old flowered couch. Lani follows to sniff me, then curls up and falls asleep at my feet. I feel so comfortable here. Everything in the house is simple and worn: another couch, a couple of easy chairs—nothing matching. These are gathered randomly around the stone fireplace. The pool table takes up the other half of the room. The floors are wood, with faded braid rugs here and there.

Harp goes into the kitchen and brings back a couple of beers. It's another thing I need to do if I'm ever going to get a social life: learn to like beer. I pull the tab on mine, take a sip. If Harp notices me wrinkle my nose at the bitterness, he's nice enough not to mention it.

"Nice place, huh? My uncle's." He smiles wryly. "He's letting me use it this winter, so I can get my shit together."

"Join the club," I say. "So what got *you* out of whack?"

"If I am out of whack," he says.

"Meaning?"

He shrugs. "My parents think there's something wrong with me because I don't want to be stressed out all the time over some high-power job I don't give a fuck about. I don't want to spend my life pleasing a bunch of greedy assholes who don't give a shit about anything but grabbing all the power they can. Not to mention all the people you have to step on or rip off if you want to get ahead."

"What's wrong with that?" I ask.

"Nothing, in my mind. *Now.* The problem is, at one point I was all set up and gung ho to do it their way. Business degree from Michigan, accepted into law school there. Funny thing is, it's my dad's fault I changed. Always the good liberal, he says, 'What you need is a few years in the Peace Corps, son. It'll broaden your horizons. Look great on the resume.'"

He laughs, sort of. "So I spent two years in this tiny village in Niger, teaching the people basic farming skills. News to me: they didn't even know our country existed. How could they want to be like us? It blew me away how much they *didn't* want or need.

"I don't mean to romanticize how they live," he adds. "Or to say I want to live that way myself. I don't even know if I could hack it. But it shocked the hell out of me. It made me think. And the more I thought, the more I wanted—"

He shakes his head. "I wanted *not* to want, if that makes any sense at all. To just *be.*"

"Like I was, skiing this morning. That Buddhist thing."

"Yeah," he says. "The problem is, unless you're a Zen master, you can't be like that all the time. Plus, you've got to eat, which means you have to make some kind of living. So I'm trying to figure out two things. How to get to that place in my head more often, and how to make enough money to keep from having to ask my parents for anything."

"So, do you meditate?"

"Too squirrelly. I turn on the Tibetan chant CD, get in the lotus position, and immediately start itching. I smoke a little weed sometimes, but that seems like cheating. The need thing, you know? I don't want to need weed to get there.

"So what about you?" he asks. "You've got the money problem beat—unless your parents are setting up a lot of bullshit rules about how you ought to be."

"My parents are wonderful," I say, blinking back the sudden tears that burn my eyes.

He raises an eyebrow. "No rules?"

"No *unreasonable* rules. There's nothing wrong with rules if they're reasonable, you know. There's no such thing as living with *no* rules."

He raises his eyebrow again, but doesn't comment.

I know what he's thinking, though. Once, he believed *his* parents' rules were reasonable. There's no point in arguing that my parents' rules really *are* reasonable, so why wouldn't I want to live by them? Though it strikes me, suddenly, that if Mom and Dad's rules and expectations had been unreasonable, I'd have been glad to go off to college. If they'd given me something really serious to rebel against, it would feel good to leave them behind and make my own way.

Which gives me that old familiar plunging-elevator feeling. I mean, I must be even more fucked up than I realized to even *consider* that it might be a bad thing for me to love Mom and Dad the way I do. But it's the kernel of truth I see in the thought that really scares me. I *do* have to separate myself from them to make my own life—and not in this chickenshit way I'm doing it now. Somehow, I have to figure out which parts of them I'm *not.*

"Another beer?" Harp asks.

"No thanks, I still have some."

"You don't like beer," he says. Just like, earlier, he said, "You're lonely."

He takes my can, still half-full, and disappears into the kitchen again. When he comes back he's got a mug of hot chocolate, whipped cream piled high on the top. It's wonderful, creamy and sweet, and the two of us sit quietly, Harp having another beer, me savoring my hot chocolate.

"Listen," he says after a while. "I really don't know shit about anything. You want to keep that in mind about me. So—" He grins and leans over to wipe the whipped cream moustache from above my lip. "Want to play some pool?"

We rack the balls again and again, concentrating so hard on the game that I'm surprised to glance at the clock and see it's well past three in the morning. Even more surprised to realize that, all that time, I didn't think about anything but the balls on the table, how to position myself for the best shot. I didn't once feel stupid or self-conscious. I didn't feel anything. I just *was*.

I like this idea that you can learn to be empty of *yourself*. That when you're empty in the right way, it doesn't make you feel lonely or sad. In fact, when you surface, reenter your skin, what you feel is this weird, pure, clean happiness. Amorphous happiness that really isn't about anything at all. When I wake up the next day, near noon, I make a list of the moments in my life when I was really, really happy. Reading them over, I realize that in almost every one of them I was empty in exactly the same way I was empty while skiing and playing pool with Harp.

Craig, my boss at the restaurant, gestures me into his office when I clock in for my evening shift, nods toward the chair beside his desk. I sit down. He's a nice guy, overworked, always worrying about his wife and kids and how he's going to give them everything they want and need.

"Emma." He clears his throat. Then clears it again. "Uh. I hope you won't take this wrong, but, well..." *Again*. "I need to talk to you about Harp."

"Harp?" I sound like a ventriloquist's dummy.

"Yeah," he says. "Listen, I know this is none of my business. And Harp is an interesting guy. Smart. No question about that! He's got a real good heart. I can see why you'd—" He blows his breath out through his lips.

"Emma," he says. "Jimmy, the night guy, mentioned he saw the two of you leave together last night. He was a little worried when he looked out and saw your car still in the parking lot—pretty late. And, well, I'm a little worried about that myself. Harp's quite a bit older than you, Emma. And he's, well, he's not—"

"He has a pool table at his house," I interrupt. "I went over to shoot a few games with him. That's all."

Craig doesn't look convinced.

"We're just friends. Really." I stand up, smooth my black waitress pants. "I need to get out on the floor," I say. "There's a group of ten coming in any minute. Thanks, though. I appreciate your being concerned."

But I don't, really. The tight band of anxiety that settled itself across my chest when Craig called me into his office bursts into rage that makes me feel light-headed and dangerous. What's with him anyway, I think. Trying to make me feel embarrassed and ashamed about a perfectly innocent relationship. What's with *me*, letting him sucker me into feeling that way?

"Are you okay?" one of the waitresses asks.

"Fine," I say. "Why?"

"You look upset. Did Craig say something to upset you?"

I shake my head, pick up the Specials sheet, and pretend to study it until she goes away.

Harp's not here tonight, and I'm glad. Whatever happiness I had felt this afternoon, thinking about how our time together had made me discover something that might help me change my life, collapsed with Craig's words. I'm right back to where I always am when there's a male involved: second-guessing myself about every little thing, scrambling for a plan to make him think I'm cool, trying to convince myself that I don't care if he likes me or not.

Seventeen

Then there he is, leaning on my Jeep, when I come out of the lodge. Lani's lying beside him, her head between her stretched-out paws, and she lumbers up and comes toward me, tail wagging. When I ruffle her neck she leans toward me for more, so I drop to my knees in the snow, put my arms around her and nuzzle against her big face.

"We're going for a walk," he says. "Night's good. I don't have to keep her on a leash." He smiles. "She gets twice the walk I do that way. Anyway, I thought maybe you might want to walk with us."

I glance back toward the lodge, and there's Jimmy, the night guy, standing at the door.

"If you're too tired, that's okay," Harp says. "We can do it another time."

"No." I stand up. "I'm fine. I'm not tired."

We walk out to the end of the road, Lani disappearing into the woods—sometimes reappearing ahead of us, sometimes loping to catch up with us from behind. She stops and barks now and then. Once, she throws herself into an untouched patch of snow and rolls around on her back, her big front paws limp with pleasure. She looks so sweet I can't resist falling backwards beside her, waving my arms and legs in an arc to make a snow angel. I lie there a long time, looking up at the full moon, feeling like—if I wanted to—I could float right up into the stars.

I don't want to, though. I want to stay right here on earth, breathe in the cold, crisp air, hear the snow crunch beneath my feet as Harp and I walk back toward the lodge together. Halfway there, he stops, puts his hand on my arm to stop me, too. He points, and I see three deer, caught in moonlight, at the edge of the forest. They seem frozen there, not quite real. Then Lani makes a funny little sound in her throat, not quite a bark, and the deer bolt, leaping across the meadow on their impossibly thin legs, graceful as dancers.

I suddenly think of Jules in the middle of New York City, and, at least right now, I wouldn't trade places with her. I'm happy to be who I am, where I am. I'm over being mad at Craig, who was just trying to be helpful. Grateful for the happiness bubbling up inside me again, allowing me to believe that last night with Harp was real. He *is* my friend, because here he is beside me. I don't want or need him to be anything more than that.

And, over the next few weeks, being with him, things begin to seem possible. We spend every night after work hanging out at his house, playing pool, watching movies, talking about everything under the sun. At the restaurant, I hang out at the bar between customers, continuing whatever conversation we started hours before. I tell him funny stories about my awful semester at college. My Friday night dates with Freud, Matt and Tiffany constantly making out in our dorm room, and how Tiffany was determined to jump-start my love life. The mortifying coffee date with Gabe Parker.

"You liked him, though, didn't you?" Harp says.

I shrug, blushing.

He laughs, but doesn't press me, which only makes me like him more. I'm happy when I'm with him. I never worry about what or what not to say, or feel embarrassed by what I just said; it's exactly the way I used to feel when I was with Josh.

I even tell Harp about Josh. Everything. Even seeing him with Heather right before I bolted for Michigan and how bad it hurt, even though I knew Josh and I would never be anything but friends. I was happy to be friends with him again. It was enough. I thought I'd accepted that. But maybe not. Maybe I never could.

"Well," Harp says. "The way I figure it, you never fall out of love with that first person. It's like a scar, you know? It heals over after a while. You can live with it, cover it up if you don't want someone to see it. But it never goes away.

"Things end," he says. "It's the way life is. The guy's nuts for not loving you, Emma. But it's nothing *you* did. Most guys never know who the really cool girls are. You need to quit running that trip on yourself and move on."

"But *how*?" I ask.

"Tell me one thing you want," he says. "Don't think. Say the first thing that comes to mind."

"A dog," I say. "A big, slobbery yellow dog that loves me."

"Then get one," Harp says. "That's moving forward."

"But I can't get a dog. My mom's totally not a dog person. If the idea of *any* kind of pet comes up she always says she can't stand the idea of being responsible for one more living being. There's no way she'll—"

"So?" Harp says. "Get your own life, then. Put a dog in it. What's so hard about that?"

I'd never thought about life that way before, like it's a big box into which you put everything you want. I could start small, I guess. Get an apartment, get a big yellow dog to live there with me. I imagine running with it, playing Frisbee, rolling around in the grass. I see it in the passenger seat of my Jeep, its big head stuck out the window to catch the wind.

"There's that girl with the great dog," people would say as I drove past.

Who knows? Maybe getting a life really is that simple: making a place of your own, living day-to-day in it surrounded by what you love. Maybe it's also true that I'm cool, like Harp assures me I am. Also pretty, funny, and smart. The day we road-trip to Traverse City to buy me a pool cue, I actually begin to believe it. To believe that, in time, I might even be happy.

And, duh. It occurs to me for the first time that I don't have to be happy at IU before I can be happy somewhere else. Getting it together *there* is not some kind of test. It didn't work: so move on. As for the Gabe thing, *whatever* it was. Yeah, I liked him. So what. It only matters in that place, and if I'm not *in* that place, ever again, eventually it will just be one small thing that happened to me along the path of becoming who I am. I mean, what's *wrong* with not going back? Staying in Michigan—maybe forever?

Harp helps me pick out the cue and a tooled leather case to carry it in. After we try it out in a bar for a couple of hours, he says, "Hey, let's go to the beach." It's a gorgeous day, cold and crisp, blue sky and sunshine. He says, "Why think of the beach as a place to go to only in the summer?"

"Really!" I say, though until that second I had.

We drive over to Sleeping Bear Dunes, a place I love. Mom called it "Ocean Michigan" when we were little, and I still think of it that way. Lake Michigan *is* like an ocean: so big you can't see across it, and those wonderful white sand beaches. Today, there's nobody but Harp and me. All I hear is the sound of the waves breaking and receding and the sound our boots make cracking the thin crust of ice. I love the way the snow is swirled in patterns on the sand, making the beach all tan and white, like a huge animal hide.

In some places the wind's blown the sand into ridges, and where the snow's crusted on them, cracking and melting here and there, the sand beneath shows through in mysterious, stick-like patterns. Hieroglyphs, I think. Secrets left here for me to decipher.

It's freezing cold, and windy; my face burns. But I never want to leave. Harp and I stand at the edge of the water for a long time, watching some ice balls caught in a scoop of shoreline. They're all sizes, from snowball size to the size of a snowman's torso, but none of them quite round—which is probably why they roll in the water so crazily, bobbing like drunks, bumping against the thick curve of ice that stops a few yards short of the beach. I'm hypnotized by them. A wave comes in and soaks them brown. Then it recedes, sucking the water away with it, and the ice balls are white again. It makes me think of sucking all the juice from a snow cone.

I can't help it. I throw my arms around Harp and say, "This is so wonderful. In my whole, whole life I've never seen anything like this. Thank you so much for bringing me."

And he hugs me back a long time. We just stand there in the freezing cold, the two of us, like lovers. It feels strange when I have that thought. Sure, I've had some fantasies about Harp. But because he's older, because he knows so much more than I do, because he's been such a help to me, it's never occurred to me that Harp might think of me as someone he could love. The more I think of it, though, the more it seems to me that these past few weeks together have been moving toward this moment. And I feel my heart open to what might happen next between us.

Eighteen

I wake up early the next morning, full of energy. There's new snow on the ground, and when I open the window I can hear the distant rumble of the big ski cats already out grooming the slopes. I pop in a can of cinnamon rolls, put on my ski clothes while they bake. I smile at myself in the mirror, thinking about how I'll drag Harp out of bed, feed him breakfast, and make him go skiing with me.

But when I get to his house, he's gone. *Gone.* I know

because the door is locked; Harp never locks the door. I sit down on the porch steps, as if the wind's been knocked out of me, the stupid cinnamon rolls cooling in my lap.

"Fuck!" I say, over and over. "Fuck, fuck, *fuck*." Going back and forth between feeling furious, mortified, and heartbroken. How could he *do* this? What's the matter with me that guys can't even stand to be my *friend*?

I don't know how long I sit there before throwing the cinnamon rolls into the woods and heading back to my Jeep. I'm freezing by the time I get home, though. Shaking from the cold. I can't cry. I can't do anything but make a fire in the wood stove and huddle up to it, shivering.

All I can think of is that in a few hours I'm going to have to go to work, where everyone will feel sorry for me. I can't wimp out, I have to go. I'll just have act like Harp leaving is no surprise to me. No big deal. Like I knew he was going all along.

Right. As soon as I see Craig standing at the door, looking as worried about me as if I'm one of his own daughters, I start crying. "I'm really sorry about this, Emma," he says, ushering me into his office, closing the door.

"Really, we were just friends," I say.

Craig nods.

"Well, I thought we were friends, anyhow. I guess I should have listened to you."

He gives a little shrug. "Hey, you live and learn. Thing is, the guy's FUBAR, Fucked Up Beyond All Repair. You're a nice girl, Emma," he says kindly. "You'll find someone a lot better than that."

Out on the floor, the other waitresses hover over me. Like Craig, they all assume there was more going on between Harp and me than there actually was. Sex, that is. God. Would they feel more or less sorry for me if they knew that the idea of having sex with me is probably what made Harp bolt?

I get through the weekend okay; then Monday and Tuesday nights I call in sick. I *am* sick by then. Sick at heart. I lie in bed for three days straight, just lie there. I don't read or even listen to music. It's a bad kind of nothing, though. Not *shunyata,* because I can't stop thinking. *Isn't there one person in the entire world who wants to be with me?*

Then, after three days of feeling like I want to die, I wake up and a voice inside my head says, clear as anything, "Simplify your life."

I don't know why I do what I do next. It's not exactly like I decide. But I get up and shower, gather every stitch of clothing I brought with me from home except the jeans and sweatshirt I'm wearing, put them in plastic trash bags, and haul them out to my Jeep. Then I drive to Traverse City, dump the bags at Good Will, and go shopping. I buy black jeans, black combat boots, black turtlenecks and sweaters, a black ski jacket and pants, a black-and-white gypsy-looking dress, all new socks and underwear—everything black or white.

I can't give myself full credit for the idea to do the black-and-white thing. I got it from reading a book about Georgia O'Keeffe, whose clothes were all either black or white because she didn't like to have to think about what to wear. I thought it was cool when it read it, and it seems like a good plan to me now. I go one step further than Georgia, though. I walk into a beauty shop and say, "Anyone have time to buzz my hair?"

Every single person in the shop turns to look at me. Even the ladies under the dryers lift up the hoods and offer their opinions. "But, honey, your long hair is so pretty," they say. "Are you sure you want to do something that drastic?"

"Absolutely," I say. "I'm tired of thinking about hair. I'm tired of thinking about anything."

I love the chop, chop, chop of the scissors. I love watching long strands of my hair fall to the floor, I love watching my face—a whole new face—appear. Why didn't I do this sooner, I wonder? Hair is stupid. What's the point in having hair? For whom? I feel light and free when I leave the beauty shop. For days afterwards I glance in the mirror, totally shocked to realize that the person I see there is myself.

Once again, I am a human dynamo. This time it's different, I tell myself. This time it's real. I get up early, cross-country ski so fast that, ten minutes onto the trail, I'm soaked through with sweat. All dressed in black, I feel sleek and dangerous, like a James Bond girl. Then pretty soon, it gets even better than that and I feel nothing at all.

After skiing, I go inside and study my French the rest of the morning—a promise to myself that, in time, I will live in a world wider than the one I'm living in now. I make myself think in French all day, which turns out to be a stroke of genius because, to translate my thoughts, I have to make myself think slowly. I can't indulge myself in that awful spiraling of dark thoughts that always lead me to the same place: *I'm so lonely. Will there ever be a time I won't be lonely?*

Sometimes those thoughts come anyway; and when that happens, I make my mind take a right-angle turn into something simple. A childhood memory, clear as a snapshot: *La petite jeune fille en skis descende la montagne très rapidement.* Or I run through the various steps to do something I've done a hundred times, like tuning my skis. If controlling my thoughts doesn't work, I just start naming the things all around me. *Le table, le livre, la lampe, la fenêtre. La porte, la neige, le ciel, les arbres.*

Le restaurant. There, I'm usually too busy to think. If there's dead time, I concentrate on describing the customers. *La famille bonheur avec deux enfants charmante. La grosse femme avec la lipstick très rouge. Les yuppie skiers d'enfer.*

I carry a little French dictionary in the pocket of my apron so I can look up words I don't know. Sometimes I walk into the kitchen and say things like, "*Les sheeseboorgeres sont très, très sublime!*" The other waitresses think it's hilarious. We all get to saying, "*Sacre bleu!*" when something goes wrong. And "*Au revoir, mes amis,*" every night when we leave.

Je vais bien, I tell myself. *J'ai une vie.*

I'm doing fine. I have a life.

Then Mom calls and says, "Emma, Mary Clark called and said there's a beige Honda Civic in our driveway at home. Do you know anything about that?"

At which point, everything comes crashing in on me, and I burst into tears and tell her everything.

"You're *where*?" she says. "You're *what*?"

Before I know it, she's made arrangements for me to fly to Steamboat Springs the next day. I feel horrible giving zero notice, just like Harp did. It's an awful thing to do, and I apologize to Craig about a million times when I go over to tell him.

"It's okay, Emma," he says. "Really. It'll be good for you to be with your parents."

He's so nice about my going that he even takes me into town the next morning so I can catch the limo to Traverse City instead of parking my Jeep for who-knows-how-long in the airport parking lot. In fact, he says, if I pay his expenses, he'll drive it to Indy for me and come back on the Greyhound; he has a friend there he'd like to see.

"Yes!" I say, and hug him hard. Then I get on the bus and promptly start to cry *again*. I cry the whole way to the airport. Then I cry again when the plane lifts off and I look out the window and see the snowy forests and meadows I loved so much as a little girl. The plane banks and turns westward. The shoreline of Lake Michigan with its long white stripe of beach seems like the shoreline of my childhood. We're flying away from it so fast. In moments, it's no more than a pencil line along the horizon. Then it's gone completely. Everywhere I look there's either cold blue water or hard blue winter sky.

Nineteen

When I come through the gate at the airport both Mom and Dad look right through me, their eyes peeled for the person I used to be. I have on my black clothes, of course. Jeans and a big turtleneck, combat boots. Not to mention my haircut.

Then Mom does a double take. "Your hair," she says, faintly.

"Jesus!" Dad says. "Emma."

If they're still pissed off at me, the shock makes them

forget it—at least for the moment. Or maybe talking about what a disaster I am is just more than they can handle right now, considering how quickly it becomes obvious that they're not doing so great either. They bicker the whole way back from the airport, which they hardly ever do. About where we should have dinner, whether snow is forecast for tomorrow, what kind of ski pass I should buy.

Who cares? I want to say.

The condo they've rented is all stone and glass, with high-beamed ceilings. The walls are white, hung with Navajo weavings. The carpet's white. Butter-colored leather couches and easy chairs are gathered around the stone fireplace, or slanted toward the big antique armoire that hides the TV and stereo system. There's a tall silk plant in one corner of the room, silk flower arrangements on the end tables, baskets full of magazines like *Architectural Digest, Town and Country, GQ*. Things Mom and Dad would never read. In fact, the only clue they're living here at all is the clutter of books on the coffee table—Mom's art books, Dad's detective novels—and Mom's easel set up on the sun porch.

When they've given me the tour and agreed on a plan for dinner, Dad goes off skiing and Mom settles me into the extra room, with its king-size bed and full bath, its own TV and little balcony. Then she fixes some hot chocolate and we sit down by the fire in the living room.

I can see her easel from where we sit, and ask what she's been working on.

"Oh, this and that—" She waves her hand vaguely. "But still nothing I can really care about. Mostly I sit and draw. Anything. Just to be moving my hand. But I'll hit on something in time. I will. The thing is," she says, "in a whole new place, a new life, really, you don't realize what you're seeing, what's important, until later. Then suddenly you know what to do with it. You know where it belongs."

But she doesn't sound like she believes it.

"Mom, I'm sorry about—" I begin.

"Emma, *I'm* sorry," she says. "We're sorry—your dad and I, for not . . ." She waves vaguely again. "Honey, I'm just glad you're here. This stupid money. Really. It's got us all out of whack."

"It's not the money," I say. "I was miserable at school before the money."

"You'd have stayed, though," she said. "You'd have adjusted."

"Maybe." I shrug.

"You withdrew, right? Before . . ."

Before I'd have failed all the classes I'd signed up for, she means—and is afraid to ask. I nod.

"Well, then . . ." she says.

Oh boy. I see in her face that she's going to go chirpy on me, which makes me feel worse than I already do because it means she's wracked her brain and come up clueless about how to deal with the fact that dropping out of school is just the tip of the iceberg of what a wreck I am.

She smiles, takes a sip of her hot chocolate. "You've got plenty of time to decide what you want to do. You can go back to IU in the fall; you could transfer—out here, maybe. You could take some time off; maybe travel." She reaches over, gives my arm a squeeze. "We'll get this money stuff sorted out. All of us."

I ought to feel relieved that she's giving me a pass, at least for the time being. I mean, did I really want her to grill me about what I plan to do with my life when I have no plan and can't even imagine anything other than holing up here, safe, for as long as I can get away with it? So why is it that her being so reasonable makes me feel even worse than I did before?

Late that afternoon, I sit out on my balcony with my laptop, reading e-mail after e-mail from the intrepid Tiffany, who kept being my friend, kept sending me e-mails at least once a week even though I hadn't answered a single one of them—or even known they were there, waiting to be answered, until now.

I can't help being cheered up a little by her familiar, over-excited voice reporting every bit of gossip she's heard since I left. *I miss you so much,* one of the early e-mails concludes. *Our room seems so empty without you. You left your Pink* Try This *CD behind, and I play it all the time. I know I should send it back (especially since I STILL don't like it all that much and Matt REALLY, REALLY hates it), but I'm not because when it's playing, it's like you're here. Plus, I figure if I keep it you'll have to come back and get it. You're too poor to buy a new one, right? (Ha, ha.) Matt says hi, by the way. Love, Tiff.*

There's nothing about Gabe Parker in any I've read so far. She's getting smarter, I guess. Or she's just gone underground on the issue, biding her time. But her e-mails make me think about him anyway. I see him in my mind's eye, sitting in the booth at the Daily Grind that day, waiting for me. The way he looked up and smiled at the sight of me. "Emma?" he said.

Oh, for God's sake, he was not smiling at the sight of *you,* I remind myself. He was smiling because he thought you were going to give him a great story. No, let's be totally honest here. He was smiling because he's a nice person. Didn't he follow you out to the street, trying to be nice even after you made a total fool of yourself in the café? Didn't he even try to be nice during the Winnebago debacle?

Which, naturally, makes me think that Josh was nice that day, too. I remember how he followed us all up the steps, into the Winnebago, rather than hurt Gramps' feelings. How he tried to call me when I left Bloomington and I deleted the message without even listening to it—not to mention the six e-mails he'd sent in that first week I was gone, which I deleted when I opened up my laptop an hour ago and saw them there. Probably, in one of them, he told me he'd brought the car back to Indianapolis and left it in the driveway, since he didn't feel right about keeping it after what happened.

I put my laptop aside, partly because I'm afraid that if I keep reading Tiff's e-mails there will be something about Gabe or Josh, partly because I just can't face the fact that I can't really go forward until I go back and figure out how to think about . . . everything. I was dumb to think I could. Even if things with Harp hadn't worked out so badly, even if I had been able to make my own life in Michigan, all those bad feelings about Josh would still be there, inside me. Every single stupid thing I said or did when I was with Gabe Parker would still be looping through my mind.

I sit back, breathe in cold, sharp mountain air. The condo is slope-side, within easy walking distance of the main chair lift; and watching the skiers drift down the mountain like bright bits of confetti, I remember our first trip here, when I was six. The mountains seemed like a fairyland to me, as if I'd awakened into them from a dream; and it occurs to me that, even then, long before I knew how large and awkward the real world would ultimately make me feel, their vastness was a comfort to me, a promise of belonging. Now I sit in the last warmth of the winter sun and wait for that feeling to overtake me again.

The sun goes in, and it grows cold. But I stay out anyway, watching the twinkly white lights blink on along the walkways lined with shops and restaurants, and the skiers coming down from the mountain tired and content. The little balcony seems like the right place for me. Not on the slopes or in the bars or restaurants, where happy people entertain themselves; not inside the glitzy condo, one more place I don't belong.

Twenty

As the days pass, the only thing that makes me feel grounded is skiing with Dad. He wakes me in the early morning, just like he did on Michigan Saturdays when I was a child; and for a little while each day there's only the shush of the snow beneath my skis, the smell of pines, the feeling that any second I might lift off and soar into the bright blue sky. We ski tirelessly, like we used to, stopping only to grab a bite at lunchtime, maybe for hot chocolate if we get cold.

In the afternoons, we race—NASTAR, the amateur racing program we did every winter weekend when Jules and I were kids. We don't talk, except about skiing: the run we just took, our race times, whether the snow that's starting to come down in big, fat flakes all around us is light enough to ensure powder in the morning.

Then one afternoon we're reminiscing about racing up in Michigan, and get to watching this cute little girl on the course. She's six or seven, all bundled up in a bright red ski outfit. So proud of the two bronze NASTAR medals pinned to her jacket.

Dad gets a kick out of that. "Two medals!" he says to her. "You must be pretty fast."

She grins a toothless grin. "I got one for trying really hard," she says. "Yesterday I almost won, so my dad gave me his medal. Then today, I really won. So I got another one."

"That is so sweet," I say afterward, going up on the chairlift.

"Are you kidding?" Dad says. "It's bullshit! Why the hell would her dad give her a medal she didn't earn?"

"To make her feel good?" I say. "To encourage her to keep trying? What's so wrong about that?"

"It's dishonest," he says. "It makes both medals meaningless. Don't you remember how you felt the first time you won a bronze medal, what a big deal it was?"

"Sure," I say. "But maybe earning every goddamn little thing isn't the most important thing in the world. Maybe once in a while it's okay just to make your kid feel good."

We get to the top right then, and I catapult myself off

the chair and huff away. I'm so mad I fly through the gates and beat his time by three seconds.

"You know I'm right," he says, back on the chairlift. "You know there's no point in having a medal you didn't earn. Tell me that gold medal you just won wasn't all the better because you kicked my butt doing it?"

"Who cares about a gold medal," I say. "Who cares about winning a million medals? I'd ten times rather feel like I wasn't such a loser all the time."

Dad looks pained. "For Christ's sake, Emma, you're not a loser. You're just going through a tough time. You need to lighten up a little. Enjoy yourself."

"Lighten up," I say. "Okay. I'll get right on that."

Furious, I ski away from him, away from the race hill, and slam down through the first mogul field I can find. Once in the middle of it, I feel pure, like a machine. I don't think about anything. My body knows what to do and it does it again and again the whole way down. My legs are burning by the time I get to the bottom. I stop, bend over, breathing hard.

Dad slides to a stop beside me. "Great run, Emma," he says. "I mean it. That was a great run. You were unconscious!"

But I ski away from him again, all the way down to the base. Then I take my skis off, heft them onto my shoulder, and head for the condo.

"I'm sorry," Dad says, catching up to me. "Really. I didn't mean to upset you."

I shrug.

"You're not speaking to me?"

"Why bother, when you have no idea what I'm trying to say?"

"Fine," he says. "Fuck it. Be miserable."

"What's wrong with you two?" Mom says when we stomp in. "What happened?"

I just sink into one of the ridiculous leather couches, fold my arms across my chest, and watch Dad get pissed all over again telling Mom about the little girl's medals.

"It's not about the stupid medals," I say. "Okay?"

"Then what is it about?" Dad asks. "For Christ's sake, we win fifty million dollars and suddenly everyone's depressed? You're right. I don't have a fucking clue."

Mom and I sit there, mute, until he leaves, slamming the door behind him.

"I know what you mean about the medals," she says after a while.

"Yeah, well, do you know how Dad can be so incredibly obtuse?"

"Actually," she says, "I think I do. The thing is, Emma, he's so—himself. He's so comfortable in his own skin. It's a wonderful way to be—"

"Maybe," I say. "But he thinks everyone should be that way. He thinks you can just decide to feel good about yourself. That I can decide that."

"I know," Mom says. "He thinks I can, too—though, God knows, I've spent the better part of a lifetime trying to disabuse him of the idea. But Emma, you know how you can understand something in your head, how you can absolutely believe it, and no matter how hard you try you keep on acting, thinking in the same old ways?"

"Yeah. Unfortunately, I have no problem whatsoever with that concept."

"Well, there you go," Mom says. "Your dad's not perfect, either. And ever since we got the money, he's been like a kid in a candy store. But he'll come down from it. He can't ski forever. Eventually, he'll have to figure out what to do with himself, just like the rest of us."

She means to make me feel better, saying that. But as much as Dad drives me crazy sometimes, I count on his relentless enthusiasm. It scares me to think of him being any other way. "The thing is, he was right about the medals," I say. "That's what made me so mad."

"Maybe," Mom says. "But you were also mad because he wasn't listening to you. Fine. He's right about earning your own way. But feeling good about yourself helps you be able to do that—and feeling good about yourself doesn't automatically happen just because you're competent. Which is basically what you were trying to say to him, wasn't it?"

"Yeah."

"Then you were right, too, weren't you? He should have done a better job of letting you know how proud he was of you, growing up. We both should have. Emma—" Her voice wobbles. "Dad and I both think you're wonderful. You know that, don't you? You know how much we love you?"

Then we're both crying.

"I know you and Dad love me," I say, when I can get my breath. "*I* don't love me. It's *my* problem." I let her put her arms around me and hold me, like she did when I was a little girl.

I should tell her about Harp now. Try to explain what happened between us and how it made me feel worse about myself than I ever have. But it seems like such a long story, so stupid and confusing, that I can't think how to begin.

Trouble is, I can't think how to stop thinking about it. For days, I swing back and forth between believing that maybe I really am a perfectly okay person like Harp said, just confused (maybe even a person Gabe Parker could like), and replaying my failures with Harp—and Josh, too—certain that they're just the first two of however many heartbreaks I'm bound to suffer until I finally wise up and accept that I'm destined to spend the rest of my life living all alone with my competent, out-of-it, dilettante self.

I also think about something I read about karma in a book Harp lent me: that you choose your troubles based on lessons you need to learn. Could that be right, too? Could I actually be choosing to be screwed up, choosing to be a human pinball machine of emotion? Choosing not to be loved? I run that one by Mom, who looks at me with that expression she gets when she's standing at her easel, paintbrush in her hand, trying to decide where to make the next stroke.

"Well, take a look at yourself," she says carefully. "Your clothes, your hair. You look great, but so—extreme."

"Yeah?" I say.

Mom shrugs. "You're always talking about not being

pretty, yet you refuse to make any effort to look pretty. You cut off all your beautiful hair. You dress in black—"

"I did it to simplify my life," I say. "I told you that. And anyway, why should I spend all my time trying to look pretty just to attract some stupid boy? I hate that. If boys don't notice me, if they don't like me the way I am, screw them. Who needs them?"

"Emma," Mom says. "I hate to tell you this, but the way you look now absolutely screams for attention. Personally, I think you look wonderful. You know, very chic. But to most boys, you probably look, well, a little alarming. Why would you want to alarm them?"

"I don't want to alarm them," I say. "I just don't want to bother with them if they can't handle the real me."

"Okay," she says. "I can see that. But don't you think you might be putting off a lot of perfectly nice guys in the process, guys who'd like you just fine if they felt comfortable taking the chance to get to know you? It's hard for them, too, you know. Dating isn't only hard for girls. And think about this: trying to look avant-garde is ultimately no different from trying to look conventionally pretty. You do realize that, don't you? That it's the same impulse at work? The same extreme attention to appearance?"

My heart sinks: I hadn't, till this moment.

"Bullshit," I say nonetheless. "I look the way I do because I like looking this way. I can't believe you think I should dress to make boys happy."

Mom looks pained. "I didn't say you should dress to make boys happy, Emma. You know me better than that.

I'm saying, be honest with yourself. That's all. It's not easy, I know. And I know we went overboard making such a big deal about you and Julie being smart and independent. We should have made sure you knew we thought you were pretty, too."

"But Jules *is* pretty. And smart. It's not like it turned out to be a problem for her."

"Julie has her own problems," Mom says. "We all do. And for God's sake, Emma, you're pretty too. Don't you realize that there are probably a million girls out there not nearly as pretty as you are who think they're gorgeous because their parents made a big deal of telling them so? They're probably upset about how nobody ever told them they were smart."

Well, I'm too tired to think about that, too tired to think about anything. In fact, I'm suddenly so completely exhausted that I fall asleep right there where I sit. When I wake up, it's night, and I can hear the low murmur of my parents talking in the kitchen.

"... pack up, get a few hour's sleep," Mom says. "If we leave early and drive straight through, we'll get there about as quick as we could by flying..."

I can't make out the next words, so I get up and go toward them. Dad's sitting on the edge of his chair, bent over, his forearms crossed on his knees. Mom's pulled another chair beside him. Still half-asleep, I look at them and feel relieved to see them close, her hand on his knee, their heads bent in earnest conversation.

"At least he made it back from Florida," Mom says.

"Christ, who knows when someone would have found him in that damn Winnebago if it had happened on the road."

I thud fully awake then. "Gramps?" I ask.

They both look toward the doorway, where I stand.

"Margaret called a while ago," Mom says. "She thinks he may have had a heart attack."

"Gramps?" I say again.

"He's okay now," Mom says quickly. "Of course, he wouldn't let Margaret call an ambulance, wouldn't go to the doctor—so we're a little concerned. But you know Margaret: such a worrywart. He's probably perfectly fine."

Margaret's a worrywart, all right. But I'm not fooled. Margaret or no Margaret, I know Mom always believes the worst thing will happen: her pretending that Gramps is fine is absolute testimony to how certain she is that something's terribly wrong with him. I look at Dad and know he doesn't think Gramps is fine either.

I turn and walk back into the dark living room. I look at the rumpled afghan on the chair, at my boots that Mom placed neatly side-by-side. I go to the window and press my forehead against the cold glass. Beyond it there's only the dark mountain, snowflakes swirling. I close my eyes. My life has been on a skid-path ever since we got rich, and now this. Gramps had a heart attack.

As if those two things were equal, I think.

As if winning fifty million dollars was a tragic event.

Twenty-one

Gramps is in his garage when Dad and I get there, Waylon Jennings blaring on his little radio, his beat-up tools and a half dozen greasy engine parts in a clutter all around him. He's working on the snowmobile. He and Dad never did get it running right up in Michigan.

He doesn't hear us come in. The music is loud and he's hard of hearing, anyway. He's sitting there, holding the carburetor in his hand, staring at it. Dad smiles, really smiles, for the first time since Margaret's call. I smile, too—and feel the knot of anxiety give a little inside me. Gramps' bemused expression is so familiar. This whole scene is familiar, reassuring: Gramps in his wreck of a garage figuring out too late that he has no idea what the hell he's doing.

But when he looks up and spots us, fear flickers in his eyes. He holds up the carburetor with a sheepish grin. "Hey, when all else fails, follow directions," he says. Which is what he always says when he gets to this point in a project.

Clever, I think. How he avoided asking us why we're here.

Dad avoids it, too. He finds the owner's manual under a pile of junk on the workbench. "Okay," he says. "What are you trying to do with this mess?"

"Goddamn carburetor," Gramps says. "I can't get any rpm's out of the son of a bitch. I know it's not electrical, and it's breathing air. Got to be the carburetor. Clogged high-speed jet."

They work a while: soak the carburetor in cleaner, then run a wire through the clogged place. I watch, which is what I've done ever since I was big enough for Dad to set me on the barstool Gramps keeps at his worktable and not have to worry about me falling off of it. I'd listen to them talk, wait patiently for the moment they'd turn and, laughing, tell me some story. How Dad used to stay out late and climb into his bedroom window when he was a teenager, and one night Gramps waited in the bushes and scared the shit out of him when he crept around the corner into the backyard. How Gramps once ran a drill bit right through the palm of his hand, stared at it for about two seconds, then turned the drill back on, pulled the bit off, wrapped his hand in an oily rag and kept on doing whatever he was doing.

It cheers me up a little to remember that he refused to go to the emergency room to have his hand looked at, just like he refused going the other night. Still, I watch him now, looking for any sign of what Margaret described when she called us in Colorado. He looks a little tired, maybe; other than that, he looks all right. He's wearing a jacket, though, which worries me a little. Even in the dead of winter, Gramps works in the garage wearing just a flannel shirt.

He looks up. Maybe he can feel my eyes on him. "Emma," he says. "I'll tell you what, that Winnebago runs like a dream. I pulled it right up on the beach down near Tampa. Sat in my leather seat with my feet up on the dash, drank a beer and watched the sun set over the ocean. It's the life, all right." He winks. "Couple of gals were out there one day, sunbathing, and I gave them the tour. If I hadn't been heading back home the next day, well, who knows?"

"Did you feel okay while you were gone?" Dad asks. "You didn't have any—episodes down there, did you?"

Gramps picks up the carburetor, examines it, wipes it off with a rag. "So that's what you're doing here," he says. "Goddamn it. I told Margaret not to call you."

"Don't be pissed off at Margaret," Dad says. "You scared her half to death the other night. What happened, anyway?"

Gramps makes a disgusted sound and starts polishing again. "Yeah, okay, it was probably a little heart attack," he says. "I got your mother's medical book down and took a look at it after Margaret left. There's a pretty good chance that's what it was."

"Oh." Dad takes a step back. He looks as shocked as I feel. In a million years, I'd never have thought Gramps would admit he might have had a heart attack, and I realize that, till this moment, I haven't really believed it could be true. I feel nauseous, dark and fuzzy at the edges— kind of like I felt once in grade school, coming to after I got conked in the head with a swing.

Dad looks at Gramps, takes a deep breath, and blows it out through his lips slowly like air hissing from a punctured tire. "Shit," he says finally, almost to himself. Then, "Why wouldn't you let Margaret call an ambulance if you thought you had a heart attack? For Christ's sake, Dad—"

Gramps sets the carburetor on the garage floor with a clunk. "Listen," he says. "If you came all the way from Colorado to call a goddamn ambulance for me, forget it. I'm not going to the hospital. No way. When your mother died, I swore there was no way in hell I'd die in a goddamn hospital."

"You're not dying," Dad says.

But his voice cracks, and that scares me more than anything.

"I mean it," Gramps says. "I'm not going to the goddamn hospital to die." He takes his glasses off to peer at the small print on a can of motor oil on his workbench, then mutters, "Fifty to one. Not enough oil. Burn a piston."

"Dutch," Dad says in a low voice. "Dad. Will you please listen to me?"

Gramps shrugs, looks up. "Yeah, okay. Shoot," he says.

"All right. No hospital." Dad holds his hands up, in surrender. "I'm not asking you to go to the hospital right now. But you need to see a doctor and find out if you really did have a heart attack. How to avoid having another one, if you did."

Gramps snorts. "I had a goddamn heart attack, okay? And I know how to avoid having another one: crap health food, no beer, sit around and watch the goddamn TV like an old fart. To hell with that. I'm leaving for Arizona in the Winnebago next week, just like I planned. So don't talk to me about doctors and hospitals. I'm not going."

Dad says, "It could be something else, you know. There's all kinds of weird shit it could be. Would you just see the fucking doctor? Indulge me?"

Gramps shrugs again.

"I'm going to call Dr. Crandall, okay? See if—"

"Doc's dead," Gramps interrupts. "Couple months ago."

That stops Dad for a second. Then he collects himself and goes on. "All right, then. How about you come home with Emma and me? And if anything happens between now and whenever we can get in to see a heart guy and find out what's wrong with you—if you have another one of those ... spells—you'll let me call an ambulance."

"I *said*—" Gramps begins.

"I'll spring you," Dad says. "You go to the hospital if it's an emergency, but you don't stay. All right? I swear to

God, I'll spring you. I'll get you out and take you home with me."

"No matter what the docs say?"

"Yeah," Dad says. "No matter what."

Gramps concentrates a long moment on putting the carburetor in place. Then he turns to me again. "You heard him, Emma—"

I nod. I can't speak.

"You won't let him back out on me."

"No." It comes out in a whisper.

"Okay, then. If you swear you'll spring me."

"I'll spring you," Dad says.

"Okay, but I'm not going anyplace till I get this goddamn snowmobile running."

Dad groans. "Fine. But would you give me the fucking manual, so we can do it *right*?"

They spend the next few hours doing what they've always done together. Tear the engine down completely and bicker about how to get it back together again. Drink beer, laugh a lot. At one point Dad says, like he always ends up saying, "Goddamn it, Dutch, you can't fix a thing by beating the shit out of it." Gramps gets mad and bounces a wrench off the garage wall.

As the afternoon unfolds, I'm utterly present in each moment. It's a little like *shunyata*, I think. And for the first time, I can think of Harp without feeling foolish or mad. He'd understand how I can feel so completely happy watching Dad and Gramps the way I always have—and at the same time know, absolutely, deep inside me, that Gramps is going to die. And soon. He's not going to Arizona in the Chieftain, or anywhere else. Ever. I'm pretty sure Dad and Gramps know it, too. Yet it's as if this time together lengthens instead of shortens because of it. The familiar seems more familiar, more secure. The jokes bouncing among us seem funnier than usual, the moment the engine finally starts more satisfying, more dear.

It's about five o'clock when they finish. Gramps goes inside to throw a change of clothes into his duffel bag. Margaret comes out of her back door and waves Dad and me over.

"I hope you convinced him he needs to see a doctor," she says. "Lord, he was white as a sheet when I got to him in the driveway. And so cold. I turned the thermostat up to eighty degrees and he still couldn't get warm."

"He's going home with us," Dad says. "He promised to see a doctor, though he's still dead set against going to the hospital."

"It's what he kept saying to me the other night." Margaret pulls out the linen handkerchief tucked into the cuff of her gray cardigan sweater, dabs at her eyes. "And it wasn't that I couldn't sympathize with him. Mercy, I've seen all I want of hospitals myself. But I was so frightened."

"Well, he seems okay now," Dad says. "He seems better. Margaret, listen, I can't thank you enough for taking care of him—"

"My goodness, it's the least I could do," she says. "He bought me a brand new car, for heaven's sakes! And he's been such a help to me since Ernie died. I don't know what I'd do without him."

She blinks back tears, puts her hand on mine. "He's not mad at me, is he, honey? He explicitly told me not to call you."

"Gramps?" I say. "Mad?"

That makes her laugh.

"He knows you did the right thing," Dad says. "Of course, don't ever expect him to tell you that."

"Well, I know Dutch pretty well," she says. "He doesn't have to tell me every second how he feels."

She walks over with us to say goodbye to him and he hugs her, patting her on the back a few times, the way you'd pat an anxious child.

"Keep an eye on the Chieftain," he says.

Margaret assures him she will.

And as we pull away I think, I swear, if it could make Gramps well, I'd let him drive me down to Bloomington in that stupid RV right now—to the Phi Delt house, if that's where he wanted to go. I really, truly would.

Twenty-two

We're quiet, driving home. Gramps dozes off and Dad and I listen to NPR on the radio: *All Things Considered.* Arabs and Israelis killing each other, genocide in Africa. Politics as usual in Washington. A lengthy feature about keeping bees.

Maybe it's the weirdness of nature that reminds me of driving through Kansas on the way home the day before, Mom rapturous at the sight of the prairie. It *was* beautiful, the rolling hills buttery yellow in the morning light. The sky as blue as a plate. We stopped once, to stretch our legs, and walked out into it. The dried grasses were knee-high; they crackled beneath our feet. Beyond us, a vast herd of buffalo grazed.

Mom said, "Do you realize we're seeing what the pioneers saw, coming across the prairie more than a hundred years ago?" She stopped short, and Dad and I, following, crashed into her.

"What's that?" she asked.

"What?" Dad said.

But I heard it: a low rushing sound, like the inside of a seashell.

Mom listened, perfectly still, then she turned to us, her face lit with joy. "It's the buffalo," she said. "A thousand buffalo munching on that dry grass! And not a mountain in sight." As if those two pieces of information were, in fact, one thing.

Who knows? Maybe they are. Maybe that's all life is: a bunch of stuff sitting side-by-side in the universe, not really meaning anything at all. *Emma*, I say to myself. *This is no time to be thinking like that.* I can't help it, though. Just like I can't help thinking about how strange and sad our own little universe would be without Gramps in it.

He's slumped over in the front seat, fast asleep. He looks pale. I'm so thankful when we pull into the driveway, and he wakes up, grumbling.

"Christ, I hope there's something to eat inside," he says. "I'm starving."

Of course, there's not. Mom spent the day doing what she always does when she's been away: wandering through the house, as if reacquainting herself with it, with all the objects she loves. So we order out for pizza. But Gramps doesn't eat much when it comes.

"You okay?" Dad asks. "Are you sure we shouldn't try to talk to a doctor tonight?"

"Nah." Gramps shakes his head. "Just tired, buddy. Think I'll turn in early. Get some rest so I'll be in good shape to get the shit beat out of me tomorrow. You know how those docs love to give you every goddamn test ever invented."

We set him up in Jules' room—the guest room now—and leave him there, surrounded by her dance posters and all her worn-out pointe shoes tied by their faded pink ribbons to a grid beside her dressing table. The last thing I say to him is, "So, Gramps, if you get it in your mind to get up and dance—"

Then, in the morning, he's dead.

I know it instantly, by the sound of Dad's voice.

"Dutch?" he says. "*Dutch*?"

But it's the long quiet that comes afterwards that makes me get up and go to the doorway of Jules' room, where I see him sitting next to Gramps on the bed. He touches Gramps' forehead, his hands. Pulls the blanket up to his chin and smooths it, as if that could make a difference now.

The floor creaks behind me, and there's Mom, her hair sticking out every which way,

"Mac? Oh, no. Mac—" She goes past me, bends to put her arms around Dad.

I'm watching again, which it seems I'm destined to do. I can't move, can't speak. I just look at the two of them, and Gramps so still on the bed. Dust dances in the shafts of sun streaming through the window. Sun puddles on the carpet. I can hear birds chattering outside. The sky is offensively blue.

Quietly as I can, I retreat to my room, get back into bed and wait for Mom and Dad to come in and tell me Gramps is gone. I'm not crying, exactly. It's more like tears are just leaking from my eyes.

Right now, they're talking in low voices. I can't hear what they're saying, only the rhythm of their words. Slow, halting. In time, they come to me. They look tired, sad. Older.

"Emma." Dad sits down on the bed beside me.

In a small voice I say, "I know."

While Mom and Dad make arrangements, I pace around the house in figure eights. Living room, dining room, kitchen, hallway. I pass by the closed door of Jules' room, where Gramps lies, on my way to the den. Then through Mom and Dad's bedroom, Mom's studio, my own bedroom, and back through the hallway to the living room to do it all over again. I remember how Jules and I used to do the same figure eights when we were little, how we'd get out of control—running, yelling, inevitably ending up hurting ourselves or breaking something. It was Gramps, half the time, who got us whipped up into those frenzies, got all three of us in trouble with Mom before it was all over.

It's not *fair* that he's dead. He was such a good-hearted

person, he loved life so much. Why couldn't some cranky, couch-potato old person have died instead? And why did he have to die now, just when he was getting such a kick out of being rich? The only one of us purely enjoying it. I think of him heading up the snowy hill in the Chieftain on his way to Florida and it makes me so sad I have to go outside and shock myself in the cold air to keep from crying.

I feel a little better when they've come to take Gramps away and there's not that *presence* of him in Jules' room. So wrong. Nothing like the real Gramps ever was. Dad retreats to the garage, Mom to her studio. Pretty soon, neighbors will start showing up with those casseroles that always appear at traumatic moments. They'll say how sorry they are; we'll have to tell the whole story of what happened again and again. The very thought makes me tired, and I go back to bed and sleep until I hear Jules' voice—at which point I drag myself out of bed and into the living room.

"Oh, Emma," Jules says, and hugs me. She looks bad. Pale, her eyes red-rimmed. She doesn't seem to notice my drastic hair. Just sighs, and heads for her room to put her stuff away.

Uh-oh, I think when she opens the door and I see the tangled sheets and the pillow still hollowed out where Gramps' head had been.

"Oh, God," Mom says. "Oh, no. I completely forgot—"

"He died in *my* room?" Jules asks.

Then before anyone can answer her, she sets her suitcase just inside the door, goes back into the living room, and sits down on the couch like a zombie. When Mom finishes changing the sheets, she comes in and fusses over her. Does she want some tea? Is she hungry?

"No, no," Jules says to everything.

"I'm so sorry," Mom says about ten times.

About Jules' room, she means. About not thinking to change the sheets before Jules got home. About Gramps dying there—as if she's responsible for that.

"So," I say. "How's Will?"

"He's fine."

That's all. Nothing about why he didn't come with her, which seems kind of strange to me, since at Christmas they were so lovey-dovey they couldn't stand to be out of each other's sight. When, just a few weeks ago, she told me they were talking about moving in together. But I know better than to press her.

We're all a wreck. It doesn't help a bit to know that Gramps died of a massive heart attack. It was inevitable, the coroner told Dad when he called. If Gramps had let Margaret call the ambulance that first night, he'd have been at the hospital when he died, that's all. Instead of at our house, where he had always loved to be.

Dad keeps repeating this, like it's supposed to make all of us feel better about Gramps being dead. Mom sits down on the arm of his chair and puts her hand on his shoulder, as if to ground him. As if she's half-afraid he might fly up and disappear to wherever Gramps has gone.

After a while, Dad speaks in a wondering tone. "You know something? All the time Dutch was in the world, I never really thought anything could hurt me. Jesus, I knew he was a klutz. I knew that. But he was my dad. Some part of me never quit believing that he could do *anything*."

"Oh, Mac," Mom says, and puts her arms around him.

I want to go and put my arms around him, too. I want to say, "Dad, I know what you mean. I feel the same way about you." But I can't move or speak. I just keep thinking about how, some day, I'll lose him just like he's lost Gramps now.

We're quiet for a while. Then we start telling stories. Dad remembers the first time Gramps went skiing and got going so fast that he took out all the people in the lift line when he got to the bottom. "Sorry," he said, brushing the snow from some fat guy's jacket, grinning that shit-eating grin. "Haven't had Lesson Two yet: How to Stop."

Mom remembers the time he put on Grandma Hammond's sweater by mistake and Dad had to cut him out of it. "He was in the shower," she says. "The doorbell rang and he got out and put on the first thing he saw. You know how Grandma always left his clothes out on the bed when they were going out. It was right there by his trousers, he said afterwards. As if that explained perfectly why he'd put on a lady's sweater, size small."

It seems strange to be laughing, knowing Gramps is dead. Wrong. But Gramps, of all people, wouldn't be upset with us for that. If he were here, he'd be laughing himself, trying to one-up our stories.

I can just hear him. "Did I ever tell you about the time my Uncle Vernie took me water skiing at Lake Celina?" That was one of his favorites. "Drunk as a skunk," he'd say. "Truth is, the liquor probably saved his life, since the first thing he does is step off the goddamn pier and fall ten feet into the boat. He isn't moving. Christ, I think he's broken his neck. I'm about to yell for help when he sits up. 'Watch that first step,' he says. 'It's a pisser.'" He'd wait for everyone to laugh, then go on. "Then, like a fool, I put the water skis on and let him take me out. The lake is low, a whole line of dead trees sticking up above the water, and Vernie starts weaving in and out of them like they're a goddamn obstacle course." He'd shake his head. "I'll tell you something," he'd say. "I'm goddamn lucky to be here to tell you this story."

He always told stories exactly the same way. I can actually hear his voice inside my head, which makes me feel a little better. I'll always be able to hear it. Remembering those goofy stories, I can make him come alive again inside me.

"Well." Mom stands up. "I don't know about you guys, but I don't think I can stay awake another second. I'm going to bed."

"I'm with you." Dad follows her into their bedroom.

Jules looks stricken. Clean sheets have made absolutely no difference to her, I can tell. She's totally freaked out by the prospect of sleeping in the bed where Gramps died.

So I say, "Hey, would you sleep in my room tonight? I know I'm being a big baby, but I'm way too weirded out to be alone."

She agrees, casting me a grateful glance.

She falls asleep quickly beside me, but I lie awake a long time. I think about how I used to climb into bed with

Jules sometimes when I was little and had a bad dream. How, still sleeping, she'd turn and wrap her arms around me. I always felt so safe when I was with her.

Tonight, it's enough just to have her breathing, not two feet away from me. The sound of the radio turned down low: WTLC, the soul station we've both listened to since Jules started high school. The hip, whispery voice of the late-night deejay takes me back to that different time, and the house settles in around me, utterly familiar. Our house, alive with the thousands of nights we've all spent in it, together.

Twenty-three

Apparently Jules is feeling better the next morning, because we get to the subject of my hair. Mom and Dad have gone to make the funeral arrangements; Jules and I are eating breakfast at a little café in the Village. I'm making my usual mess, sprinkling sugar all over the table while attempting to get some in my oatmeal, getting jam on the sleeve of my sweatshirt.

"I see *some* things never change," Jules observes. Then,

of course, she has to remind me how I never failed to spill something in a restaurant when we were little. "You'd be reaching for the menu or the ketchup, or one of those comment cards." She laughs. "Remember how you always insisted on filling those out? Your spelling was always so creative." She makes her voice like a child's. "The habuger wutz gud, but I donut lik the bens."

"Ha, ha," I say.

"Speaking of creative." Jules raises an eyebrow. "Your hair?"

"I decided to simplify my life," I say, attempting nonchalance.

"That's it?"

"Yeah."

"Well, thank God. You *aren't* enlisting in the Marines then."

"Screw you," I say.

Jules grins. "Hey, it's—dramatic, I like it. But what do you mean, simplify your life?"

"It's a long story," I say. "Remember, I told you I met that guy—Harp—at the ski area? Well, he sort of got me into thinking about Buddhism—"

"And you got a crew cut?"

"More or less," I say.

Jules takes a bite of fruit. "A love interest?" she asks. "This—Harp?"

I blush, which pisses me off. "Hardly," I say, then turn the tables on her. "Speaking of which, where's Will?"

She looks at me with an odd, caught expression.

"Are things okay?" I ask. "I mean, with you and Will?"

"Of course," she says shortly. "He has a job, you know. He can't just drop everything and go someplace at the drop of a hat."

Gramps' funeral isn't just *someplace*, I think. It isn't *at the drop of a hat*. But I let it pass. I heard that big-sister tone in her voice: what could *you* possibly know about my love life? Like I'm nine and she's a hotshot freshman in high school. In fact, she acts half-mad at me after that. Like she used to act when I said something dumb and embarrassed her in front of her friends. When I ask her if she wants go to the mall and help me look for a funeral dress, she says she's too tired.

So I go by myself. I find a dress right off: a simple black lightweight wool dress. Long-sleeved, fitted in the bodice, it flares gently and falls to my ankles. It looks good. Grown up. I buy black heels and a small black Coach bag to go with it. Then I wander in and out of stores for a while, ending up where I always do, looking in the window of the pet shop. Two yellow lab puppies play in some straw, rolling and nipping at each other. When I knock on the glass, one of them stops and looks at me, panting.

I think of Harp again, how he looked at me that day and asked me what *I* wanted. He ditched me, sure. But for a little while, he knew me in a way no one else ever had. I think of the cold winter day we stood on the beach together, remember the feel of his arms around me, and I long for that now. Someone, anyone just to hold me.

The yellow puppy barks, scratches at the window as if

to beckon me. I go inside, breathe in the furry, fecal animal odor, and the puppy puts his paws on the retaining wall of the display window and cocks his head. I set my shopping bag on the floor. I lift my hands to his face and feel his soft fur, his rough, wet tongue licking my fingers. "Hey, Harp," I whisper, surprising myself.

The puppy twists eagerly, as if he recognizes the name.

"May I help you?" a sales clerk asks.

Get a life, put a dog in it, the real Harp said. Suddenly, it occurs to me that it could work the other way, too. Get a dog, get a life to put it in. I ask, "Do you ever put dogs, like, on hold?"

"Hold?" the woman asks.

"Well, yeah. I mean, what if I wanted to buy this puppy, but couldn't take him today? The thing is, I just moved back to town and I don't have a place to live right now; but my grandfather died and the funeral's tomorrow, so I can't find a place till after that. So if I wanted to buy the puppy, do you think it might be possible for me to pay for him now and then leave him here a couple of days until I find an apartment?"

The woman goes back to the office to consult with the manager, who agrees that I can leave the dog for three days if I'll sign a statement releasing them from responsibility for any accident that might occur.

I shouldn't do it, I know. I think of my parents, upset enough already about Gramps, and feel almost nauseous. But the puppy yaps urgently at me. He jumps wildly, as if trying to jump into my arms. And I can't help it. I lean over the restraining wall, pick him up and draw him close to me. He's so warm, so needy. He nuzzles my neck, burrows against me, as if to convince me that he belongs here in my arms.

"Okay," I say, abandoning whatever shred of common sense I ever had, and a few minutes later I leave the shop with the receipt and a copy of *The Natural Dog* in hand. I'll just keep it a secret, I think. Until the time is right.

The next morning, the day of Gramps' funeral, I get up early, put on some old sweats and my running shoes, and go outside. It's sunny, but cold for March. Still, the bushes in the yard are red-tipped, promising spring. I walk briskly toward the canal, thinking of Gramps, acutely conscious of the visible puffs of vapor my breath makes in the air. I think, too, about the time I took this same walk all by myself when I was barely three. I was going to feed the ducks, I said, when Mom found me nearly two blocks from home. I was carrying my breakfast toast. The ducks might be hungry, I thought, and I had decided to go feed it to them. I knew the way to the canal perfectly; I'd been there dozens of times. I didn't understand why Mom was so upset about it, why she was crying.

I don't *actually* remember that morning myself. But Mom's told the story so many times that it seems like a memory to me. There are other stories about me, too. How I constantly escaped from the baby pool at the swim club by attaching myself to some family and walking with them past the lifeguard, out the gate. How I cried the first time I skied in powder because it was too slow. I love the image of my small, brave self. I miss that self so much. Where *is* she? I feel sick at heart to think that the happy, fearless little person I used to be might be gone forever. Like Gramps is.

I walk faster, glad to be outside, alone, in the beautiful morning. At home I'd just sit around, getting sadder and sadder. I'll walk an hour, I decide. Think of something happy. Like how it will be walking this same path in a few days with my puppy. Harp. I smile, remembering the way he twisted, burrowing into me. But then I remember I have one day, tomorrow, to find a place to live. And whether I am or am not lucky enough to achieve that, I'm still—and soon—going to have to tell my parents what I've done.

Suddenly, another memory surfaces—a real one this time, my own—and I'm a little girl again, waiting for Mom and Dad on the pier at Mackinac Island. Jules and I had been allowed to explore the shopping street alone and Dad's last words to me were, "Don't waste your money!" It was legendary already, how I spent money on the weirdest things. So I was determined to impress my parents that day by being practical, finding something sturdy and useful to buy.

What I bought was an umbrella hat. Red, white, and blue striped, it sheltered my face from both sun and rain. And it was collapsible, like a real umbrella! It fit neatly into my backpack. I put the hat right on my head, mortifying Jules, who walked ten steps behind me the rest of the afternoon and was now sitting on a bench far away from me reading one of her Nancy Drew mysteries. Sweating, I noticed. While I was shaded by my wonderful new hat. I couldn't wait to show my parents how sensible I'd been.

The second I caught sight of them walking up the pier, I jumped up and ran toward them.

"Oh, *Emma*," was all Mom said, but I knew from the tone of her voice and the expression on Dad's face that the hat had been a mistake. They weren't mad, it was worse than that. They were amused, in that wry throw-your-hands-up way that made me feel like a big fat baby.

But Gramps loved my umbrella hat, I remember. He was the one person in the whole world who always believed that every single thing I did was just fine. And now he's gone.

I hurry along the bumpy dirt path with my head down so that the joggers and bikers who pass me can't see my face. I pass the old, hollowed-out tree where the geese nest, and a few stride after me, squawking and hissing.

I whirl around, hiss back, and the geese stop short. "Freud?" I say. "Okay, which one are you? Don't fuck with me, man! I saved your life."

The geese regard me with their beady little eyes, then turn and wobble down the steep bank toward the water. I hiss again and they flap their wings and speed up. "Assholes," I mutter. "Chickenshit bullies." Geese are disgusting creatures, I think. Everyone in my psych class thought it was hilarious when I insisted on rescuing Freud; my parents were annoyed. And who could blame them? I see now that rescuing the goose was just one more dumb thing in a long line of dumb things I've done. It's not even like I'm a vegetarian, a person with a moral imperative. I just got it in my head to save the goose and nothing anyone said could deter me.

And now Gramps is dead.

Which has nothing to do with the goose, I remind myself. But I can't shake the feeling that if I hadn't insisted on saving Freud, if we hadn't gotten rich because of him, Gramps would still be here. I was so happy the day I found out Dad won LOTTO CASH, intoxicated, thinking of everything the money could buy; but now the money seems like a physical presence in my life, a disapproving voice reminding me to think twice about every little thing I do. Reminding me that I'm just a dumb kid who's never been responsible or properly appreciative and who doesn't have a clue about anything, let alone what to do with a million dollars. Before it's all over, I'll probably end up buying something even more stupid than the umbrella hat—but at a hundred-thousand times the cost. I think of the car I bought for Josh sitting reproachfully in our driveway, where I guess he left it—a pretty good start. That's the problem, after all: the way the money allows me to make even bigger, stupider mistakes.

Suddenly I don't feel like walking anymore. I cross the bridge at Meridian Street and head back home. In the little park across the street from our house, energetic Yuppies in power suits stand around drinking coffee from Starbucks mugs and chatting with one another while their dogs romp in the grass: a chocolate lab, a couple of Dalmatians, a Weimaraner. Some mutts. The Dog Club, Mom calls them. They gather every morning, rain or shine; greet one other with easy familiarity, part half an hour later with cheerful regret, clapping their hands to call their dogs back to them so they can move on through the day. I imagine them in their Pottery Barn interiors, checking their Blackberries then tucking them back into their worn-just-right Coach briefcases, climbing into their BMWs or Jeep Cherokees, and heading downtown.

Is this the kind of life they always wanted, what they planned?

Once long ago, when asked what I wanted to be when I grew up, I said I wanted to be one of those ladies on a parade float, waving. It's just one more amusing thing about me, one more story my family likes to tell about what a goofy little kid I was. Mom and Dad would probably bring it up right now if I asked them what they think I ought to do with my life, and I stomp up the porch steps as annoyed with them as if they actually said it. As if they're already making up an amusing story about the time I went into a pet shop and put a dog on hold.

In fact, they're in the kitchen, half-discussing, half-arguing about Gramps' funeral.

"I told you," I hear Dad say. "Dutch was a great father, now he's gone. What kind of funeral we have doesn't mean a thing to me. People like my parents always have church funerals. It's just what you do."

"I know. It's just—it won't be about *him*. Can't we at least read the poem?"

I know which poem she means: that Dylan Thomas one about not going gentle into the good night. She read it to Dad yesterday. "Isn't this Dutch?" she said. "Isn't this the way he was? He never gave up. He was so alive." But Dad's face looked blank, like it always did when she tried to read him a poem.

"It's so beautiful," she says now.

"I don't want anything beautiful," Dad says. "I mean it, Abby. The goddamn funeral doesn't have a thing to do with Dutch, as far as I'm concerned. Or how I feel about Dutch. I only want it to be over."

They both get quiet after that. I tiptoe backwards, open the front door, close it loudly, and head for the kitchen with a cheerful expression on my face.

"Hi, Emma," Dad says glumly.

He's dressed in suit pants and a white shirt, his tie untied and draped around his shoulders like a scarf. It's the way he looked every morning when I was growing up. He'd drink his coffee, then tie his tie, button the collar buttons over it, and say to Mom, "Turn my collar down, will you?"

Now that once-ordinary scene replays itself. I watch Dad tie his tie, watch Mom stand behind him and turn down the collar of his shirt just right. I can smell the starch in it, almost feel cool, stiff cotton as her fingertips slide beneath it. And I have to leave the room because I can't bear to remember the way things used to be.

Twenty-four

We get to the church about an hour before the funeral service is to begin. Mom and Dad and Jules go on down the aisle toward the open casket, but I just stand at the back, breathing in that sickly-sweet smell of funeral flowers, wondering why they smell so different from the flowers in a vase on your dining room table. And *do* they smell different—or is it one of those weird psychological things? I'm trying to avoid remembering the other funerals I've been to. Grandma Hammond's, right here in this church. Grandma and Grandpa Deere's. That first awful moment of looking down into the casket, the person you love there and not there.

I don't want to go to the front of the church where Gramps lies, but Margaret arrives and throws her arms around me, then holds my hand so that I have no choice but to follow her down the aisle. Teary-eyed, she hugs Mom, then Jules.

"Oh, your wonderful grandfather," she says. "He was so, so good. Just look at him there. I swear, he looks so peaceful. Like he's fast asleep."

"Can you believe she said that?" I whisper to Jules when Margaret has liberated her and gone on to fuss over Dad. "Gramps looks *dead.*"

"Emma," Jules says. "Shh."

"Well," I say, "he'd have said the same thing himself."

Which is true. And he'd be right, too. The skin on his hands is blue-white, like marble. They've put that awful dead-people's makeup on his face. Even his lips look wrong. Too red. Not smiling. And he's so still. Alive, he was never still; he never went two minutes without laughing. His hair never looked neat either. Usually parts of it were sticking out because of the way he was constantly running his hands through it. Now it's combed so nicely. The only thing that seems right is his black Harley T-shirt: the tackiest one he owned, with a huge bald eagle on the front and gold lettering that says "Ride Free." It was Dad's idea for him to be buried in it. He said, "I'll be goddamned if I'm going to send him into eternity dressed for church."

Now he stands beside the casket, his hand on Gramps' shoulder. Occasionally, he reaches up and smooths Gramps' hair or runs the back of his hand along his cheekbone. I go over and put my arm around him and he pulls me close, never taking his other hand away from Gramps. We stand there, Mom and Jules just behind us, until it's nearly time for the service to begin. They closed the doors to the sanctuary so that we could have some time alone with Gramps, and I can hear people milling around in the vestibule, waiting for the doors to be reopened. The man from the funeral home appears and puts his hand on Dad's shoulder. Dad nods.

He steps away from me then, bends over the coffin and kisses Gramps' forehead. "Okay, this is it, Pal," he says, patting Gramps' shoulder as if he's a little kid on his way to camp. "I love you, Dad. I love the hell out of you and don't you forget it." Then he steps back and kind of shakes his head. "Okay," he says again, to no one.

By this time I'm sobbing. I brought a smooth rock from Lake Michigan, one I've had a long time, and I tuck it under Gramps' cold hands so he can take something of Michigan with him. Mom and Jules take a last look. Then the funeral guy closes the lid and arranges a wreath of red roses on top of it.

Gramps is in there, I think. Forever. But I can't make it seem real.

The church service doesn't seem real, either. Mom's right. It doesn't have much to do with Gramps at all, just hymns and prayers and a lot of talking about how thrilled he must be today, reunited with his beloved Evelyn in heaven. All eternity ahead of them, living with Jesus.

It's gotten chilly while we were inside the church and, at the cemetery, gusts of wind blow my thin dress coat open and make my ears ache. It creeps me out the way the tips of my high heels sink into the muddy ground as I walk toward the grave, like the earth itself is trying to pull me into it. I'm grateful when Jules grabs my hand and squeezes it—like she used to do when I was little.

It makes me remember what good care she took of me then, how she always knew just what I needed. She was in charge of me a lot, probably too much after Mom got so obsessed with painting and spent hours in her studio, working, while Jules fixed our lunch, got our things together to go swimming, or made us a tent out of chairs and blankets in the yard. And I was such a pain in the butt most of the time. I spent my bus money on video games, so we both had to walk home from the mall. I lost my jackets, and we'd both end up half-freezing because Jules had to give me something of hers to wear. I was constantly making messes. God. No wonder she ditched me when she got to high school.

Now she sits down beside me on the rickety folding chair, and I lean over and put my arm around her shoulder. "Hey, Jules." I whisper. "I love you, you know?"

"Yeah," she whispers back. And her face does that quivery thing. She has to press her lips together, blink her eyes about ten times to keep from crying.

When the burial is finally over, we go back to the church for the dinner the ladies of the hospitality committee prepared. Mountains of mashed potatoes, mushy green beans, slabs of ham. People chit-chatting, even laughing. People cornering us to speak tragically of our loss.

I absolutely cannot deal with it. When nobody's watching, I slip out into the empty Sunday school room across the hall. Illustrations of Bible stories hang on the walls; there's a felt board with "Jesus Loves the Little Children" spelled out in blocky red letters on it, and I have to resist the urge to move them around to see what really offensive words I can spell. I sit down on one of the kid-size chairs—maybe the very one I sat on when Grandma Hammond brought me here years ago and I drew the picture of Jesus with blue hair that got the Sunday school teacher so upset at me. Thinking of it still makes me mad. Nobody knows what Jesus looked like! He might have had blue hair, for all that stupid lady knew. It's about as likely as his having been a blond white guy. Though I have to admit that, right this second, I wish for the easy answers that come with believing in Him.

On the way home in the car, Mom and Dad commiserate about all the stupid things people said to them. "It's getting tiresome the way nobody seems to be able to look at us anymore without seeing dollar signs," Mom says. "At a funeral, for God's sake! I quit counting how many times people shook their heads and said, 'All that money you and Mac won—'"

"'I guess you'd give it all back in a heartbeat if it could

bring Dutch back,'" Dad finishes. "About one more time and I would have said, 'Fuck him. No way.' Just to see what they'd say then." He laughs, but it doesn't sound right, and Mom reaches over and squeezes his arm.

"Well, it's over," she says. "Thank God for that."

They fall silent then. Mom dozes in the front seat; Jules dozes beside me in the back. I'm wide-awake. Somehow I've got to tell them about the puppy. I've got to tell them now.

I'll offer to stay in Gramps' house, I've decided. Actually, it's not a bad idea. I can help by cleaning things up, getting it ready to be sold—and while I'm living there, I can look around for a place of my own. It seems like a sensible plan.

Still, my heart rattles wildly as I lean between the two front seats and say quietly, "Dad?"

He glances back at me.

"I'm thinking maybe I could move into Gramps' house for a while," I say. "I mean, it's not a good idea to let a house sit empty—right? It would be good for someone to be there."

"You don't need to do that, Emma," Dad says. "Thanks, though."

"I want to," I say. "Uh. The thing is—see, I bought this puppy yesterday, and—"

"You *what*?" he asks.

Mom jolts fully awake, and turns to look at me.

Jules acts like she's still asleep, but I can feel her watching me through slitted eyes.

"I bought a puppy," I say. "It's on hold at the pet shop. I went in yesterday, after I got my dress for the funeral, and I saw him there. He's so cute. You won't believe how cute he is. A little yellow Lab. He was playing in the window and came right up to me—"

"And you just *bought* it?" Mom asks.

"Sort of," I say. "Yeah. I explained to the manager about Gramps dying and the funeral and all, and she said, okay, I could pay for the puppy and leave it there for a few days as long as I signed this thing that said if anything happened to it they weren't responsible. I'm going start apartment hunting first thing tomorrow morning."

Mom's face bears an expression of utter disbelief. "Emma," she says. "Sometimes I think your dad and I were out of our minds to give you all that money. Your grandfather just *died*, for God's sake—and you go and buy a puppy? You don't *think*. Or maybe you just don't give a damn. Maybe that's what really scares me. If you'd thought about it one second, you'd have realized there is no way that you're going to find an apartment and move in tomorrow. You'd have realized that you're going to have to bring the puppy home."

"I did too think," I say in a wobbly voice. "I wasn't going to bring it home. I was going to get a motel room until I found an apartment. But then I thought of living in Gramps' house. I *could* help, you know? I'd keep it clean for when people come to look at it," I babble on. "And mow the grass when it gets warmer."

It gets real quiet then. Clearly, Mom is finished talking to me. So I say, "Dad?"

"Abby?" he says. But she won't talk to *him* either.

I feel bad, putting him in the middle. But at this point, what can I to do?

"Dad," I persist. "Please?"

"Goddamn it, Emma," he says in a tired voice. "You shouldn't have bought the puppy. You know better. But since you have, yeah, I guess you'd better take it out to Dad's and stay there till you find a place of your own."

His words resonate in the dark silence that falls among us all the rest of the way home. A place of my own. This is what I said I wanted, but until Dad spoke the words I didn't truly understand that, buying the puppy, I'd taken the first real step away from him. Mom, too. And Jules. The only life I've ever known.

Twenty-five

A week later, I'm sitting in Gramps' kitchen, arguing with Margaret about *The Natural Dog*. "The book says rewards are the answer," I tell her. "And also keeping in mind the various aspects of your dog's various learning capabilities."

"What on God's green earth does that mean?" Margaret asks.

"I'm not exactly sure," I say. "I guess, remembering

a dog's not a person. You know, so you can't teach it like you'd teach a person."

Of course, she pounces on that. "*Exactly* why you need a newspaper. That's how I trained Butch, and that's how I trained every other dog I've ever had. There's no way around it. A little whack doesn't really hurt them. You just have to convince them that messing in the house is connected to something unpleasant. Something they don't like."

But I can't make myself whack Harp. Or rub his nose in the mess he's made, which is the other thing Margaret says I should do. She knows it, too, and goes for the jugular. "Honey, it's starting to smell bad in here," she says. "I hate to be a bossy old lady, but you've got to let that puppy know who's in charge. And soon."

I watch her walk back to her house, Butch following obediently behind her. As if on cue, he stops and pees against the big oak tree before trotting through the back door she's holding open for him. I kick the floorboard and mutter a few choice phrases I know would shock the shit out of Margaret if she heard them.

There's no way I'm going to admit to her what I hate admitting even to myself: the reward system does not appear to be working. The few times Harp just happened to pee outside, I praised and petted him and gave him a Milk Bone treat or his special squeaky toy, but so far he's still clueless. I just need to be firmer, I tell myself. I lift him from his bed, fast asleep, and take him outside, where he instantly becomes fully awake and ready to play.

"No way, dude," I say. "Pee." I point to the grass. "This is where you pee. Outside. *Not* in the kitchen."

Startled by my harsh tone, Harp looks up at me, his little head cocked, his eyes liquid and pleading for my approval, and I remember the part in *The Natural Dog* about how puppies can be traumatized, just like people. You can screw them up so bad you have to take them to a dog psychiatrist. Even then, they might not get over it. That makes me feel so guilty that I kneel down and ruffle Harp's fur and let him lick me.

But I know I have to do something. In an hour or so, Mom and Dad will be here to start sorting through Gramps' things, getting the house ready to put up for sale. No way are they going to be as polite about the smell as Margaret's been. I leave Harp to play in the fenced-in yard, go in and fill a bucket with hot water and ammonia, and wash the kitchen floor for about the hundredth time. The average puppy pees once an hour. I didn't need *The Natural Dog* to tell me that. At least I had the good sense to take Margaret's advice and put a barrier at the doorway so Harp couldn't get out of the kitchen and pee on the carpet. And to replace the plaid cushion in his cute wicker bed with a couple of old, crumpled-up sheets that can be thrown in the washer when they get smelly.

This is not turning out quite the way I planned. For as long as I can remember, I've wanted a dog. A dog would love me no matter what I did; a dog would always be glad to see me. I used to imagine myself rolling around in the yard with a yellow lab just like Harp, hiking through the woods with it, curling up on the sofa with it to watch TV. Even sleeping with it.

Actually, I *have* been sleeping with Harp—on the kitchen floor. Because if I don't he stays awake half the night whining.

Still, I totally adore him. Harp is my dog; I knew it the second I saw him in the pet shop, and I still feel exactly the same way. Just watching him cavorting in the backyard, barking at squirrels, makes me happy. Now, as if he knows what I'm thinking, he bounds over to me, tilts his head expectantly, then yaps a couple of times. I swear he's smiling. I open the sliding glass door to let a little fresh spring air into the kitchen, then throw myself down on the warm grass and let him crawl all over me. I wrestle with him a while, then sit him in my lap, holding him by the collar. He yaps and tries to twist out of my grasp, nipping at my wrist with his sharp little puppy teeth.

"Ouch," I say, yanking my hand away from him. "Ouch! Okay, that's it. I know conversation is not one of your various learning capabilities, pal, but you and I need to talk. What are we going to do here?"

Harp yaps at me one more time, then nuzzles his head into my lap and falls fast asleep.

"Well, shit," I say. I can't stay mad at him for two seconds. But it's exhausting, being a dog owner. I close my eyes, let the warm spring sun wash over me. I'll just lie down in the grass a second, I think. Rest. The next thing I know, I hear Mom's voice.

"That damn puppy," she says.

When I open my eyes, she's wiping something off of her shoe. And she does not look happy. I sit, clutching Harp, who's been sleeping on my chest. When I set him down, he rushes toward Mom, barking. "Harp," I yell. "Stop that. Harp!" I look at my watch, glance at the sliding glass door, which is wide open. "Jeez, I guess I fell asleep. I meant to—"

But it's too late to explain. Harp's bed is next to the door and as soon as Mom steps in that direction she wrinkles her nose. "Emma," she says ominously, and goes on inside.

I follow her. "I know. It smells horrible. I'm sorry. I was going to clean it all up before you came. And the dog poop in the yard. I really was. But Margaret got me so upset when she came over. She says I have to hit Harp with the newspaper to get him to learn about peeing and all that, and I just can't. I can't. It's too mean. And smushing his face in it—"

"Well, what *are* you going to do then?" she says. "Reason with the puppy? You know, Emma, if I'd reasoned with you every time you took a fast break for the deep end of a swimming pool, you'd probably be dead right now. Drowned." She sits down at the kitchen table and puts her head in her hands.

I look at Mom, who refuses to look back at me. I look at poor, traumatized Harp, who gives a little bark and nudges the sliding glass door with his nose. I open it and, amazed, watch him trot out into the yard and pee, just like he's been doing it this way all his life.

"Thank you!" I shout. "Thank you, Jesus!" And do a

little dance around him, dropping Milk Bone treats at his feet. I feel about ten years older than I felt when I got up this morning. But I feel—in charge. Of Harp, anyway. But it makes me feel like maybe, *maybe* I can see my way to taking charge of myself, too.

I need to find my own place. I made the leap, it was my choice. Now I have to land somewhere and start moving forward. Plus, it's depressing to be in Gramps' house; I keep coming upon things that make me feel even worse about his being gone. Like the newspaper from the last day of his life, folded to the comic section. The photo of Dad in his Little League uniform that he taped just inside the drawer of his bedside table. I can hardly stand to go into the garage at all, because it's so full of him. His Harley, his workbench cluttered with various automotive parts that he never figured out what to do with. Its smells like Gramps out there: some combination of soap and dust and motor oil.

But it's where Dad fled when he heard Mom start yelling at me, so I go out there and dig in to the major task of helping him clean it out. We don't talk. Both of us thinking our own thoughts, we go through an old battered cabinet where we find a drawer with nuts and bolts and screws, all thrown in together. In another drawer, there's a jumble of instruction manuals—for cars, snowmobiles, chain saws, lawn mowers—all of them heavily fingerprinted with grease. These are Gramps' fingerprints, I think, pitching the manuals into the trash. Nobody in the world will ever have these same fingerprints again.

Methodically, we throw things away. Boxes and boxes

of things. Other things we set aside for Goodwill: dozens of pairs of brown work gloves, bright orange mechanic's jumpsuits, boxes of clay pigeons, rakes, shovels, hoses. All through the process, Harp snoozes peacefully on some old towels in the corner of the garage.

After a while, Mom brings out some lemonade. And Harp's water dish, a kind of peace offering. She sits on the seat of Gramps' Harley. "It's so strange taking a house apart," she says. "Like dismantling a universe. All those beautiful antiques your mother spent a lifetime collecting, and here they are gathered together in the middle of the floor, like refugees. And that old sofa in the living room. I remember sitting on it and feeding Julie a bottle!"

It's nearly six o'clock by the time we finish, and we decide to go for Mexican food at a place in the Village we like. It's a nice evening, balmy, and we decide to eat outside where we amuse ourselves by watching a bunch of skanky high school boys practicing tricks on their skateboards.

"Freshman boys," Mom says in a melancholy tone of voice. "Oh, I know. By this time of year I was always up to my ears with kids. Ready for summer. But watching these goofs makes me miss my students. I miss *having* students. Knowing them, watching them grow."

"I think I know of something that will cheer you up," Dad says.

"What?" Mom looks wary.

"You'll see," he says mysteriously.

"Dad," I say. "Remember? Mom doesn't really like surprises."

He beams. "She'll like this one. I guarantee it. Come on, you'll see."

I climb into the back seat of the car with a sense of impending doom. Five minutes later, he pulls up in front of this big white frame house—two stories, with green shutters and a brick sidewalk. Surrounded by a wrought iron fence, thick with ivy. Mom's favorite house in the world. And there's a FOR SALE sign in front of it.

"Is this amazing, or what?" Dad says.

Mom just looks at him. "You're bringing me here because—?"

"You've always been crazy about this house. Now we can buy it."

It's ominously quiet for a long time. Then Mom says, "Mac, are you crazy? In less than five months we become millionaires, we quit our jobs, Dutch dies—and you want to talk about *moving*?"

"You hire a moving company and move," Dad says. "What's the big deal about that?"

"I can't think about moving," Mom says. "I can't think of one more single thing than I'm thinking about now. Okay?"

"But you love this house," Dad says. "It's what you've always wanted."

"It's what I used to want," she says. "I wanted it so bad I could *taste* it. I'd drive by it sometimes at night, when the lamps were on, and I could see inside to the living room and I'd imagine us all there. It scared me, it seemed so real. Like it was a life I'd lost. Or the life I should have had. But you didn't give a damn about houses then. You thought buying a big house like this would be stupid. Jesus, wouldn't it be even more stupid now? Buying a big house like this for just the *two* of us?"

"I thought it was stupid then because we couldn't afford it." Dad says. "Now we can. Who cares if it's just for the two of us? We can have whatever house we want."

"Well, it's too late," Mom says. "The last thing I want to do is buy a big house and have to decorate it, buy stuff to fill it up, get used to living in it." She turns to me. "Am I missing something, Emma? Or is it not at least a little insane to think you can just *decide* to buy what's probably a million-dollar house like you'd buy, I don't know, a *kitchen appliance*?"

"It's kind of—sudden," I say. "But, Mom, everybody knows how much you've always loved this house. Why wouldn't Dad think you'd like to have it?"

She doesn't answer.

I think it's over at this point. Finally. I think, surely, Dad has the sense not to pursue this any further. But I am completely, totally wrong.

He says, "Abby, listen. I know I've been driving you nuts ever since we got the money. I know you're afraid I'm going to spend the rest of my life just fucking around. But I've been thinking. You know how I've always said I wanted to build kit cars? Custom cars. Do it right, make them perfect? Well, when I drove by this morning and saw the house was for sale I noticed it had a four-car garage—"

I look at the house again, notice the big garage for

the first time and have the feeling I'm about to see a train wreck.

"It would be a great place to set up in," Dad goes on. "I could do one at a time in the beginning. See what happens. If I like it, if I can sell them."

"Oh," Mom says. "The four-car garage. So that's what this is really about."

And I wish I were anywhere but here. I don't want to hear this ugliness between them, don't want to be scared by it, to think for the first time in my life that there might be something really wrong between them.

I *really* don't want to hear Dad say, defeated, "Abby, I don't need to pay seven-hundred-and-fifty-thousand dollars for a fucking four-car garage. I can rent one for a hell of a lot less than that if I decide I want to build the cars. I just thought the house would make you happy."

Twenty-six

"Emma, I'm so sorry," Mom says when she calls the next day. "Your dad and I arguing in front of you like that. I know it upset you. We were both exhausted. Physically and emotionally. We all were, after having to go through all those things in the house."

I'm still in bed, paralyzed with said exhaustion. Mostly emotional, in my case.

"Emma?" Mom says. "Honey, are you okay?"

"Yeah," I say. "Fine. So, are you and Dad speaking yet?"

She's quiet a moment. "Not exactly," she says. "Emma. About the house. I lay awake all night thinking about it and, the truth is, that house was the house *I* wanted to have grown up in. You know, a 'Father Knows Best' house. Where everyone's always happy, where everyone always knows exactly the right thing to do. That's why I had such a thing for it, when I was younger. But see? What I've figured out is that there is no such house. Anywhere." She laughs, kind of. "Which seems like progress to me. I don't need the house now. And one thing I know for sure is that I don't want to move, at least right now. I was telling your dad the truth when I said I couldn't face the hassle of that."

"Mom, what *do* you want?" I ask.

She thinks a moment. "I want to paint," she says. "To get back to the place in my head that lets me paint. I want to get sane, get a life. I want to quit worrying about what to do with all this stupid money."

"Then, go paint somewhere," I say. "You always do that when you get whacked out. What's the big deal about doing it now?"

"You're right," she says. "Probably that's what I ought to do."

I meant she should go up to Michigan alone for a few weeks. Or maybe rent a condo someplace beautiful and warm. So I'm speechless, consumed with guilt, when she calls me a few days later to tell me she's on her way to France.

"You were so right when you told me I should just

go away," she says, undeterred by my shocked silence. "I thought and thought about it. Then yesterday, when it was raining, I went out for a long walk and thought some more. It was so weird, like an omen. In the Village, there were all these people hurrying around under their umbrellas and I thought of that Caillebotte painting in Chicago. You know the one—

"Oh, he was such a dislikable, *pigheaded* man," she rattles on. "Do you know he refused to include a single one of Berthe Morisot's paintings in his private collection? Which, you may remember, ended up being the collection that *defined* Impressionism. Because she was a woman! I can't help it, though. I still love that painting of his, and I just stood and closed my eyes and pictured it in my mind. Those beautiful umbrellas! The shine on the cobblestones, the silvery air.

"Like the air would be in Paris right now, I thought—and knew, instantly, that Paris was where I needed to be. That I needed to be alone for a while. To remember who I am, figure out where I'm going."

All I can think to say is, "Dad?"

"We talked," she says. "I feel bad leaving so soon after Dutch died, but I need to go. He knows that. He knows I can't be any help to him the way I've been. Maybe you should come home. If you want to come home, that is. I'm sure he'd be glad for the company."

When I remind her about Harp, she acts like having him in the house is no big deal, which freaks me out more than the news that she's already at the airport. Driving home, I play the Red Hot Chili Peppers—loud—hoping to distract myself from thinking about the fact that Mom has been reduced to taking advice from *me*. When "Give It Away" comes on, it seems like some kind of cosmic message.

Of course, Dad's in his garage. He's sitting at his workbench, all the kit car catalogs he'd sent away for spread out before him. But he's not really looking at them. He seems oblivious to the Corvette he'd so determinedly tracked down, parked beside him, gleaming.

"You okay?" I ask.

"Yeah, great." He shrugs, half-laughs. "I'll tell you something, Emma. I'm beginning to wish we'd never gotten all that goddamn money. We were doing fine without it. We had a good life. Now we don't know *what* we're doing. I hang out in the garage, fucking around with cars like a teenager. Your mom's bolted for a whole other country. Hell, for all I know, she might decide to stay there."

"She'll be back," I say. "She can't speak French. I mean, seriously, how long will she be able to stand not being able to express her opinion?"

But he doesn't laugh. And to tell the truth, it doesn't seem all that funny to me either.

I have just about as much luck cheering Jules up when she calls a while later. "I just got home and there's this weird message from Mom about leaving for Paris this afternoon," she says. "What's going on, anyway? Emma, are Mom and Dad getting a divorce?"

"They're not getting a divorce," I say. Like I'm absolutely sure.

No way am I going to tell her about opening Mom's dollhouse an hour ago and realizing that in the past few weeks she'd papered the walls, laid tiny strips of plywood flooring in each room, painted the trim around the doorways. She'd furnished the living room, put a little brass bed in the bedroom, and made a tiny cross-stitch quilt to cover it. She made an attic room for the children filled with books and toys; a studio for the mom that has a tiny easel with a painting propped on it, a tiny palette and paintbrushes, a wing-back reading chair. She'd set a tiny red convertible in the attached garage, near the workbench with tiny tools on it.

And when it was finished, perfect, she'd put the mother at her easel, the father on a stool at his workbench. She sat one little girl on a rocking horse, the other one on one of the beds reading a miniature *Green Eggs and Ham*. Then she closed it up, and left—as if she were leaving that part of her life behind her.

"It's not like she's never gone away before," I say to Jules. "She was always going away to paint when we were kids."

"But she's never just *up* and left. And *Paris*? She's never gone to Paris to paint! Did you talk to her?"

"Yeah," I say. "She called me, too. From the airport."

"And?"

I tell her what Mom told me and also that I've come home from Gramps' house so I can keep Dad busy while she's gone.

"What do you mean, busy? There *is* something wrong between them, isn't there?" She sounds mad at *me*. Kill the messenger, I guess. I can't blame her for being upset.

"Jules, I really don't know. I'll let you know as soon as I find out anything, okay?"

No answer.

"Okay? Jules? Listen, I'm going to make Dad take Harp to obedience school with me. We'll go to movies. Watch basketball on TV. Whatever. Really, I'll keep you posted—"

More silence. Then she says, "You know, Emma, things aren't so great here either."

"What?" I say. "What things?"

"Everything," she says. "Okay, everybody made a big deal about not asking why Will didn't come for Gramps' funeral, and I figured we had plenty to upset us without dragging out all my problems. Well, he didn't come to the funeral because I didn't tell him Gramps died."

"*What*?" I say. "Why? What's the deal? He liked Gramps. They got along great at Christmas. Why wouldn't you tell him?

"I'm stupid is the deal. I didn't want him to feel, you know, *obligated*. But all I did was hurt his feelings, and it wasn't the first time either. Lately, we just haven't been getting along very well. It's my fault," she says. "I don't know what I want. I mean, I want *him*—I know that. Sometimes I think he's all I want; but that can't be a good thing. I don't care about networking, or auditions. I just want to be with Will. But then when I'm with him, I get clingy and bitchy. I act like it's his fault I'm so confused. My God, half the time I can't even make myself go to dance class anymore.

"I don't know *what's* wrong with me. Will says I need

some time alone. To think. So we're not—" Her voice gets wobbly and she falls silent.

"God, Jules," I say. "I'm really sorry. It'll work out, though, don't you think?"

Silence.

"Jules?" I say.

"You *always* think that, don't you, Emma? That everything works out fine for me. That everything's easy for me."

"No," I say, though it does often seem that way to me. "I just meant—"

She sighs. "I know what you meant," she says. "I'm sorry. I told you I was messed up."

"Are you okay there, all alone?" I ask. "I mean, really?"

She sniffs.

"Jules?"

She sniffs again, so I try to make her laugh. "Too bad our communication skills have been so crappy lately," I say. "You and Mom could have gone to France to be alone together."

"I don't want to go to France," she says miserably.

"Well, what do you want?" I'm starting to feel like some kind of bogus genie, asking people what they want when I have absolutely no power whatsoever to give it to them. "Do you want to come home?"

"Emma," she says, like I'm five. "I *am* home. I'm a grown-up, remember? I have my own life."

She doesn't sound very convincing. But I know better than to argue with Jules when she gets huffy. I tell her to go out, do *something*. I've heard Mom tell her that plenty of times when she calls, feeling low. "You're eating, aren't you?" I add for good measure.

"Yes, I'm *eating*."

"Not only frozen yogurt?"

"Not only frozen yogurt," Jules says, finally amused.

I'm worried about her, though. I consider going to New York to try to cheer her up. But I can't ditch Dad; and to take him along would be even worse. He hates New York. Baghdad with theater, he calls it. A few days there and who knows what kind of shape he'd be in?

What would Mom do, I wonder? She's never been much good at things like making dinner or chauffeuring people around, but I have to say that—barring the past months—she's gifted at disaster. Emotional traumas are her specialty. She'll drop everything and, pretty soon, under that spotlight gaze of hers, whatever you're freaked out about will come out in a rush. An hour later, she'll have thought of ten things you can do to try to make it right. Or, if it can't be made right, ten different ways to see it so that, suddenly, it seems like, however things turn out, you'll survive.

"Interesting," she'll say. And pretty soon you start to see that it is.

I could call her. She'd come home on the next flight if she thought we really, truly needed her. Instead, I muddle along, checking the mail every day for a postcard or a letter from her, hoping there will be something in it to help me figure out what I should do. Finally, one of those crinkly blue airmail letters arrives, but it turns out to be mostly about a painting by Cézanne, that she stood and looked at for an hour.

It was a still life, she wrote. *A square table, covered with a red and yellow and blue patterned tablecloth. On it, a blue ceramic bowl, a wine bottle with a yellow cork, a basket of yellow-green apples, and two apples sitting in front of it. The way the composition of the painting listed to the left, the three cropped paintings on the blue background—the way they seemed to have been placed randomly there—all this interested me. The pleasure in looking for so long was to discover the way the lines of the table didn't quite match up, the way it was slightly tilted forward so that, if the apples were real, they'd roll right off of it. And I understood finally what Cézanne knew: this is the way the world actually is, everything at a tilt, improbable. As real and not real as the red blush at the bottom curve of the biteable apples made only of paint. Yet, at the same time, he thrusts life at you. Here, touch this apple. Eat it. Live.*

Whatever *that* means.

Okay, I tell myself. Suck it up. You're on your own.

Twenty-seven

Apparently, I'm also in charge of Dad.

When he reads the letter, he says, "You know, if it were only me, I think I'd have been perfectly happy to put the goddamn money in the bank and just be worthless for the rest of my life. Hang out in my garage. Go skiing when I felt like going skiing. Ride my Harley. Read. I should be ashamed of that, I suppose. Sometimes I think I'm just a dumb, happy person. I don't want to go to France. I never did. I don't give a goddamn about Cézanne, or whoever. I feel like I fail your mom that way. I know those things are important to her. I feel like if it were just her with the money she'd want to live a whole different way."

To tell the truth, it scares the shit out of me. But I say, "Dad, there's no point thinking that way." Then spend the next week just trying to keep him occupied. We go to shoot-em-up movies, the kind Mom refuses to see; we go bowling, work on Harp's obedience skills. We go out to eat every night, nothing that's good for us. We don't talk much. What is there to say?

The first really warm day of spring, nearly seventy degrees, I get the idea we should put the top down on the Corvette for the first time and take a drive. He shrugs but agrees to it, and we head out of town. We drive down toward Brown County and I lean back, my face lifted to the sun. The woods are greening up, brushed with redwood and violets, and the Corvette takes the turns nicely on the winding road. We stop and browse through the junky shops near the state park, eat way too much at the Brown County Inn, a homey place with red-checked tablecloths that specializes in fried chicken dinners.

Dad says, "Your mom and I once drove from trash can to trash can in the state park on a Sunday afternoon and collected enough beer cans and pop bottles to pay for dinner here when we were first married. You'd get a nickel apiece for them then. Dinner was maybe five bucks each." He sounds melancholy, like he'll never, ever see her again.

Back in the Corvette, we're halfway to Bloomington before I realize that's where he's going. *Shit.* That's my first thought. I do *not* want to go to Bloomington. What if I see—

Then I get this shocking little twinge of... something. What if I *did* see... Tiffany or Josh—maybe even Gabe Parker? My heart starts knocking inside my chest, and not only with dread. Which surprises me.

Thirteen miles, the sign says. Pretty soon the forest and fields give way to the clutter of strip malls and housing divisions. Instinctively, I shrink down in my seat as we pass the College Mall, then the fraternity houses on Third Street.

"Take a walk?" Dad asks.

No! I want to say. Maybe I don't *only* dread seeing Tiff or Josh or even Gabe, but that doesn't mean I want to see them now. I don't feel up to trying to explain that to Dad, though, so I get out of the car and set forth, my head down to avoid looking into the faces of the students hurrying to class.

If Dad notices that I'm acting weird, he doesn't mention it. I swear, it's as if he's looking for Mom, half-hoping he'll find her here, just the way she was on the day they first met. Wandering through campus, he tells me funny stories about living in the fraternity house, things he and Mom did together. I've heard them a million times before, but I don't mind, because I can hear Mom chiming in, correcting, expanding them, and it's as if she *is* with us. She'll come back, I think. Eventually. How could she not?

Of course, there's the ritual tour of the Commons,

where they met. Afterwards, we check out the bookstore, where I lose myself for a little while selecting a pile of novels—then I wander into the area where the textbooks and school supplies are kept and get sideswiped by a sudden, intense desire to be a student again. I miss learning stuff. I miss studying late at night, the excitement of making connections. I miss notebooks, pens, and highlighters. The way, if you study hard enough, you can reduce a whole semester of knowledge into a list of sentences and then some kind of anagram—each letter, like a seed, that makes all you know bloom in your mind.

I want to go back to school! The sudden certainty makes me feel light-headed, but also puts me off guard so that I forget the no-eye-contact thing—and, wouldn't you know it, at the exact moment Dad and I leave the bookstore, there's Tiffany coming out of the bakery across the corridor.

"Emma!" she shrieks.

Of course, she has one of those huge cookies with a smiley-face on it. Which crumbles and goes all down the back of my shirt when she throws her arms around me.

"Oh, my gosh! Emma! I didn't even recognize you at first. Your hair! It's—well . . . and you're so thin! God, I've missed you *so* much. I mean it. I'm so *glad* to see you." She steps back and wags her finger at me. "So. Why didn't you answer all those e-mails I sent you?"

"Uh—"

"You got them, didn't you? I told Matt, I hope you *got* them. Like, maybe you didn't get service way up in Michigan, where you were."

"I got them," I say. "I'm sorry. I'm an asshole."

She rolls her eyes at my language. "You haven't changed one bit. Well, that's a relief." Then, turning to Dad, she does a total Dr. Jekyll and Mr. Hyde. "Hello, Mr. Hammond," she says primly. "I didn't mean to, like, ignore you, but I just cannot *believe* it's Emma right here in front of me. My goodness, Matt—that's my boyfriend—Matt and I were just talking about her the other day. He's riding in the Little Five Hundred, you know. For Phi Delt. And we were saying, why don't we get Emma to come down for that."

She swivels her head around like a chicken to look at me again. "And suddenly you just—appear! Like you're always saying: *cosmic!* So why *don't* you come?" she says. "I'll hardly see Matt all weekend, and I need you to keep me company. Really. I *do*. Please! It's this Saturday. You can come down Friday and stay in our room."

Our room. For a second, I believe it still is. Honestly, when Tiffany gets on one of her talking jags, she can get me so confused I don't know whether I'm coming or going. Then I remember that if I go to Little Five with her, I'm bound to see Josh and Heather.

Not to mention Gabe Parker—which makes me feel like I just hit my emotional crazy bone. Hard. It all floods back into me: the coffee date, the Winnebago debacle—the way I *felt* in his presence. The very scary fact that I really, really want to see him again.

But there's no way I'm actually *ready* for it. I give Dad a pointed look, like, *save me*.

But he just laughs. "Go," he says. "Jesus, get out, do something. Quit hanging around with old farts like me." He looks as amused as I've seen him look since Mom took off for France.

What can I do? I tell Tiff, "Yeah, okay, I'll come."

Twenty-eight

Sure enough. I walk through the door of our room—upon which Tiffany has spelled out WELCOME HOME, EMMA in daffodil stickers—and within five minutes she informs me there's a big dance at the Phi Delt house tomorrow night, a beach party, and we'll all be going together.

"Wait a minute," I say. "What exactly do you mean, *together*?"

"Hel-*lo*. As in a double date?" Tiff says. "Me and Matt, you and Gabe? It was his idea," she adds. "Gabe's."

"Really," I say. "How did he know I was coming?"

"Um—" Tiff blushes. "You're not upset, are you?"

"Just—*wondering*."

"Okay, Matt *mentioned* it to him," she says.

I suppress a groan. I'd prepared myself to *see* Gabe. I'd even planned what I would say to him. Well, more like what I wouldn't say. But I'd thought that seeing him would just be a matter of... well, seeing him. Not that I'd be going on a *date* with him. I'm in no way prepared for that. Plus, Josh and Heather will be there.

I could strangle Tiffany for setting this up without my permission. But trying to stay mad at her would be like trying to stay mad at Harp. So I sink onto my old desk chair and let her rattle on about what a great time the four of us are going to have at the Phi Delt beach party after the race, all the while feeling nearly sick with dread.

They've brought in truckloads of sand to make a beach in the yard, she says. Rented dozens of chaise lounges and some of those cute little striped cabanas. Right now, the spring pledges are blowing up all the kiddie swimming pools they bought at Wal-Mart. Those will be the ocean. It's only too bad that both Matt and Gabe and are riding tomorrow, she concludes—because this evening they'll be carbo-loading with the other guys on the team.

"Gabe's riding?" I say stupidly. "He smokes like a fiend."

"Yeah?" This is distinctly Valley-girl in tone.

"Never mind," I say.

I'm thinking about how my dad used to light up a cigarette after running a 10K race, how funny he thought that was; but I don't dare mention this to Tiffany for fear she'll catch on to the fact that Gabe Parker being a cyclist and smoking is perversely appealing to me.

Later, the two of us go out for strombolis, then drive around campus in my Jeep. There are people everywhere: mobile parties and evidence of all kinds of mischief. Greek letters are stenciled in bright colors on the porch steps of rival fraternity houses; tree limbs are hung with streamers of toilet paper; vendors hawk X-rated T-shirts on the street. At the Acacia house, a bunch of guys with fire hoses shoot water in huge arcs onto the sidewalk and send some girls screaming. Tiffany leans over and honks the horn when we pass them, and a couple of them wave and holler at us to come back. But we speed on, pass under the huge banner across Third Street that reads "Little 500: The World's Greatest College Weekend."

We luck out and find a parking place just off Kirkwood. We get some frozen yogurt and walk over to Dunn Meadow, where a local band is playing Sixties music, much to the approval of a crowd of people my parents' age and older. They clap and hoot and yell out requests. Tiff and I sit on the grass watching the Frisbee players. Most of them have dogs with them: big, rangy mutts that wear bright bandanas around their necks and leap and twist to catch the Frisbees their owners throw. I have a sudden image of myself among them with Harp, and I like the feel of it. So what if Josh is stupid enough to fall in love with girls like Heather, so what if Gabe Parker thinks I'm pathetic. I wouldn't feel so lonely and out of it living here if Harp were with me.

Meanwhile, Tiffany talks. She's joined a sorority, and gives me a blow-by-blow account of pledging, recounts all the pranks her pledge class has played on the actives, clues me in on which girls are nice and which ones are bitches. Suddenly, in the middle of telling me about these pissy red-haired twins who give demerits every time a pledge gets them confused, she starts to laugh.

"What?" I say.

"You would hate it *so* much, that's all. Being in a sorority."

I start to apologize, assuming I'd somehow let her see how dopey it sounds to me.

"No," she says. "It's *okay* that you'd hate it. My gosh, Emma, we're nothing the same; but I love that. Really. Ever since we've been friends, I can't help it—whatever I do, I wonder what *you'd* say about it, and it starts to seem funny to me."

Well dang, I think. Who knew Tiffany actually had a clue about me? All I can do is look at her; for once, I'm completely without a smart remark.

Then she surprises me again. "Listen, Emma, I know you're worried about Josh Morgan being at the party. He will be, okay? But not with Heather." She hesitates, then forges ahead—but not in that chirpy, in-denial-about-reality voice she's always used talking about my love life (well, lack thereof) in the past. Downright matter-of-factly, she says, "He's been doing a lot better. His grades are up. And—well, he's been dating this girl in my sorority. Amy. She's nothing like Heather. I mean, she's a nice person. Which is good, right?"

"Just peachy," I say. "And we're all going to this party *together*?"

"You and I and Matt and Gabe are going together," she says, firmly. "Josh and Amy will be there, that's all. If it gets weird, we'll leave. Okay? I swear."

I don't answer.

"Emma? I just thought you needed to know. You're not mad at me, are you?"

"No." That's all, because I couldn't begin to explain what I *do* feel—even to myself.

Tiff looks anxious. "You know, when we talked?" When you left? When you were on your way to Michigan?"

I nod.

"You said you weren't leaving because of Josh. You meant that, didn't you? I mean, you're not still—?"

"*No*!" I say. "I just don't want to see him. I know I have to some time. But I don't want to deal with it—"

"Emma, could you *please* just tell me what happened between you?" she asks, quietly.

This time I surprise *myself*—and tell her the whole truth about it.

"I just want to *kill* him," she says, her eyes brimming over with tears when I'm through.

I shrug. "It's over."

"Emma, *is* it?"

"Maybe," I say. "I think maybe it is."

The next morning, we sleep till ten o'clock. Matt's still incommunicado, bonding with his teammates. Tiffany, of course, needs sufficient time to prepare for our upcoming social event, so I go out and get us some bagels. When I get back, she's showered and dressed in a pair of khaki shorts and a Phi Delt T-shirt. She's sitting on the bed, her toweled head in her hands, reading the arrest list in the *Indiana Daily Student*. She grabs the bagel I hand her, takes a bite, and munches thoughtfully.

"God," she says. "I know three people on this. Remember that Kristin girl, down the hall? She's one of them. Ha. And she goes to church every single Sunday."

"Then she's saved," I say. "A little earthly trauma like an arrest shouldn't freak her out too much."

Tiffany snorts.

I watch her dry her hair, then pull it back and make a perfect French braid. All this she does in silence, with intense concentration. She does her makeup next, wielding her half-dozen or so brushes with the deftness of a painter. She looks beautiful when she's through, tendrils of errant hair curling at her temples, her cheeks dewy and pink.

I had showered and dressed in black shorts and a white T-shirt before going to get the bagels. But I'd let my hair air-dry in the Jeep, so now I spritz it down with water, borrow Tiff's hair dryer, and step up to the mirror to get the cowlicks under control—at which point, it occurs to me that Gabe Parker's never seen my hair buzzed. Did Tiffany clue him in to the fact that the girl he's stuck taking out tonight is even weirder than the girl he remembers?

Obsessing about Josh and his new girlfriend, particularly about the moment I'm going to actually have to come face-to-face with them and say ... something, has distracted me all morning, but now the anxiety I have about seeing Gabe again comes back full force—and deepens when I get to the stadium, see him standing with Matt and the other two guys on their team, and feel just like I felt when I first caught sight of him that day at the Daily Grind. Josh is there, too—in the Phi Delt pit, doing some last minute adjustment on the bike. And I *am* okay about seeing him. Or maybe it's just that I can't stop looking at Gabe.

God. When I met him, it was winter; he was wearing khakis and a sweatshirt. Now he's wearing biker's garb, and his strong, muscular body makes me feel faint. I'm not exaggerating. Tiffany's beside me, waving madly, calling out Matt's name, and it's all I can do to keep from grabbing her hand and yanking her down to sit on the bleachers beside me. But I just sit there like a prisoner. Matt looks up eventually, and waves back. Gabe smiles and waves, too. But I adjust the bill of my baseball cap and pretend to be looking the other way.

There's plenty to see. The stands are filling up, each team block on the north side of the stadium recognizable by its concentration of bright T-shirts. Fraternity pledges take turns running their huge banners up and down the bleacher steps. An occasional Frisbee whizzes overhead like a little spaceship. A beach ball is kept aloft by hundreds of reaching hands.

In the center of the track, people bustle about importantly among the red-and-white-striped tents. Student

Foundation members mostly, dressed like executives in navy blue suits. There's a long table, the Little Five Hundred trophy on it, glittering in the sun.

The bikes, thirty-three of them, have been laid out in rows of three on the cinder track. The riders are gathered behind the last row, stretching or running in place. Gabe stands off to the side a bit, tapping his fingertips thoughtfully, his expression intent, as if pondering some deep philosophical question.

Then, at some unseen signal, the lead riders move to their places beside their bikes, the others to their pits, and the festivities begin. "The Star Spangled Banner," of course; and "Back Home Again in Indiana." Then skydivers float down beneath rainbow parachutes to land on the grass—one, two, three, four, five—right in front of the podium.

"Gentlemen," the president of the university says. "Mount your Roadmasters."

They do. The pace car moves into place ahead of them, hundreds of balloons stream upwards, and Queen blasts out over the sound system as the riders start on the parade lap.

"I want to ride my bicycle…"

The whole crowd roars the song as the cyclists make their first circle around the track, then speed up, preparing for the green flag. A weird nostalgia overtakes me, and I think of all the stories my parents told me about the Little Five Hundred, almost as if they're my own memories. Then, as the bikers approach the starting line, Tiff grabs my arm and I'm up shouting, part of the madness, making a memory all my own.

Twenty-nine

Afterwards, back at the dorm—shades of the coffee "date" with Gabe in the fall—Tiffany tries to shape me up for the party. Since it's a beach party theme, she's wearing very short shorts and a cute little pink top. When I opt for my usual jeans and a T-shirt, she raises an eyebrow.

"That's it? That's what you're wearing to a beach party?"

"Yeah," I say. "Is that a problem?"

She just looks at me.

"Okay, I guess I could go for the Hawaiian look." I grab a red carnation from the vase of them Matt had sent her for one of their various, known-only-to-them anniversaries, and hold it to the side of my head. "Got any Scotch tape?

"How about Valium?" I add, when the phone rings to alert us to the fact that Matt and Gabe are waiting downstairs for us.

"It's going to be fine," Tiff says. "Come on. Really."

I just moan. Walking down the hallway toward the elevator I feel like Harp must feel, being dragged on his leash somewhere he doesn't want to go. But, hey, look on the bright side, I tell myself when the elevator doors open and I see Gabe; at least he's fully clothed.

"Emma?" he says, as if seeing a ghost.

Clearly, Tiff did *not* tell him about my new look.

"*C'est moi.*" I run my hand across my head, attempt a jaunty expression.

"I like it," he says. "It's—"

"Could *short* be the word you're looking for?" I say, grateful when he laughs.

Tiff and Matt have been hugging all this time, having been cruelly separated for more than twenty-four hours. Now she gives Gabe a hug, too. "You guys were so great," she says.

"Come on, we sucked," Matt says cheerfully. "Except for Gabe. If we'd let him ride the whole race, we might have done okay."

"Like that movie," Tiff says. "*Breaking Away.*"

"Yeah," Gabe says, lighting up a cigarette. "But scratch the Puccini. I'd do it smoking."

Matt punches him in the arm. "He *could* have ridden it alone," he says as we set out for the party. "No shit. He's that good."

Gabe shrugs, embarrassed. "I grew up in Speedway," he tells me. "I hate auto racing, so what do I end up doing? Racing bicycles. I don't know, I guess *something* about the place must have been contagious."

"Emma ski races," Tiff says, proud as a mom.

"Jeez, not seriously," I say. "Just NASTAR races with my dad. That's hardly—"

"Pooh," Tiff interrupts. "She has medals: gold ones. I've seen them."

"Your grandfather said that," Gabe says. "That day we—" He stops short. "Uh. Emma, I heard. I mean, Josh—"

"... told us about Dutch dying," Tiff finishes for him. "He found out from someone you guys knew in high school."

"Probably Lisa Cochrun," I say. "She knows everything."

"Maybe," Tiffany says. "All I know is, I felt really awful when I found out. It was so fun that day he came. I hate it he didn't get to take that big trip he was planning."

"He was a cool guy," Gabe says.

I nod, blinking back tears because I can't help remembering what a shit I was the day they met.

We walk up Fraternity Row, Tiffany holding up everyone's end of the conversation. Gabe smokes, moodily it seems to me. I wrack my brain trying to think what to say to him.

"So, did you do any Little Five reporting for the *IDS*?" I finally ask.

"Nah," he says. "I don't work for the paper anymore. I changed my major."

"Why?"

He grins. "It's your fault. Remember, you said that thing to me when we went for coffee? About how there was no Pulitzer Prize for being nice?"

"But I was kidding," I say, stricken. "I mean, it was funny. That's all I was trying to say. You got me talking about my parents and the lottery, just like a reporter would, then you were like, 'No problem if you don't want me to write the story.'"

"And I *didn't* write it," Gabe says. "That's the point."

"You didn't write it?"

He shakes his head.

"Emma, wouldn't I have *sent* you the story if he'd written it?" Tiffany looks hurt. "My God. I never dreamed you thought Gabe had written a story about you and I just didn't bother to send it to you."

"Duh," I say, thankful when she giggles at me, appeased.

But I feel bad. I only half-read all those e-mails she sent me, just like I only half-listened to whatever she was saying when we lived together. Plus, there's wrecking Gabe's career plans to feel guilty about.

"Hey, you did me a favor," he says when I apologize for that. "You made me realize I don't really like poking around in other people's lives. I'm no good at it. So I'm an English major now. I figure, how can I do any damage to made-up stories written by dead people?"

"I'm an English major," I say. "Well, I *was*—"

"Yeah," he says. "I remember. So, are you coming back in the fall? To be an English major again?"

"I don't know," I say. "Maybe."

We walk the rest of the way to the house without talking, but it's a more comfortable silence. At the fraternity house, the party's cranking up. I stand, taking it all in, while Gabe goes to get some drinks. The windows of the frat house are open and you can hear the band from halfway down the street. The front sidewalk is lined with plastic blow-up palm trees. The yard, front and back, is completely covered with sand and dotted with striped cabanas and lounge chairs.

"Surf's up," some dipshit yells. Dressed in baggy shorts and the ugliest Hawaiian shirt I've ever seen, he holds a mug of beer aloft and splashes through the long row of baby pools that make up the ocean.

And there's Josh, with—I guess—Amy, heading toward me.

She's elfin, with copper-colored hair, freckles, and intelligent brown eyes. Nothing like the Heathers he's always been attracted to. When Josh introduces her, she surprises me with a quick hug.

"I feel like I know you," she says. "I've heard so much about you from Josh."

Josh looks anxious, like he thinks I'm going to be mad

(madd*er*) because it's obvious he's told her the whole story. "It's really good to see you, Emma," he says. "Really. Listen, sometime could we—"

Thank God, Tiffany arrives and starts talking before he can finish the sentence.

What a *great* race, she says, too bad we didn't win—though it wasn't for the lack of a great mechanic! Josh was awesome with the bikes, *everyone* said so. And isn't this the coolest party, ever? How many little swimming pools *are* there, anyway? How long did it take to fill them up with water? Not to mention shovel all that *sand*?

Josh looks stunned, which sort of amuses me.

"Well. Sorry, you guys, but I've absolutely got to steal Emma," Tiff concludes, linking her arm with mine and guiding me firmly away from them. "Gabe's been looking all over for her," she calls over her shoulder. "See you guys later,"

Usually, I don't drink. Mainly because—as Harp (the person) so astutely observed—I don't like it. But also because I've always figured I was weird enough *without* alcohol. Why take the chance of getting drunk and doing something even stupider than usual? But tonight, some degree of intoxication seems, well, the sensible thing. So I take the cup of sangria Gabe offers me, drink it down, and wait for the effects to overtake me.

Meanwhile, we go inside and dance. That helps. You don't have to talk when you're dancing. And it's so crowded that I don't have to worry about whether I'm dancing *well.* Matt and Tiffany drift away from us, probably out to one of the cabanas, which I heard somebody say are equipped with army cots. Probably Josh and Amy have claimed one, as well. But fortunately, I've had a couple more sangrias, so I don't really care. I don't even panic when Gabe suggests we go for a walk. It's grown chilly and I wait, humming along with the band, while he goes up to his room to get us a couple of sweatshirts.

Walking along together, it seems to me that things have turned out okay after all. I didn't make a total fool of myself seeing Josh. And it's been easier than I thought it would be with Gabe. Not that I think he's falling madly in love with me or anything like that. Just that maybe he's not embarrassed to be with me, maybe I'm not as much of a dork as I thought I was.

We're even talking. We talk about books, some. And movies we like. We goof around a while, reciting our favorite parts of *This Is Spinal Tap*. Then he asks me what I've been up to since I left Bloomington—as if assuming I'll be back in the fall.

"Skiing," I say, which is certainly part of the truth.

"Nice," he says. "I've always wanted to try that."

"You should," I say. "Cyclists are great skiers. You know, because of their legs? Cyclists have great legs," I babble on. "So they pick it up easily."

"Really," he says.

Even the three, or is it four, sangrias I've drunk cannot save me from being mortified by his bemused response. Jesus, how did I end up talking to him about his *legs*? But do I stop there? No. I keep right on, tell him about this girl I know, a ski racer, who had a snowmobile wreck and saved herself by lifting the snowmobile off her body with her legs.

"That's how strong skiers' legs are," I say.

He laughs. "Yeah? What about speed?" Then he surprises me, running the flat of his hand over my hair. "I mean, speaking of body parts. Athletically, that is? Did you cut off all your hair to make you faster?"

I'm rattled by his touch. All I can do is keep talking, and I segue into the story of how I decided to simplify my life. Well, obviously, not the whole story. I leave out the part about being ditched by Harp. By the time I'm finished telling it, we're all the way down to Tenth Street.

Gabe nods toward the little shopping area a block away. "Want to get some ice cream?"

"Sure," I say.

And it goes downhill from there. First, I insist on paying for my ice cream, which embarrasses him. Then, to make up for it, to make him laugh again, I tell him all about Harp: buying him on impulse, the grim scene at Gramps' house resulting from my misguided belief in the premise of *The Natural Dog*, and my efforts to train him ever since—including walking him every evening on the Monon Trail, where he continues to resist the whole concept of walking on a leash in the most annoying but amusing ways.

"You could be a stand-up comic," he says. "Really."

But that's not the worst thing. He adds, "I've had a really good time tonight, Emma. This was a good idea Matt had."

"Oh," I say. "Yeah."

Of course, it wasn't his idea to ask you to the dance, I tell myself. You knew that.

And suddenly I start feeling sick. Maybe it's Gabe inadvertently admitting that Matt bullied him into taking me to the beach party, or maybe it's the sangria finally catching up with me—and Rocky Road ice cream on top of it. Whatever. The world starts spinning around me. Walking back, I keep stumbling and bumping into him—partly because I feel a little better when I close my eyes.

The next thing I know I wake up, way past midnight, freezing, on a chaise lounge near the ocean at the Phi Delt house.

"Jesus, I should have warned you about that sangria," Gabe says when I sit up. He's sitting on a lawn chair beside me, smoking. "They mix up every fucking thing you can imagine to make it. I'm really sorry."

"It's not your fault," I say. "I drank it. Just tell me I didn't throw up, okay?"

"Sure. You didn't throw up," he says. "Should I tell you if I'm lying?"

"You're not capable of lying," I say. "That Pulitzer Prize thing. Remember?"

"Yeah, okay. You threw up," he says.

"Shit. I knew it." I sit up too fast, and my right eye feels like someone's sticking little knives into it. "Shit," I say again and draw my knees up so I can rest my head on them.

"Hey." Gabe smushes out his cigarette and leans toward me. "Emma. Are you okay?"

"Fine. Fabulous." I wave my hand weakly toward the

deserted ocean of baby pools beyond where we sit. "Except for that fucking tidal wave. It gave me a killer migraine."

He shakes his head and smiles at me. "Are you ever *not* funny?" he asks.

Sometimes, I want to say. When I'm not mortified. When I'm not trying to be cool.

But of course I don't say that. I let him walk me back to the dorm, grateful for the way he talks the whole way about *The Things They Carried*, this book he read in a lit class and fell in love with. It's about Vietnam, he says. "I'll be reading one of the stories, horrified by the war stuff in it—and at the same time laughing my ass off. I mean it, that book kills me. I've read it about ten times, trying to figure out how something could be so depressing and hilarious at the same time. I mean, how did he *do* that?"

It doesn't seem like any kind of trick to me, which only makes my head hurt more. Depressing and hilarious: that's the story of my life. What I don't understand is why, if you feel that way, you'd want to write it down. It seems to me your energy would be far better spent trying to forget.

Something else I don't say. Maybe I'm getting smarter, learning how not to be so... my weirdest self *all* the time. Maybe next time I feel attracted to someone, I'll be able to break him in gently as to who I am. I just wish I'd started to have a clue about some of this stuff before I met Gabe.

"So," he says, when we get to the dorm.

"Listen. Thanks," I say. "You know, for—"

He shrugs. "Hey, I wasn't in the greatest shape myself. It might just as easily have been me who—"

Barfed, we're both thinking.

I feel sorry for him. He looks embarrassed for having brought us back to *that.* The truth is, he's not much better at this dating thing than I am. I'm going to have to be the one to give him the exit he needs now.

"Well," I say. "It was really great to see you again. But I'd better get some sleep. I've got to get up, get back to Indy before noon. I promised my dad—" I wave my hand vaguely in lieu of an actual plan.

"Oh. Sure," he says. "Okay, then. See you."

And he's gone.

Thirty

Please, please, please, please, *please* don't let Tiff be back yet, I pray, standing in the elevator with a bunch of girls who look as bad as I feel. But when I open the door and she's not there, it's as if I tumble backwards in time to last fall and I'm the miserable, lonely person I was then—which seems even worse than being the miserable, lonely person I am now.

At least I'm a rich miserable, lonely person now, I say to myself, still apparently unable *not* to be a comedian.

I don't even turn on the light, just lie down with my clothes still on and try to sleep. But there's laughter along the hall outside and the smell of spring drifting through the open window, and I feel so restless. Plus, I realize I'm still wearing Gabe's sweatshirt. I lift my arm and breathe in what must be the scent of him. I can't stop thinking about how great it was, the two of us walking along Tenth Street together for that little while, feeling like I could say anything. Was that *real*? Or was he just being nice when he said he had a good time with me?

And so what if he *was* telling the truth about that. Whatever good time we might have had occurred *before* I threw up and passed out and he had hours to sit in the yard on a lawn chair all by himself remembering the other times we were together and what a dork I was *then*.

What time is it in Paris, I wonder? What's Mom doing? If I were to tell her about what happened tonight and how I feel about Gabe Parker, what would she say?

It seems to me at this moment that there's not a single person in the world, not even Mom, who'd be able to understand how I feel—about anything. When Tiff finally comes in, near three o'clock, I pretend I'm sleeping.

"Emma?" she whispers. "Emma?"

I give a little moan. "Mmmm?"

"How was it? Did you have a good time with Gabe?" She giggles. "God, are you as tanked as I am?

"You are," she says when I moan again. "Okay, I'm wasted too. See you in the morning."

But there's no way I can face talking to her about my date with Gabe. I'm not mad at her for telling me it wasn't his idea. I know how she is. She wanted it to be his idea, so she twisted her mind around somehow and actually thinks it *was.* I'm just embarrassed—about everything. I don't want to talk about Gabe. Or Josh and Amy. I just want to go home, find a good book and exit to a whole other universe for a while.

I can't go till the sangria's totally worn off. But I know Tiff. She sleeps like the dead; she'll be out cold till at least noon. So I let myself drift off to sleep, knowing the sun will wake me. When it does, around seven, I get out of bed and scribble a note on the back of a concert flyer on her desk. *Tiff, Didn't want to wake you up. But I need to be home before noon, so I'm heading out. Thanks for everything. I'll call you! Love, Emma.*

I leave it on her bedside table, and consider leaving Gabe's sweatshirt for her to give back to him, but I don't. I turn it inside out, though: my little secret. Halfway home, I stop at a Bob Evan's for breakfast, where I sit in a booth for nearly two hours reading a bunch of outdated *People* magazines that have collected in my Jeep, passing the time so I don't get home too early.

When I pull into the driveway, Dad's waxing Gramps' Harley, and the sight of it sends me to a whole new low. I love that turquoise bike as much as Gramps did, even though it's the absolute tackiest thing you'd ever want to see, all got up in silver and fringe.

"Emma!" Dad calls, and throws the wax rag in my direction. It lands just short of Harp's nose, and he opens his eyes, gazes at it suspiciously. Then he picks it up in his teeth and trots over to me, his tail wagging wildly, and drops it at my feet like a gift.

"Good boy," I say, ruffling his warm fur.

"Good boy, hell," Dad says. "He ate a whole box of chocolate donuts yesterday and then threw them up all over the living room carpet. That little shit! Knocked them right off the kitchen table. He's got spirit, I'll say that. Did you have a good time in Bloomington?"

I shrug, which he takes for an affirmative.

I walk over to examine the newly waxed bike and I can see myself, all wavery, in the gleaming turquoise tank. The chrome sparkles. The silver fittings on the saddlebags wink in the sun. Dad steps closer to the bike, then back, squinting like Michelangelo assessing the Sistine Chapel. He picks up the rag and rubs here and there.

"Can I sit on it?" I ask.

"Sure," he says.

I throw my leg over the tank and get on, remembering how Gramps used to lift me up and put me on the seat when I was little. How I'd sit there, Emma Hammond, girl biker, for as long as he'd let me. Today Dad saddle-soaped the leather seat and it feels soft and warm against my bare legs. The very weight of the bike beneath me is exciting. I lean over and put my hands on the handlebars, just like I used to do then.

Dad smiles at me. "Do you remember asking Dutch if you could have his motorcycle when he died? You were maybe eight."

I remember, all right. Mom's horrified reaction to my request was my first real clue about what dying actually meant. She hustled me off into the kitchen and, kneeling so we were face-to-face, holding me tightly by the arms, she told me never, *ever* to ask such a question again. It was a terrible thing to talk about someone dying as if all it meant was a bunch of things going up for grabs as a result. It became one of those embarrassing family jokes afterwards. Jules would say, "Can I have your new skis when you die?" Or your Lenny Kravitz CD, or whatever.

Gramps and Dad thought it was funny, though. "I was kind of surprised he didn't leave it to you in the will," Dad says now. "Though he probably just assumed I'd remember and give it to you when the time came."

"Wait a minute," I say. "What are you saying?"

"You want it?" He nods toward the bike.

Yes, I want it! But the words stick in my throat. I can almost feel Mom beside me, hear her voice saying, *What in the world are you thinking about*? She'll be furious with Dad if he gives me the Harley, making things even worse between them.

"I don't know," I say. "Mom—"

He shrugs. "Your mom's not here, is she?"

That hangs between us for a few seconds. Then he says,

"I wrote her a letter, told her what I had in mind. I told her I'd make you dress right: boots and leather jacket, all that. You'd have to wear a helmet. And you'd have to let me give you some lessons before you take the riding test for your license, too.

"I've been thinking of taking that trip west that Dutch and I always used to dream about," he goes on. "Thinking maybe you might want to go with me. We could spend a couple of days riding around here, so you can get used to the bike. Then head out. Margaret will keep Harp for you; I already asked her. What do you say?"

I look at the bike, think of how Gramps would never, ever roar up the driveway on it again. That, somehow, gets all mixed up with Gabe being so nice about what an ass I made of myself last night, and I feel paralyzed with sadness.

"Emma?" Dad says.

"Yeah, I want to go," I say, blinking back tears. "I just—"

"I know," he says. "I wish Dutch could go, too. But we'll have a good time. And he'd like it that we were going together. You know that."

"Yeah," I say. It's true. But I don't want to go on the trip because I think Dad and I will have a good time, or because I think it would please Gramps to know I was his substitute. Gramps is dead, way beyond pleasure or disappointment. I want to go west with Dad because going will put a half a continent between me and Gabe Parker's humiliating kindness. But then, I figure, Dad's motives aren't totally pure either. Yeah, he wants us to have a good time together. But he also won't be sorry about putting half a continent between himself and home, where every single thing reminds him of Mom.

"Can *I* have it when *you* die?" That's the first thing Jules says when I call to tell her about our plans. "Let's see," she goes on when she's finished laughing hysterically. "That ought to be... *when* did you say Dad wrote Mom that letter?"

"Very funny," I say.

"Mom *is* going to be pissed."

"She is not," I say, feeling five.

"Is too." Jules laughs again. "Well, anyway, becoming a biker chick ought to cancel out whatever points you got on account of saving that stupid goose. Speaking of which—"

"What?"

"The *money*," she says, like I'm a dunce. "You know something, Emma? The other day I finally just sat Will down and said, 'What's the matter with us, anyway?' And we ended up talking about everything. He was totally paranoid about the money. He was, like, 'All my parents ever cared about was money, and I don't want to end up like them.'

"God. And there I was, constantly trying to foist it off on him. 'Let me invest in the gym,' I'd say. 'Let me pay for dinner.' I couldn't figure out why he'd get so upset every time I bought him a present. It hurt my feelings, you know? And I still don't exactly understand why he's so freaked out about it. I mean, we don't have to be like his parents just because we have a lot of money. We can be any way we want—

"Anyhow, we decided what I could do for him is work at the gym," she goes on. "That way, he and his partner can get by not hiring another person for a while. He feels comfortable with that. And I like it there, you know? We can schedule ourselves to work a lot of the same hours. Plus it's like dance, in a way—only it's about being strong and healthy instead of being strong and thin. Not that I mean to stop dancing," she says. "For myself, anyway. I still have some thinking to do about that."

I'm glad for her. She's doing what people are supposed to do when they grow up: figuring things out, slowly making her own life. But that life seems so far away from what our life together used to be.

As for me, I feel like I'm in limbo: the past irretrievable, the future frightening, unknown.

I call Tiff, like I said I would, but she seems distant. We don't mention the beach party. She doesn't try to convince me how Gabe actually really likes me, but is shy. In fact, she doesn't mention Gabe at all. She talks about how finals are coming up soon. I tell her about the trip I'm taking with my dad.

She's tired of trying to prop me up, I suppose. Who can blame her? But I miss the Tiffany who drove me crazy most of the time. I feel sad when we hang up, like I've lost something that, till now, I didn't quite realize I had.

Dad gives me my first lesson on the Harley on Monday morning, and, over the next few days, riding is the only thing that makes me feel okay. We set out early, take the old winding highways down through southern Indiana, spring bursting all around us. I love the sound of Gramps' bike, low and throaty, and the way, when we pull up for a late breakfast at some small-town diner, the old guys sitting there get a kick out of the fact I'm a girl. I wear Gabe's sweatshirt under my leather jacket, and I like thinking that even though he's probably lost to me, too, some part of him is with me, seeing me in a way I'd like him to see me: adventurous, real.

Back home at night, Harp curled up in bed beside me, I think about Mom. Nearly a week's passed since Dad sent the letter, and every time the phone rings, I'm certain it's her. Surely she'll call and let us know that what we're doing is okay—won't she? If she thinks it *is* okay. I half-want her to call and say, no way you can have the bike. It's too dangerous, whatever. Anything to make me believe that she means to come home eventually and shape Dad and me up, after all.

Sometimes I go sit in her studio, add seven hours to whatever time it is, and think about where she might be. Having coffee and croissants in a café; in the Gare d'Orsay, breathing in some painting she loves; sitting on the steps of Sacré-Coeur at midnight, all of Paris laid out at her feet. Two letters come that she wrote before she would have heard from Dad. She'd met up with an English woman on a side-trip to Provence, and they'd gone to Cézanne's studio together. Later, she'd gone alone to the little village, St. Mammes, where Sisley had painted. There were no tourists there, and she had wandered through the town marveling at the way the paintings in her guidebook appeared before her in a sequence of little scenes.

She calls, finally, the day before we leave. I'm just back

from taking Harp to Margaret's house, already missing him, thinking of the way he sat at my feet, tilted his head, and looked at me with those liquid eyes all the while I was talking to Margaret. He knew something was up. I felt so guilty I considered telling Margaret I'd changed my mind, I wasn't taking the trip with Dad after all, but I knew she'd never stand for it. I'm in a blue funk by the time I walk in the door and hear the phone ringing.

"Emma?"

"Mom, hi," I say, but there's that funny little glitch you get sometimes on overseas calls, so I guess she doesn't hear me.

"Emma?"

I wait a second, then say, "Yeah, it's me—"

"Everything's okay?"

"Yeah."

Even I can hear in my voice that it's *not*, and I feel myself sink a notch lower when Mom says, "Well, that's good." Pretending she believes me. "Listen, I got your dad's letter yesterday—"

That time warp thing happens again.

"... okay with me," she goes on, about the bike trip, I assume. "It's for you to decide, really. Each of us has to do that, you know? Decide what's right for ourselves."

I have to say I don't like the sound of that. I'm half-afraid she's going to tell me something she's decided about herself, something I'm not going to want to know. Which she does, sideways, talking about her trip to Monet's house at Giverny. She went there to paint—which you can do, if you arrange it ahead of time. She rented an easel and set it up in the garden, but the tourists were too distracting. Even though she chose an out-of-the-way corner, they stopped and peered at her through the spring flowers as if she were part of a museum exhibit.

"So I took a break and went over to the house," she says. "I was upstairs in Monet's bedroom, looking out the window at masses of tulips, every color you can imagine. Just glowing. And blue forget-me-nots. The fruit trees were covered with blossoms. They looked like prom dresses. Or pink clouds—

"I said to myself, this is what he saw. And then the light changed and *I* saw—I suddenly understood—that, yes, of course, he was obsessed with light, but the paintings are about so much more than that. Think about it, Emma," she said. "Haystacks, poplars, water lilies. How can they be so beautiful and make you feel so sad?"

She doesn't give me time to attempt an answer.

"Because light's a metaphor! The paintings are about life itself, how you try to hold on to what you love, all the while knowing that each moment carries its own tiny death within it. Everything, *everything* is alive and dying at the same time. Nothing lasts."

It falls quiet between us. There's a little crackling on the phone line. Maybe she says something else I don't hear.

"Mom?" I say.

"I'm here," she says. "Oh, Emma, this time has been so good for me. Being alone, thinking about hard things.

Have a wonderful trip with Dad. You think about hard things, too, while you're away."

"He's not here right now," I say. "Want me to have him call you when he gets back?"

She's quiet a moment. "I don't think so," she says. "Just tell him to have a good time. And I love him. You, too, Emma." Then she bumbles a kind of apology, tries to reassure me that things will work out fine.

We hang up and I go to the garage and sit on my bike. It's waxed, gassed up, and ready to go in the morning. Even my saddlebags are packed. We're leaving at six a.m.; in Paris, it will be one o'clock in the afternoon. I close my eyes and try to imagine Mom there, but all I see is Dad and me on our Harleys, riding farther and farther away from her.

Thirty-one

Our engines start up, shattering the early morning air. "Harley's *sound*," Dad always says when anyone asks him why he loves them so much. "That's what they're all about."

Now I know exactly what he means. Sitting on my bike, ready to go, I *am* the sound: the low, throaty burbling of the exhaust, the clacking valves, the thump, thump of the big pistons. The raw power of the engine rumbles right up through the seat of my jeans and flows through me, as vital as blood.

Dad guns the Sturgis and grins, gives me the thumbs up, and we're off. The weather's perfect, a tinge of early warmth promising to heat up to an almost-summer day by noon. We stop for breakfast at Bedford, then arc west toward Illinois. The highway winds through the Hoosier National Forest, through the rich farmland in the southern part of the state. It smells green. Occasionally, a farmer waves from his yellow tractor. Kids wave, too, when we pass through little towns.

"Everyone loves a Harley," Dad says.

We get to Emporia that first day, just the other side of Kansas City. My arms and shoulders ache from having been locked in the same position. The sudden absence of wind makes me feel light, slightly unbalanced, and I can still feel the vibration of the engine inside me. I go to sleep, feeling it. Ride all night in my dreams.

The next evening, near dark, we roll into a little town near the Kansas-Colorado border, check in at a mom-and-pop motel, and ask the desk guy where we can get a decent meal. There's a bar a couple of miles down the road where they serve great steaks, he tells us. But when we get there, a man standing at the door, smoking, says the whole place is reserved for a private anniversary party. "Twenty-fifth," he says. "My sister's twenty-fifth, in fact." He's a nice guy, a Harley rider himself, but I can't see any point in Dad standing there talking about bikes with him when we can't eat here and, according to the motel clerk, there's no other decent restaurant for miles. I'm starving. The kitchen windows of the restaurant are open and I can smell steaks cooking. I'm just about to try to talk Dad into riding up to the interstate to see if we can find a McDonald's, when the guy—Dave—says, "I'll tell you what, Mac. I think I can get you guys in on this deal tonight. Wait here, okay?"

"*Dad*," I say, when he's gone inside. "We can't crash somebody's twenty-fifth wedding anniversary."

But Dave sticks his head out the door and motions us to follow him; and before I know it, we're sitting with the guests of honor at the main table. Dad springs for champagne for everyone, and the corks pop as introductions are made. There's Dave's wife, Marilyn. Bob and Linda, whose anniversary it is, and their sons, Randy and Bob Jr.—about my age. Dave's and Linda's parents, Bud and Lil.

All through dinner, there's a constant parade of people out to see the bikes. Linda and Marilyn love the fact that mine is turquoise. Randy and Bob Jr. have never met a girl who rides, and they keep looking back and forth between me and the bike with bemused expressions.

One young, really drunk guy—Jack—looks at Dad's Sturgis for a long time.

"You ride?" Dad asks.

"Nah," he says. "Not any more. I cut a deal with the state of Kansas. Sheriff said, 'Jack, either you drink or you drive. What'll it be?'" He grins goofily and raises his beer mug.

Dad laughs, and throws his arm around the guy's shoulders. It's one of the great things about him, I think. The way he takes people just exactly the way they are. Mom's always trying to understand them. She'd meet a guy like Jack and talk you to death about him afterwards, trying to puzzle him out. Not Dad. It never occurs to him to wonder how a person got to be the way he is, or how he's going to end up.

I wish I could be that way. Right now Dad isn't thinking about what a great evening it's turned out to be or what a relief it is that none of these people know that we're rich. He isn't noticing the way the neon sign blinks in the night or the smell of the earth or the little ramshackle house across the road with the television flickering in the window. He *lives* in an almost perpetual state of *shunyata*. Moment to moment. Just being.

But standing in the parking lot that spring evening—wearing Gabe Parker's inside-out Phi Delt sweatshirt, like a widow wearing some relic of her lost love—I feel something loosen inside me, and I'm so filled up with emotion that I think I might cry. I want to remember everything: the white cowboy hats gleaming in the moonlight, the tips of cigarettes glittering like fireflies. I want to remember the sound of the band tuning up inside and how everyone insists that Dad and I stay and dance.

Which we do, until our feet are burning. Linda teaches Dad to swing dance and makes him dance with her all night because Bob hates dancing. Bob Jr. teaches me. He's a big, beefy guy, exactly my age as it turns out, and already farming with his dad. I feel small and light and graceful spinning out from beneath his hands. I feel lit up. I feel myself smiling. When the band breaks into an old Patsy Cline song I love, I sing along so loud that, laughing,

Randy picks me up and sets me on the stage with them. The singer, a hard-looking girl with a big voice, grins and leans toward me with the mike and we belt out the rest of the words together. I'm flustered and a little embarrassed when the song is over and everyone applauds wildly, yelling at me to sing again. But I feel good. I feel like *myself.*

I think about that a lot the next day, riding. Or maybe it's closer to say that memories float up while I'm riding, and I think about how they feel. I remember my friend, Renata, whom I haven't seen for ages. We were three when we met at nursery school. We played together all day, and sometimes I cried when it was time to go home because I didn't want to leave my friend. Renata had beautiful toffee-colored skin and wonderful black pigtails that stuck out from her head exactly like Mickey Mouse ears. I wanted to look just like her. The thing is, Grandma Hammond had dragged me to Sunday School a couple of times, and I guess I got some convoluted idea about what religion was, because I got it in my head that Jesus could make this happen for me. Every night, in the bathtub, I checked out every inch of my body to see if He had decided to answer my prayers.

"Mom! Mom!" I yelled one night. I pointed to my knee, all shriveled from being in the water so long. "Look," I said. "Look! Jesus is making me brown, just like Renata."

It's another one of Mom's favorite stories about me. She never fails to tell it when explaining to someone what a strange child I was. I'd always thought it was pretty funny myself. Just a funny story. But now, suddenly, it seems like more than that.

Just like Renata.

I realize for the first time that, in the past, whenever I tried to figure out who I was or what I wanted to be, it was always a matter of measuring myself against someone else. I was emotional, creative, verbal, curious—like Mom. I was a speed-demon—like Dad. I wanted Jules' body, I wanted Renata's pretty brown skin and her kinky brown Mickey Mouse pigtails.

I think of this animal mix-up book that I used to play with when I was little. There were three sets of pages, top to bottom: heads, torsos, and legs of animals. You flipped them to make bizarre concoctions. A gelephingo, for example: the head of a giraffe, the body of an elephant, the legs of a flamingo.

I felt like myself, singing at the party; but who, exactly, is that self? Is it just a human version of the mix-up game, or is it more than that? What is it about *my* self that's different from any other self that's ever been born? And, supposing I could figure that out, where would Harp's *shunyata* thing fit into the picture? Can you lose a self you haven't found yet? Do you have to find your true self to be able to let it go?

I'm still pondering all this when we stop to fill our gas tanks. So I say to Dad, "What would you say the essence of Emma is?"

He taps the nozzle lightly so that the last drops of gas will go inside the gas tank, not on it where they might mar the shine. "The *essence* of Emma?"

"Yeah. I've been thinking. Last night when I was singing with the band I was really, really happy, and I asked myself why. You know, why was I happy? And it was because singing made me feel exactly like myself. But then I thought, what *is* my self?"

Dad says, "Christ, you sound just like your mother."

"Hel-*lo*," I say. "That's exactly my point. Every time I try to figure out who I am, I end up comparing myself to Mom or you or Jules or—whoever. But who am *I*? I mean, suppose you and Mom had ditched me at birth and I was raised by a whole other family. What part of me would be exactly the same as it is now?"

"But we didn't ditch you," he says. "You are who you are."

"Dad," I say, "what I'm asking you is—"

"I know what you're asking me. But I don't know the answer. To tell you the truth, it doesn't seem that important. If singing made you happy, then you ought to sing more often. Seems pretty simple to me. Do what makes you happy, and you'll be happy. Plus, you won't have time to torture yourself with questions you can't answer."

"Maybe some people need to do that," I say. "Maybe torturing themselves with unanswerable questions is the only way they can figure out how to be happy."

"I'm sure that's true," Dad says. "I just never have been able to understand why."

It's an honest response. Still, it pisses me off the way he says it so matter-of-factly, as if he's just decided to accept the fact that he'll never understand me. I'm pissed off at Mom, too. For being so consumed by her own unanswerable questions that she left me all alone to ponder mine.

I fume the whole time Dad's in the station, paying. "You really think the world would be a better place if everyone was like you, don't you?" I say when he comes out.

"Nope. But I've got to say, it's not the worst thing I can imagine." He grins, waves his hand as if to encompass the entire planet. "Cold beer in every refrigerator, a Harley-Davidson in every garage!"

"You're so funny," I say. "Don't you ever take anything seriously?"

Dad puts his helmet back on, hikes his leg over the tank of his bike. "Many things, Emma," he says. "I think you know that. But never myself."

Well, fine, I think. Fine. He's so annoying sometimes. *Seems pretty simple to me*. He always says that. *Lighten up*. He'd have said that next, if I'd given him a chance. I get myself about half worked up into a snit; but once we get going again, there's the feel of the bike throbbing all through my body, the gray asphalt stretching forever, the foothills of the Rockies rolling out on either side, and my annoyance dissolves into the same pure happiness I felt the night before, singing at the bar. *Shunyata*. Not thinking about anything at all.

That night I dream I have a box of gargantuan crayons and I'm drawing everything around me. I make the Kansas hills yellow. I make the sky porcelain blue, the way it is high in the mountains where the air is thin and clear. I make trees the first green of spring. And flowers every color, everywhere.

I'm so happy coloring the world. I wake, afterwards, completely content, and lie in the motel bed in the darkness, smiling, remembering how much I used to love to draw. I'd spend hours and hours drawing pictures on sheets of white typing paper. Each one had a story, which I told to Mom. She wrote it on the back of the page, with the date, and put it in a drawer in her studio. Last year, when I graduated from high school, she collected the best ones and put them in a loose-leaf notebook as a gift.

Now, turning the pages of that book in my mind's eye, I remember how strange and vivid the world seemed to me then. "Basketball Players Going to the Haunted House," "Emma Riding an Alligator with a Blue Eye," "Ninjas Taking Ballet."

I can't even remember the last time I imagined anything wonderfully unreal, something all my own, and I wonder why I haven't known to miss that inner world. It's safe there, though not predictable. Jesus can have blue hair, little girls can ride alligators. They can be whoever they want to be—and not only one thing, either. Every single story is its own little life.

Thirty-two

Riding out of the mountains and into the desert, I'm amazed. It's nothing at all like I imagined it would be—not flat and brown and scrubby like the desert you always see in Westerns—but high and rolling, rocky and *red.* It's a giant's landscape. There are arches, monoliths. Mountains that time sculpted into bells or hands or towers. Mesas as flat as tabletops.

"Cowboy country," Dad says.

We're standing in a gas station in Arizona where there's a bunch of silver and turquoise stuff for sale. "Look," I say, holding up a hideous bolo tie. "Would Gramps love this, or what?"

"Yep," Dad says. "It would be right up his alley." He takes it from me, holds it in the palm of his hand, and looks at it as if it actually had belonged to Gramps, as if it were something he'd come across going through his stuff. Setting it back on the counter, he says, "You know, it's little things that get me—like dead-on knowing that Dutch would buy that damn bolo tie. I wonder why that is. The funeral, the will—even cleaning out the garage, I could handle. You'd think it would be the other way around." He shrugs, pays for our gas.

Then, walking back to the bikes, he laughs. "A while ago, back in the mountains, I was feeling kind of low, thinking about what a kick Dutch would be getting out of those narrow, winding roads. Then I thought, shit, if I were with Dutch, we'd probably be stuck somewhere in Kansas working on his bike. We never went anywhere together that it didn't break down at least once, and I'd find out he'd done some dumb thing to it that he hadn't told me about—

"He was the world's worst mechanic," Dad continues. "He knew it, too. I'll never forget the time we were in a Harley shop somewhere and a guy asked his advice on what to put in a tool kit for his Sportster. Dutch thought a minute, then he said, 'Just need one. Your Gold Card.'"

I can hear Gramps saying that and it makes me feel better. Still, back on the road, I miss him something awful, and as miles pass and the desert morphs into a dusty, barren landscape dotted with nothing but ugly cactus plants, it feels as if it's happening in direct response to what I feel in my heart. If it's possible, I miss Gramps even worse when we roar into Las Vegas early that evening. He'd be revving his engine all the way up the Strip, loving the whole tacky scene. The pyramid of Luxor, the medieval turrets of Excalibur just beyond. At the Flamingo Hilton, pink and white and orange light travels frantically up and down what looks like the blown petals of gargantuan flowers. Harrah's is a steamboat made of light: the red neon spokes of the paddle wheel give the illusion of turning; strings of white lights loop from smokestack to smokestack like long strands of pearls.

At Caesars Palace, where we're going to stay, there are limos everywhere. A red Wells Fargo armored truck is parked at the entrance of the casino, the uniformed guards loading bags of money into it. We pull up behind it on our bikes, turn off the engines, and a bellman wearing a toga—a guy around Jules' age—hurries over to us.

"Checking in," Dad says. "Okay to leave the bikes out here for a few minutes?"

The guy grins. "We'd be glad to park those for you, sir."

"I'll bet you would," Dad says, and gives him a twenty-dollar bill to keep an eye on them instead.

The frigid air of the casino is a shock after riding all day in the desert heat. The noise, too. Voices, laughter. Beeping, buzzing. Tinny, repeating patterns of high-pitched music emitting from the banks of slot machines and video poker machines, which are stretched as far as I can see. Neon loops like necklaces, bubbles like fountains. Dad segues over to a video poker machine, feeds it five quarters, and gets four aces the first hit.

"Damn! Look at that!" he says.

You're not allowed to gamble until you're twenty-one, but I give it a try anyway, hoping my biker garb makes me look old—or maybe dangerous—enough to get away with it. Nobody stops me when I sit down at the machine beside Dad—and *damn* if I don't get four aces with my first hand, too!

Well, that's that. After we check in and park the bikes, we're *committed.* I'm mesmerized by the plink-plink-plink-plink-plink of the five cards appearing on the video poker screen, the feel of my fingers tapping the keys to hold the cards I choose, then the delicious moment of suspense as the new cards turn over. The appearance of the right number or set of numbers, the face I was hoping for, the necessary heart or club, triggers a simple internal *yes.* If the wrong cards appear, I feel a kind of emotional shrug, immediately followed by the impulse to try again.

It's nearly midnight when we surface, starving. Walking over to a Denny's, we pass through a gauntlet of down-and-outs holding out plastic casino cups, hoping to benefit from someone's good luck. There are also guys handing out business cards with pictures of sleazy women on the front, and advertisements for shows and various—services. Dad takes the cards, grinning. He plunks coins from his own full Caesars cup into the cups of the needy.

Just outside Harrah's, an old woman approaches us.

Her heavy makeup is smeared, her scalp visible beneath her bleached, ratted hair. "Sir, I've had some trouble," she says. "I lost my coin purse at the Hacienda with more than thirty-seven dollars in it, and I really feel the need to have some Chinese food."

Dad takes out his wallet, hands her a fifty-dollar bill, and for a moment she stands there looking at him almost suspiciously. Then, like a squirrel, she tucks the bill away and scurries off into the nearest casino. Dad watches her go. "I like to see someone with a little imagination," he says.

I'm tired suddenly, battered by the excess of this place. Money everywhere, and all these pathetic people begging for some small share of it—which they'll probably gamble or drink away. There are slot machines in the lobby of Denny's. I watch a man hold up his tiny daughter so she can feed a quarter into one of them.

Dad eats eggs, bacon, pancakes, drinks about a gallon of coffee, and is ready to go at it again. But I go up to our room to sleep. At seven the next morning I find him at a bank of dollar machines, still going strong.

"I can't lose," he says. "Fucking aces out the wazoo—and two royal flushes within twenty minutes of each other. No shit. I'm up fifteen thousand bucks. So I came over here to play this progressive for a while." He nods to the computer readout above our heads. It says $8,676. Then $8,677... 78... 79... 80... It's up to $8,690 by the time I look back at him.

"Want to go eat breakfast?" I ask. "I'm starving."

"I ate a chili cheese dog a while ago, but sure I'll go with you. Just a minute. Let me play down to five hundred or up to ... *holy* shit!" Red lights all around the poker machine start flashing, and a siren goes off. "Will you look at this?" Dad says. "Can you believe it?"

The cards present themselves perfectly on the screen. A royal flush: hearts. They're even in the correct order. Ten, Jack, Queen, King, Ace. $8,740 blinks above the bank of machines. Within seconds a motley group gathers around, most of them clutching Bloody Marys. A casino cashier stops with her money cart and phones for someone to come make the payout. A couple of security guards gravitate to the scene, and pretty soon the casino representative, a big guy in a business suit, appears with tax forms for Dad to sign. Then he counts the money into Dad's hand. Eighty hundred-dollar bills, and twenties to make up the "small change." Dad turns and hands all of it to the woman with the cash cart. She's a small Hispanic woman, her sleek black hair pulled back from her face with a red rubber band, the same kind that binds the stacks of bills in her cart. She's at the end of an all-night shift, her brown eyes dull with fatigue, and she stares at the bills in her hand as if they just dropped right out of the sky.

Dad looks at her name tag. "Consuela," he says. "The money is for you. For your family."

"Sir," the casino representative says. "Perhaps you—"

Dad waves him away. "You enjoy it," he tells Consuela. "Have some fun. Get something you need."

The woman's fist closes over the bills, her knuckles whitening. She gazes upward, murmuring fervently in Spanish. Then she throws her arms around Dad and bursts into tears.

My own eyes burn at the kindness of his gesture, but mainly because I know how it would please Mom. She loves his impulsive, almost reckless generosity. His large, kind heart, which shows itself at the unlikeliest moments and delights her in the way it unnerves people who think they know him. I want her to be here now. I want her to have seen what Dad just did, to help her remember why she and Dad are meant to be together. But she'd hate this place. I know that, too. Being here would only make her more confused.

For some reason, that makes me mad. Why does she have to be so—I can't even say what she is, and that just makes me madder. I leave Dad and his circle of well-wishers and walk through the casino, trying not to notice the desperate, frenzied expression on the fat man feeding the five-dollar slot machine, or the fragile, gray-haired lady playing beside him, who wears thin white gloves to keep her hands clean. Trying not to hear the slap of cards, the rattle of dice, the whir of roulette wheels nearby.

I go out by the pool, where it's so quiet I can hear the spitting of sprinklers beyond the wall and the sound of water lapping against the edges of the swimming pool. The yellow-and-white-striped cabanas are empty, except for one in which a couple of women are drinking their breakfasts and another in which a man talks on a cell phone, his laptop propped, lid up, on his lap. I find a chaise lounge under a palm tree and lie back, let the sun filter through the leaves and soak into my air-conditioned skin, and try to calm myself by imagining Consuela going home at the end of her shift, bearing the news of her good fortune. I see a boxy little house, shabby but clean inside, cluttered with the evidence of children. Probably too many of them, I think, despite knowing it's politically incorrect to assume such a thing. A husband would be there, maybe. Tired and hard-working like herself, or maybe a ne'er do well. Maybe there's no husband at all. Maybe a boyfriend. Maybe she lives all alone.

There's no question that the sudden windfall of nearly nine thousand dollars will mean nothing but good fortune to her, in any case. It would mean nothing but good fortune for anyone. If you were rich, and always had been, it would be icing on the cake, maybe even proof to yourself that, indeed, you deserved everything the world had given you so far. If you were comfortable, as we were before Dad won LOTTO CASH, it would mean splurging on stuff you wanted but couldn't quite afford: an expensive pair of skis, a special trip, new carpet. Jewelry, if that's what you liked. If you were poor, as Consuela most likely is, it would translate to bills paid, maybe a new couch to replace an old, battered one, a new dress for yourself, a bicycle for one of your children. The thing is, it's definable. Nine thousand dollars would affect anyone's life for the better—but temporarily, and with limits. But winning millions of dollars demands that you change your whole life to accommodate it. It's a kind of cosmic dare.

Dad would think that was ridiculous. I think about how he looked, beaming at Consuela, completely absorbed in their mutual moment of pleasure. If I had asked him how he felt, why he gave her the money, he'd look at me the same way he did when I asked him about the essence of Emma.

If he said anything at all, he'd say, "I got a kick out of it," or "She looked like she could use it." Or he'd make a joke. "I figured I'd better ditch it. Another nine thousand bucks could tip your mom right over the edge." By now, he's probably walked away from the whole scene. He's probably found some other poker machine and is winning on *it.*

How can he and Mom be so different and so alike, I wonder? He gave the money to the Hispanic lady; she gave Christmas money to those kids at the mall. Dad would say it was the same thing: You help people when you can. But I knew that Mom believed she did what she did from some mix of guilt and confusion, maybe even a kind of atonement for or charm against her own good luck. Generosity, of course—though she didn't give herself much credit for that, since what she gave them was not something she needed or wanted herself.

Now, suddenly, I see that she had given it from love, too—a kind of love that's different from the love you feel for your family or friends or anyone you know. An abstract, amorphous kind of love, disturbing in its refusal to fit anywhere in your real life and in the way it spills beyond familiar boundaries. That's what Mom meant when she tried, now and then, to explain to me where paintings came from. Art was a place to put that kind of love, a way to be unburdened of it.

I feel that love, too. I've always felt it. I just never knew what it was. The night in Kansas, standing in the pink neon light of the bar, trying to memorize the moment: it was love that overwhelmed me. Now dozens of images clutter my brain. The mosquito on the snowy log, the snowballs tumbling in the scoop of the Lake Michigan shoreline. I see myself driving my brand new Jeep with the stereo turned up loud, sitting in the empty Sunday school room after Gramps' funeral, taking the gates on a race course with snow flying in my wake. It was all love, all of it—and more. Zooming around inside me with no purpose or resting place, like Harp zooms around the yard.

Maybe that's what is so large about me, I think. Maybe that's what doesn't fit in the real world. Not my body, but my heart—metaphorically speaking, as Mom might say. Whatever. Money or no money, I'm going to have to find something to do about it. And it strikes me that this is the first thing I know for sure about who I will eventually turn out to be.

Thirty-three

The next thing I know, Dad's standing over me holding a Dunkin' Donuts bag and two Styrofoam cups. "I had a hell of a time finding you," he says. "I wouldn't have, except after I gave up looking for you and went up to our room, I looked out the window and saw you down here fast asleep by the pool." He plunks the bag on the end of the chaise lounge. "What's the deal? I thought you wanted to go get breakfast."

"Who gave up on who?" I sit up, get a donut with

white icing and sprinkles on it. "I couldn't drag you away from the machine to eat. Then you got a little *distracted*."

"Oh, that," he says. "Want some coffee? I put some cream in it."

"Dad, I never drink coffee," I say. "Mom's the one who drinks coffee with cream."

"Oh," he says.

And he looks so pathetic, I take it from him and drink it anyway.

He sits down next to the donut bag. His eyes are baggy and red-rimmed from lack of sleep. He's still wearing the clothes he wore riding into town the day before. "Know what I feel like?" he asks.

"Shit?" I say. "You *look* like shit. If you felt like shit too, there'd be a nice, as we former English majors say, confluence of form and function."

"Yeah, that. But—remember when I ran the Chicago marathon?"

"Unfortunately," I say, "yes. Not to mention remembering the entire year before the marathon, in which you were completely and totally obsessed with getting ready to run it and drove me and Mom and Jules crazy."

"I've been thinking about how I got nearly to the end," he says. "Then sat down under the last shade tree before the Soldier Field parking lot because I thought I couldn't go on. I'd gotten through the last two miles going shade tree to shade tree. I kept telling myself, 'There's the next one. You can go that far.' Then there were no more shade trees. Just asphalt."

"So?" I ask, though I'm not at all sure I really want to know where he's going with this.

"That's exactly how I feel now," he says. "Like I'm at the last shade tree. The end of the line. When I won that progressive, I mean after the excitement of winning it, I thought, what the fuck am I doing? Eight, nine thousand dollars—whatever it was. Plus whatever I won playing all night. It doesn't mean jack shit to me. That's why I gave that woman the money. I just didn't want to look at it. I'm tired of the sight of money—"

"You finished the marathon," I say. "Eventually."

He shrugs. "Yeah. But right then I didn't know I could. Goddamn it," he says, and his voice cracks. "I miss your mom, and I don't know what to do about it."

I just sit there. I'm used to Mom dithering around, being traumatized and emotional about every little thing. But Dad? He always knows what to do and how to go about doing it. Until this second, it's never even occurred to me that he might doubt himself about anything.

Which I suppose is a good explanation for why, surprising both of us, I say, "Dad, I think you ought to go to France."

He looks at me as if I just suggested he go to Zimbabwe. Or Mars.

"Really," I say. "Why not? Mom's always wanted you to go, but you never had the time. And it was so expensive. Now—"

"I'm not going to France," he says. "Your mother went to France because—"

"... she wanted to be alone," I interrupt. "I know. But—"

"We give each other space," he says. "She does her thing, I do mine. That's how we've managed to stay married as long as we have."

"She went to Steamboat Springs with you," I say. "She hates the mountains, but she went."

"And bitched the whole time," he says.

"Dad," I say. "Let's not even *go* there, okay? Mom tried, and it didn't work out so well. But does that mean you can't try something *she* likes? Plus, has it occurred to you that what worked for you guys before you won the money might not work now? I mean, you *needed* to give each other space before. Maybe that's not what you need any more. Or maybe you don't need it in the same way. Maybe you have to find some new ways of being together."

He just looks at me. Then he says, "Emma, what the hell are you talking about?"

I don't know, exactly. I just know what I said was true—like I know, absolutely, that he ought to go to France. In any case, he doesn't give me the chance to attempt an explanation.

He stands up. "Well, you let me know when you figure it out," he says. "But forget France. I'm not going to fucking France. I'm going up to take a shower."

"Fine," I call after him. "Be stubborn. Be miserable."

He ignores me.

I brood for a while, not so much mad at him about the France thing as I am about the whole universe shifting on me again. Am *I* supposed to solve this problem between Mom and Dad? I'm eighteen, for God's sake. Aren't they supposed to be helping *me*?

It's getting too hot to sit in the sun anymore; plus, I think maybe a change of scenery will shake something loose in my head. So I decide to go check out the rain forest next door at the Mirage. Next door, ha. It takes practically a half-hour to walk over there. I have to go back through Caesars Palace, out the front doors, and down the long driveway to the street, all the while hearing some faux Julius Caesar's voice booming over the loudspeaker, trying to lure people into his empire. At the Mirage, I get onto a moving sidewalk that deposits me into a wide corridor with a gift shop on one side and a tigers' cage on the other. Habitat, I should say—like you'd see in a zoo. There are cement caves and cliffs, palm trees and greenery, a big pool for the two Siberian white tigers to play in. The whole space is jammed with people, twelve deep, all along the plate glass, as if they're watching a huge television screen.

I edge my way through the crowd, glancing at the caged tigers behind the glass. One sleeps, its huge paw draped over a rock cliff, vulnerable as a child. The other prowls. From one end of the cage to the other he goes, up the cliffs and down again. The pattern of his movement fascinates me, and I stop and watch a while, mainly to see if and how it will change. But it doesn't change. The tiger takes the same route through his cage again and again, back and forth, up and down, as if to constantly monitor the limitations of his world.

That's it, I think! That's what I was trying to say to

Dad. He's spent the last six months prowling the glass cage of the world that a 9–5 job made of his life, coming up against the edges of it—just like the tiger. The difference is, the glass walls in the tiger's cage are real. Dad's aren't. Winning LOTTO CASH took them away. Or, at least made the cage a whole lot larger.

That's why he should go to France.

By now I'm feeling pretty darn metaphysical and pleased with myself. Dang, I think, Mom would be proud of me for figuring this out. Then I think, oh yeah, Mom. What if she doesn't want Dad to come to France? What if she's perfectly happy there all alone?

One thing I know for sure: she doesn't like surprises. I look at my watch. It's eight o'clock in the evening in Paris. She might be in. I have the phone number of her hotel folded up in my wallet, and I get it out now and look at it a long time. I know that the emergency she thought we might need it for would be some kind of accident, like the one I imagined on that Sunday when she and Dad came to tell me the news about winning the lottery. I find a phone, punch in my credit card number, then the number Mom gave me.

There's a lot of clicking, then it rings: shrill, foreign rings.

"*Bonjour. Hotel de Notre Dame.*"

"*Madame Hammond, s'il vous plait.*"

Then Mom's voice, anxious. "Hello?"

"We're okay," I say.

"Emma?"

I take a deep breath. "Mom?" I say. "Would it be okay if Dad came to see you?"

"Here?" she asks. ""To France? He wants to do that?"

"Yes," I lie.

"Emma—"

"What?"

"Is there something wrong?" she asks.

"No," I lie again. "It's just—Dad wants to come, but he won't ask you if it's okay. He thinks you want to be alone."

She's quiet for so long that I'm afraid she's trying to figure out how to tell me, gently, that he's right. When, finally, she says, "Tell him, yes, come," I know it took her so long to speak because she's crying.

I promise to call back as soon as we make a plan.

This, of course, is a trickier issue than she knows. Dad's going to be furious if I tell him I called Mom; plus, I know it would be better for him to come to the conclusion that he needs to go to France himself. I want him to see what I see: that not to go would be to keep prowling the perimeter of some cage that's no longer there.

I find him in our room at Caesars Palace, sitting on the black leather couch and perusing the marked-up road maps he's got spread out on the smoked glass coffee table.

"I'm thinking I'll sleep a couple of hours," he says. "Then we can head out, ride into the evening when it's cooler. If we hit it, I figure we can get to L.A. by midnight."

"Dad," I blurt out. "I *really* think you ought to go to France."

"Emma, would you get off that?" he says. "We're halfway through this trip, and I'm supposed to drop everything and go to France?"

"Why not? Just because you marked the map one way doesn't mean you can't decide to go another. Let's just ride straight home instead. If we leave this afternoon, get on the interstate and go, we can be there in two days. You can get on a plane and be with Mom by Friday."

"Emma," he says, his voice warning me.

"What? We have to stay on some stupid riding treadmill? California, Montana, whatever. Eventually we're going to end up at home anyway—where Mom's not."

"I can't control that," he says.

"Dad," I say. "Would you just please listen?"

He gives me a withering glance, but I press on, explaining what I saw watching the tiger at the Mirage. "So," I say when I'm through. "Maybe the space you think you're giving Mom is false space, contained inside the walls of what your lives used to be. Maybe you ought to step outside the walls that aren't there any more. Going to France would be a way of doing that."

"Read my lips, Emma," he says when I'm through. "I. Am. Not. Going. To. France."

He folds the maps, puts them back in their case. Then he gets up, walks over to his bed, and lies down on it without turning down the covers. He assumes a sleep position, crossing his arms over his chest, closing his eyes. But he's faking it. Tension steams off his body and sizzles the atmosphere, like raindrops hitting asphalt on a hot summer day.

I sit down on the edge of my bed and watch him for what seems like an eternity. He's stubborn, I'll give him that. I couldn't lie there three minutes with someone staring at me like I'm staring at him. Then, astonishingly, his eyelids flutter, his whole body visibly relaxes, and he's fast asleep.

I'm still sitting on the edge of my bed, watching him, when he stirs an hour later. He's not really awake, just turning to get more comfortable so he can settle in and sleep for who knows how long.

"Dad," I whisper.

"Unh . . . " he says, vaguely inquisitive.

"I talked to Mom. About France. She wants you to come."

He opens his eyes. "You what?"

"I talked to Mom," I repeat. "I called her, after we were down at the pool."

He sits up. "And she wants me to come?"

"Yes," I say.

"Jesus, Emma," he says. "Why didn't you just tell me that from the start?"

Thirty-four

I give Dad a crash course in French on the way back, more to keep him occupied than anything else. We stop somewhere to eat and I make him repeat the words for whatever we're eating. He's a disaster. It's "oofs" for "*oeufs*" and "pan" for "*pain.*" He won't even try "*bifteck.*"

"Steak's fine," he says. "They'll know what I want."

"Yeah," I say. "And you might as well give up on *merci* while you're at it. For you, 'mercy' is appropriate."

"I'm not going because I want to talk to French people," he says.

I'm pretty much a wreck by the time I get home a few days later and put him on the plane. But I tell myself that if anyone will know what to do with him, Mom will. She'll break him in easy, maybe take him over to see the D-day beaches. And there are all those great battle paintings in the Louvre.

I feel better when I go get Harp. He goes into his zoom-mode the second he sees me, flying around in Margaret's backyard like a canine jet. He jumps up on me, dances around me a while, then goes zooming again. When he finally calms down, I take him inside where he promptly falls asleep in my lap while I eat a piece of Margaret's chocolate cake.

We chat a while. I fill her in on Jules and Will, and she's glad to know Jules is finally thinking about settling down. It's about time! Mom and Dad being in France, though—it's a stretch for her to see why anyone would want to go all the way over there when they could stay right here in Indiana. Especially in May, with the peonies about to bloom and everything shooting up in the garden.

"All that money," she concludes. "I guess you'd feel you ought to do something with it."

"Yeah," I say, and leave it at that.

It's late afternoon when I get home. Harp sniffs his way to Dad's leather chair, then hops up and noses around, like he thinks if he looks hard enough he'll find Dad somewhere in it. Pretty soon, he sighs happily and curls in on himself. What do I know? Maybe Dad *is* there, as far as Harp's concerned. Maybe all that dogs need to be happy is the scent, the memory of a person they love. Maybe they're more advanced than we are that way.

I wander around the house, like Mom always does when she comes home from a trip. But the things I've lived with all my life look foreign to me. Funny: I've always thought Mom did the house thing because it pleased her so much to be home again, among the things she loves. In part, I'm sure that's true. But now I suspect that some other part of her was marveling at the strangeness of the idea that her life was made of these objects, as much as it was made of all she felt and saw and dreamed and knew inside her.

As for me, wandering around the house I've lived in since I was born, I see that only something as familiar as the Snoopy glass I drank Kool-Aid from when I was six, or the way light at a certain time of day shines through a lace curtain and casts its pattern on the blue carpet where I played with my Barbies, can teach me how strange life really is. How you just have to work your way through it, collecting things and places you love to ground you, while at the same time you know that they work just like details in a story: they define, but don't explain you. Nothing can explain you, really—not even to yourself.

This should depress me, but in fact it cheers me up. It's weird. Letting go of the idea that I'm supposed to be able to explain every little thing about my life, plus figure out how to be a millionaire before I can go forward, makes me feel suddenly, absolutely, irrevocably *myself*. Like pieces of a puzzle have fallen into place. Not so that I see the whole picture, just one small part. But I see that one part clearly, and it feels like all I need to know for now.

That evening I walk Harp along the Monon Trail, the long asphalt path that cuts through the city where the train tracks used to be. It's beautiful out, warm and green, summer just around the corner. There are joggers, walkers, cyclists, rollerbladers. People with dogs and babies. It's festive, like a parade. For a while, Harp trots along beside me so that it looks like I'm actually in control. Then, just before the bridge over the river, he stops suddenly and lies down in the grass beside the path. I bribe him with a doggy treat I have in my pocket. He eats it, walks about ten feet, then lies down again. He gazes at me balefully, like a kid who's been dragged to the mall and is sick to death of shopping.

I kneel down beside him. "Harp, come." I make my voice firm, like Margaret's.

He rolls over, so I can pet him.

"Goddamn it," I say.

Someone laughs.

I look up, and there's Gabe Parker, grinning, leaning on his bicycle. Then Josh skids in right behind him. Harp gives a pathetic little growl and stands up, prepared to protect me. I scramble up myself. All I can think is, why am I wearing these horrible shorts that make my legs look like tree trunks? I hear Jules nagging inside my head, *you should always look decent when you go out; you never know who you're going to see.*

"I guess this is Harp," Gabe says. He leans down to ruffle Harp's fur. "Great dog."

"I still can't believe your mom let you get a dog," Josh says.

"My mom's in *France*."

"Oh," Josh looks at me, like, *forever*?

"You don't even want to know," I say.

"Okay."

We just stand there, the three of us. Harp gazes up at me, an inquiring tilt to his head.

Finally Josh says, "Uh, Emma ... " He clears his throat about ten times, moves his bike slightly further off the trail. "Listen," he says. "Gabe and I—" He glances at Gabe, who gives him an encouraging nod. "We, uh—"

"We've been riding the trail in the evenings, thinking we might see you," Gabe says.

"*Me*?"

"On account of Harp," Gabe says. "Remember? You told me you walked him here."

"Right," Josh says. "The thing is, Emma—well, the Heather thing. I feel like such an asshole about that. I *was* an asshole. *Again*. I didn't know what to do, so I didn't do anything, except take the car back to your house. I let myself think maybe it was even the best thing to just leave you alone."

"Which Amy and I told him was chickenshit," Gabe says.

"Not to mention Tiffany," Josh says. "Jesus, has *she* been on my case."

I cannot think of a single thing to say to that. Exactly where and when did this little pow-wow occur, I wonder—and all I can think is—holy shit—did it happen the night of the beach party? Were all of them there? Gabe, Tiffany, Matt, *and* Josh and Amy—all of them trying to figure out what the fuck to do with me while I was passed out in the chaise lounge? Which brings to mind, all too fittingly, the image of the way a slug will shrivel up if you sprinkle beer on it—an apt metaphor for how I feel standing there between them.

Eventually, Josh speaks. "It *was* chickenshit. I could see that. And, okay, it's sort of chickenshit to track you down here instead of coming over to your house, but I was afraid to see your parents. I still am, if you want to know the truth. Afraid to see them. Plus, Gabe, well ..."

"Me? I'm just plain chickenshit," Gabe says cheerfully.

About *what*, I would like to know.

But Josh rattles on. "What I'm trying to say here is that I'm sorry. Again. Emma, I really am." Probably to cover up the way his voice cracks a little, he gives a little laugh. "And I'm not just saying this to keep from getting expelled."

I can't help smiling at that.

"Friends?" he asks. "This time, *really*?"

I nod.

His face lights up in the grin I remember. He raises his hand, and I high-five him the way we used to do.

"And you'll clue your dad in before I come over? So he doesn't kill me on impulse?"

"Yeah, I'll let him know."

"Cool." He glances at Gabe, straightens his bike, puts his foot on the pedal. "All right, then," he says. "Later." And rides away.

Leaving Gabe and me standing on the trail together. The relief I'd felt in the moment I realized that things were finally right between Josh and me *forever* had sort of made me forget Gabe was there at all. Now my mind goes into high gear, trying to settle on some social etiquette that might work in this situation—whatever the situation actually *is*.

"I was wondering ... " Gabe nods toward a nearby bench. "Could we, uh, talk?"

I sink onto it. Gabe props his bike against it, scoops up Harp and sits down beside me. We're quiet for a long time, watching the world go by. It's dusk. In a nearby tree, a whole flock of birds starts up that wild chirping they do just before sunset. The river's turned silver.

Harp's curled up, fast asleep, between us, and I wish I could just close my eyes and fall asleep, too. Awake, I can't decide whether I want this moment to end *right now* or whether I want to go on sitting on the bench with Gabe forever.

Finally, he says, "Emma. I feel really bad about the weekend you came down to Bloomington, you know, for Little Five—"

Instinctively, I raise my hands, palms out. "I know Tiffany cooked up the whole thing," I say. "Which would have been uncomfortable enough, even if I hadn't gotten drunk out of my mind and made a fool of myself. Which was totally my fault. God. Don't think you need to apologize for *that.*"

"I haven't been riding with Josh every night so that I could apologize to you," he says.

"Oh," I say. Squeak, really.

"The thing is," he says, "after the party, Josh and I talked about some things and made a deal. We'd ride the trail until we found you. Josh would try to set things straight with you, which he really wanted and needed to do. And I—my part of the deal was—"

He takes a deep breath. "Okay. It was that I'd tell you I really like you. A lot. I did right off, that first time at the Daily Grind. And, I know. I blew it. I should have just shut up about the stupid lottery as soon as I saw you were uncomfortable talking about it. But I didn't know what else to say. And after I'd grilled you about being rich, how could I ask you out? I mean, I figured you'd think the money was what I cared about—it isn't," he concludes. "You just have to believe me about that. Do you?"

I nod. I can't look at him.

"So," he says. "What about Josh? I mean, do you still—"

"Friends," is all I can manage.

He groans. "Jesus," he says. "Emma. Could you give me a little help here?"

Now I'm the one to take a deep breath—and when I speak, the words tumble out. "Okay. *Okay,* I liked you that first time, too. Only I thought—well, I acted like such a moron. Then I did it again when Tiffany and my grandfather insisted on driving that stupid Winnebago over to the Phi Delt house. And *again* the night of the beach party."

"It was a stupid party," he says. "I wish you'd forget about it."

"I wish I would, too," I say. "But I never forget making a fool of myself. I've got a whole shitload of that kind of stuff in my head. So—"

I look at him, finally, and I can't help smiling because he looks as awkward and desperate as I feel. Either one of us could bolt any second, I think. Go back into hiding about how we feel about each other. But I don't want to bolt. I want—well, I want whatever not bolting from Gabe Parker might turn out to be.

"So you might as well get used to it," I finish. "And everything else about me, for that matter. It won't be easy, you know. I'm not exactly normal."

"So?" He puts his arm around me. "When do we start?"

We head down the trail in companionable silence as night falls, Gabe walking his bike beside me, Harp nipping at his heels—childhood, the life I've led till this moment, trailing behind me like a dream. Then suddenly, Gabe lets his bike drop to the side of the path, pulls me into his arms. He *kisses* me! And I don't think twice. I kiss him back, not one bit afraid.

About the Author

Barbara Shoup was the writer-in-residence at the Broad Ripple High School Center for the Humanities and the Performing Arts (Indianapolis) for almost twenty years. She has mentored young writers and makes many visits to schools annually. She has been the recipient of numerous awards and grants, including a Master Artist Fellowship from the Indiana Arts Commission and the PEN/Phyllis Naylor Working Writers Fellowship. She is also an assistant editor for OV Books.

Shoup's novel *Wish You Were Here* was named an ALA Best Book for Young Adults. Visit her online at www.barbarashoup.com.